MUSES &
Melodies

USA TODAY BESTELLING AUTHOR
REBECCA YARROS

MUSES AND MELODIES

Copyright © 2020 by Rebecca Yarros

All rights reserved.

ISBN: 978-0-9973831-4-0

978-0-9973831-5-7

Yarros Ink, LLC

Editing by Karen Grove

Copy editing by Jenn Wood

Cover by Sarah Hansen © Okay Creations

First Edition October 2020

www.Rebeccayarros.com

To Gina and Cindi—
some things just work
better in threes.

#unholytrinity

1

NIXON

I DIDN'T JUST WANT a drink. I wanted a dozen. Whiskey. Tequila. Vodka. Anything that would take the edge off was fine by me.

Wanted wasn't even close to the right word, but after forty-five days in a rehab center that cost more than my penthouse, I knew I didn't *need* a drink to survive—I wanted one.

Since that wasn't going to happen, I settled for another orange soda as the limo wound through the streets of Seattle. I'd devoured cases of this shit in the last six weeks, which may have amped up my sugar addiction, but at least it wasn't booze or pills, right? I cracked open the top of the ice-cold can, and every set of eyes in the back of the car looked my way. Not that they hadn't been staring since the moment I'd landed at the airport—now they were just blatant about it.

"I made sure you had plenty of that stocked," Ethan, our tour manager, said with a smile and nod that hit an eleven on the awkward scale.

Jonas nodded, watching me like I was a grenade that had

already lost its pin. "And we had your apartment cleaned out too."

As one of my closest friends and the lead singer of our band, Hush Note, he knew all too well what happened when I went *kaboom*. He'd been the one to haul me off the tour bus floor after I'd taken some unmarked pills with a groupie like a dumbass, then sat by my side in the hospital, waiting to see if I'd live through my stupidity.

That had been my come-to-Jesus moment. I had become a liability, not just to the band but to my best friends' personal lives as well…and they didn't even know the why of it.

"We figured it might help with…you know…temptations and staying clean and all that," he added, when I didn't respond.

Now they were both nodding.

"Right. Thanks." One of the reasons I kept this trip to rehab a secret was because people never knew what to say or how to act after I got out. Before I went, they were all too eager to tell me exactly what they thought, but afterwards, I got the nuclear bomb treatment. Kid gloves, forced smiles, and a lot of fucking nodding—like they thought I might go off at any second if they made a false move.

Since this was my fifth trip, and the only one I hadn't walked out on, I knew they were annoyingly proud yet terrified it wouldn't stick.

At least we were all on the same page there. I was a Class-A fuckup, whose sins were excused because I had a symmetrical face, lean body, and magic hands when it came to a guitar.

But my sins had long ago outnumbered my excuses, not that I could tell by the supportive, forced smiles on Jonas and Ethan's faces. My first sin? I was an alcoholic who dabbled in drugs with the clichéd justification of numbing the pain. *Go figure, that apple hasn't fallen far from the tree.*

"You really do look great," Ethan blurted.

"Yeah. Your eyes are clear and everything," Jonas added.

More nodding. They'd turned into a pair of bobbleheads.

Quinn, our drummer and the third musketeer in our band's trio, scoffed. "Seriously, guys. Could you make this any weirder for him?" She shook her head beside me. "Relax. He's still Nixon."

Still Nixon, just nuclear-bomb edition.

"You guys didn't have to come," I said for the fifth time since they'd shown up at the airport. Sin number two: my friends were way better people than me—I didn't deserve them. The minute they'd found out where I was and when I was coming home, they'd interrupted their happy little sitcom lives and shown up.

"We wanted you to feel supported," Jonas repeated the same answer he'd given the first three times. None of them had known about attempt number four.

"Mission accomplished. I'm supported." I raised my soda in a mock salute, then chugged half of it.

Quinn rolled her eyes, but she was used to me acting like a dick, so I didn't worry too much. These three had seen me at both my best and worst since we started the band eight years ago. From the bar stage to sold-out stadiums, we'd had one another's backs. We never aired band laundry in the press or stepped out for solo projects. We were dysfunctional as hell, but we were a family.

We turned the corner, and my building came into view.

Jonas swore, which voiced my thoughts perfectly.

A thick crowd of fans blocked the door and were currently going nuts over the sight of our limo.

"I told you we should have taken an unmarked SUV," Quinn muttered, flipping through her phone.

"How did they know?" Ethan asked.

There were always fans outside my building—Quinn's and Jonas's too—but this was ridiculous. Was that seriously a giant poster board of a missing person flyer with my picture on it?

"It's been six weeks, not six months," I grumbled.

"They had someone camped out at the airport." Quinn turned her phone so we could see the photo on a popular gossip site. It was of our hug on the tarmac just after I'd come off the private jet.

The driver rolled the partition down. "What do you want me to do?"

"Take us through the garage." Smiling for the camera wasn't on my agenda for today.

We bypassed the horde of fans and took the private entrance down into the garage. There was a reason I paid so much money to live in this building. Not that I minded fans. I loved fans. Especially the female ones—even if they were off the menu for the foreseeable future. But there was something to be said for drawing a line between my public life and my private one.

Once we were parked, I hauled my duffel bag out of the trunk and slung it over my shoulder. We all filed into the elevator, and I punched in my code for the penthouse. The buttons lit up as we passed the other floors, the silence filled by a piano acoustic of "My Heart Will Go On."

"You know, I wouldn't have stopped at the bar on my way home or anything," I said.

"What?"

"We didn't think that."

"That's not why we're here."

They all spoke at the same time.

"Right. Bunch of babysitters." I laughed and shook my head.

"We're not babysitting you," Quinn snapped, then narrowed her eyes at me. "We're loving you. Deal with it."

"And honestly, we both feel like shit since we're the ones who've up and moved on you in the last year." Jonas pulled his hair back into a low ponytail with enough frustration to snap that little hair tie of his.

"I don't feel like crap," Ethan mumbled. "I still live here."

The elevator *dinged* our arrival, and the doors opened to the opulent marble floor of my entry. Sin number three: I made ungodly amounts of money and spent it on ridiculous things because I liked nice shit.

"Look, I fully supported you moving to Boston to be with Kira," I said to Jonas as I pulled my key from my front pocket, then turned to Quinn. "And the last time I checked, I'm the one who told you to move back to Bozeman for Graham. You both deserve to be happy." They did, and now that they'd both fallen in love and into ready-made families, I wasn't going to be the one waving the "it's not fair" flag, like some whiny prick.

"What about you?" Quinn asked as I turned the key and opened my front door.

"Oh, you know me. I'm delirious." I flashed her a quick smile and walked into my apartment.

It was definitely cleaner than how I'd left it. The blinds were open, and light streamed through the floor-to-ceiling windows that looked out over the Seattle skyline and Puget Sound, illuminating every polished surface from the entry, through the massive kitchen, and into the living room, where I dropped my bag. Smelled nice too. Like lemons and cleaning supplies instead of pot and general funk.

It was also quiet for a change. I'd bypassed more than a few passed-out people when I walked out six weeks ago.

"I can't remember the last time your place was this clean." Quinn flopped onto the couch and kicked off her Vans.

"The day he bought it," Jonas answered, sinking into the massive armchair.

"It's not like I don't have housekeepers," I retorted.

"Oh, those women are saints." Quinn laughed. "You just never give them a party-free week so they can do their jobs. I would have run screaming by now, if I were them."

"I heard Ben paid them double." Ethan gestured to the apartment and took the spot next to Quinn.

"Ben." We all groaned collectively. Our business manager did exactly what he was paid to do: brokered our contracts, handled our schedule and promotion, and shoved staff in our general direction when we needed them. He was a hardass, but he'd been one of the major reasons we'd skyrocketed. He'd also been the reason we were all on the verge of burnout from constant writing and touring.

Jonas and Quinn had both agreed to slow it down after this next album...the album I was holding up because my lame-ass brain couldn't write anything decent, which only fed into excuse number three billion and two to reach for a bottle: I'd never written a song sober, and quite frankly, I wasn't sure I could.

Add that to my inability to sleep and I was two for two.

"I'm going to take a shower. How long are you guys planning to supervise me?" I questioned.

"We're not supervising you." Quinn folded her arms across her chest. "And we'll be here as long as you want us to be."

Hell. No.

"Great, so you guys have flights scheduled for tonight?" I lifted my eyebrows and picked up my bag.

They all averted my gaze.

I sighed hard. "Guys. Go home to your families."

"We will," Jonas assured me. "Once we know you're okay. Now go take your shower. We'll order up dinner. What are you in the mood for? Thai? Burgers?"

News flash! I'm never going to be okay.

"You guys pick, and don't get comfortable. You're leaving tonight." I left them discussing food and headed up the stairs to the second floor of my apartment, pausing at the picture framed in the hallway.

We were young then—eighteen and nineteen—with our arms around one another, smiling for the camera after our first show at the bar. Eight years later, Jonas was still the broody poet, Quinn, the blonde with the sharp tongue and the golden sticks, and me? I was just as fucked up as I was back then. Maybe even more so.

Funny thing about money? It only amplified who you were on the inside—it didn't fix you. It patched the cracks on the surface but generally greased the mechanics underneath so you destroyed yourself faster. I was past the point of fixing anyway. I'd only gone to rehab to keep from dragging the band down with me.

I walked into my bedroom and froze. There was a very round, very nice ass peeking out from under my bed. It wasn't the first time a fan had found her way into my bedroom, but it was the first time it had happened since moving into this building three years ago.

"Son of a bitch, how big is this thing?" she swore, rocking her ass back and forth, obviously trying to tug something free. "Bigger. Is. Not. Always. Better!"

Well, that was definitely a first.

"I'd have to disagree with you on that." I dropped my bag and slid my phone out of my back pocket to call security. Usually, I'd be down for a little anonymous hookup, but my rehab therapist had lectured me against using sex to fill the alcohol void, so Little Miss Nice Ass had to go.

"Oh!" There was a distinct *thud* followed by a muted swear as the woman wiggled her way out from under my bed. She was a tiny thing and had some killer legs under that black skirt. A cloud of long, auburn hair appeared as she shuffled back on her knees, dragging a laughably giant bottle with her.

Then I was the one cursing as she scrambled to her feet.

Giant green eyes and plump lips appeared behind that curtain of hair as she tucked it behind her ears. "Hi."

"Are you fucking kidding me?" I bellowed at Ben's gorgeous, pain in the very nice ass assistant. Over the last few years, I'd had more than my fair share of fantasies involving my bed and that little redhead, but she'd always been in it…not under it.

Sin number four: I always wanted what I couldn't have, and Shannon was definitely on the "couldn't have" list, for more reasons than I could count.

"What? I got it all out before you got back! Well, all but this one." She fisted her hands on deliciously curved hips. "Every bottle. Every can. How was I supposed to know you had the world's largest vat of champagne under your bed? What were you going to do with that thing?" She motioned toward the novelty bottle that stood nearly as tall as she was.

"Drink it with a really big straw. Now what the hell are you doing in my bedroom, Shannon?" But wasn't it obvious? I groaned at the realization. "You're the one Ben sent to handle everything."

"Welcome home." She sang the sarcastic little tune. "It's nice to see you too."

"Everything okay in here?" a linebacker asked from the doorway. How many people were in my fucking house? "Mr. Winters," he addressed me with a nod.

"It's all great, Trevor. Could you please help me with this?" She motioned toward the bottle.

"Absolutely." He crossed the floor in front of me.

"That's a seventy-thousand-dollar bottle of champagne!"

"Oh, did you want us to return it for a refund instead?" Sarcasm dripped from those pretty pink lips.

My blood pressure spiked. God, the woman simultaneously turned me on and annoyed the shit out of me. Always had. She might have a body like a Sunday drive—all lush curves that demanded two hands—but she had a mouth like a Monday morning alarm clock. She was a color-coded, alphabetized checklist with no sense of humor, and I had half a mind to tell her to drink the damned thing herself if it would help dislodge the stick from her incredible ass.

But I didn't want that bottle anywhere near me. Even the thought of it made my mouth water. I could already taste the sweet oblivion on my tongue.

"Get rid of it." It had been a gift anyway and wasn't worth messing up my entire recovery for.

"Thank you." Her shoulders dipped slightly in relief as Trevor hefted the bottle and carried it out.

"I'll get it dumped, Ms. Shannon," he promised as he hauled it away.

"A little formal there with the Ms., isn't he?"

Her brow puckered. "He called you Mr. Winters."

I wasn't nearly drunk enough for this conversation. "Right, but that's my last name. I thought we lost the whole title-before-the-first when we became adults, but I know how much you love your protocol, so hey, whatever floats your boat, *Ms.* Shannon. Now, is Ben coming too, or are you his emissary?"

How many people needed to be here?

"You are…" She shook her head. "If I'm stuck here with you, then at least tell me you know that Shannon isn't my first name, right?" She tilted her head and folded her arms under her breasts. I couldn't say if she had a nice set or not, considering she was always buttoned up to her throat like a librarian. Not that it mattered—I didn't sleep with girls on staff.

Wait…her name *wasn't* Shannon?

"It isn't?" I narrowed my eyes. I'd been calling her that for the last four years.

"No!" She shook her head, all indignant, like I was the one rifling through *her* bedroom. "And yes, Ben sent me to make sure all the…contraband was out before you got back. He's on his way over."

"Well, I guess you failed that one." I snorted. "But you wiggled it free so at least you're not *stuck here* anymore. And I don't really care if you stay or not, but I'm getting in the shower, so if you don't want an eyeful, I'd get out." I pulled my shirt off and headed for the bathroom.

Her gaze widened and flickered toward my torso, but she marched out.

By the time I finished my shower and got back downstairs, Ben stood in my living room, the dark skin of his forehead wrinkling with concern as he thumbed through his phone, *Ms.* Shannon at his side. She even looked small next to Ben, who wasn't a huge guy. She didn't come up to my collarbone, even in heels.

"So, if we cancel San Francisco," he began.

"We're not canceling San Francisco," I cut him off.

Chaos erupted.

"We have to cancel every show this fall."

"You won't be ready."

"We're not putting you through this."

I stuck two fingers in my mouth and whistled, which had the desired effect of shutting everyone up. "Okay, this is the point where you all stop making decisions for me." I stared down my well-meaning bandmates. "That's never been how we've operated, and we're not starting now."

Jonas rubbed the bridge of his nose and sighed. "We're just worried about you, Nix. We want to give you the best shot at staying clean. Canceling four shows is nothing in the scheme of things. We'll reschedule. You're more important."

"We're not canceling," I reiterated. "I did a six-week program instead of the full twelve because I wanted to make sure that I could handle myself in the real world before the fall dates. Did you honestly think I would dump myself into rehab and *not* think about what we had coming up?" I was a selfish prick, but I wasn't that selfish.

"We weren't sure exactly *what* went through your head." Quinn leaned forward, bracing her elbows on her knees. "You didn't fill us in. And no, don't look at me like that—we're thrilled you went. We're just trying to figure out how to best support you."

My jaw locked. My reasons for going to rehab were mine and mine alone, just like the reasons I drank. "I should have told you, but I'd already walked out of rehab the week before, and I didn't want to disappoint you if I did it again."

They all sagged, like I'd just deflated their balloons—like I'd already failed.

"Look," I said softly. "This sucks. I'm not going to lie. I haven't been six weeks sober since I was eighteen. But next week, I'll be at seven weeks, and the week after that, I'll be at eight. I chose to go. No one forced me. I didn't need an intervention. I made the decision myself. That should tell you how serious I am, and quite frankly, you're all starting to really piss me off by assuming you know what's best for me. If you want to parent someone, then go home to your kids."

They stared at me with open mouths.

"So, that means you don't want to cancel the shows?" Ben asked, still holding his phone.

"No. I don't. It's bad for business and would lead to a massive PR issue. I'm assuming you kept the rehab quiet?" If he hadn't, I was going to fire his ass, right here and now.

"Of course. Publicity stepped in and posted from quite a few beaches around the world on your social media, with bullshit captions like 'living my best life' and 'water soothes the soul.'"

I would never say cheesy shit like that, but I let it slide.

"Right. Then I'm not going to cancel dates. End of story." I shoved my hands in the front pockets of my jeans.

Ben studied me for a few moments, then turned to Shannon. "You have everything you need?"

"Yep. My stuff's in the guest room, and the doorman knows not to let anyone up without an escort." She glanced my way, then quickly found some lint on her sweater to brush away.

"I'm sorry, what?" My eyes narrowed. Why the hell would she have her stuff in my guest room? *Stuck here.*

"Shannon will be with you for the remainder of the fall dates," Ben stated. "I have too much going on to handle you personally, and well, she's the only one on my team who can handle your bullshit without wanting to sleep with you."

"Absolutely not." My eyebrows hit the roof. What was more insulting? That she wasn't attracted to me? Or that she thought she was actually capable of *handling* me?

"This isn't up for debate, Nixon." Ben turned to face me directly. "If you want to cancel the dates now, I'll support that decision. We're here to make sure you stay clean. But if you want me to keep those dates on the books, then Shannon is staying by your side to make sure you don't go off the rails. That's the deal. Take it or leave it." The asshole wasn't kidding.

I turned a glare on Quinn and Jonas. "Oh, I get it now. You two don't have to babysit me because you're having *her* do it." I pointed at Shannon, or whatever her name was.

"*She* is a lawyer, not a babysitter," Shannon snapped.

"Even better."

"Nix." Jonas stood. "I'm in Boston and Quinn's in Montana. It's killing us that we're not here for you, and if you want us to, we'll stay."

Quinn stood and slid her sticks into her back pocket. "We'll stay as long as you need us," she promised. "But please don't ask us to abandon you, because we won't."

I ripped my hands over my hair and fought the urge to break something. There was no way I was pulling Jonas and Quinn away from their families, and if I threw Shannon—whatever her name was—out, those two would stay.

I glanced at Shannon.

Four years and I really didn't know her first name?

"Fine," I barked and strode to the Jeff Frost photo hanging on the wall. The hinges were soundless as I swung it open like a door, revealing the small safe behind it. I punched in the code, opened the door, and took out the small bottle of pills I'd stashed there three months ago. The bottle felt heavy in my hand, even though I knew it weighed next to nothing. Everyone watched as I took it to Shannon and pressed it into her hand. "There you go. That's the last *contraband* in the house, and I just freely gave it to you. Now what is your damn name?" My tone quieted as I struggled to keep a cap on my anger.

Her eyes flared, and my stomach pitched as we locked gazes. Those eyes weren't just green, they were *emerald* green and brighter than any jewel I'd ever seen. I blinked and stepped back as her fingers closed around the bottle.

"Thank you," she said softly. "Zoe. My name is Zoe Shannon."

Zoe.

"Well, Zoe, I'm assuming you know where the spare towels are, seeing as you've searched my entire apartment." I turned to my friends. "Now, the rest of you can get the fuck out. I love you, but I don't really like you at the moment." I grabbed a box of whatever takeout was on the coffee table and left them all sitting in my living room as I climbed the stairs.

Ironic. They were all so concerned for my sobriety, yet they'd just saddled me with the one woman who could drive me to drink.

My lips lifted slightly. At least they'd given me something to do between shows. It was going to be a shit ton of fun to see just what it would take to get under her skin.

2

ZOE

"HOW'S THE EGOTISTICAL ASSHOLE?" Naomi asked through the phone. My best friend was more than aware of my general feelings about my current roommate.

"Still an egotistical asshole. How's my brother?"

"Taking your nephew to daycare," she answered. "He's gained two pounds this month, by the way—Levi, not Jeremiah."

"Glad to hear it's my nephew and not my brother growing." I sipped my coffee and looked out over the Seattle skyline from my seat at the patio table, then turned slightly to appreciate the magnificence of Puget Sound.

"Shit," she muttered. "Speaking of your brother, that's him on the other line. I'll call you back after my shift?"

"Don't stress. We'll catch up when you're not working. Love you."

"Love you!"

I hung up and sighed. I missed my family.

Naomi would freak if she saw Seattle from this vantage

point. Nixon Winters might have been a giant, flaming jerk, but he had great taste when it came to real estate. The view was breathtaking. Then again, when you made millions a year, you could afford a great view. It was nothing compared to the Rockies, though.

My fourth-floor apartment sported a view of a brick wall, but that was okay. It was all part of paying off my student loans, and I was almost there.

This little section of his enormous deck had become my morning haven over the past week, giving me a tiny slice of much-needed calm in the swirling vortex of chaos that was Nixon. I flipped open my planner to today's date, then placed my phone next to it, making sure the schedules matched as I reviewed the day's appointments.

"Not that he'll actually stay on schedule," I grumbled to myself.

We'd cleared Nixon's calendar of all professional appearances until the first show, which was in a little over three weeks, but he demanded to stay busy. Knowing that idle time was an enemy in this stage of his recovery, I couldn't blame him, but the man had seriously dragged me to an axe-throwing range yesterday. He had a call with his rehab therapist at ten, but other than that—

"Why do you do that?"

I startled, fumbling my coffee, but I managed to avert disaster as Nixon appeared behind me. "What are you doing up so early?"

"It's eight thirty." He rubbed his sleep-mussed, carelessly sexy hair with one tattooed hand and carried a steaming cup of coffee—black, of course—with the other as he walked out onto the deck. Shirtless. He was shirtless.

Lord, help me.

It didn't matter how many times I'd seen him run around the stage half-dressed, the sight of his inked, ripped torso never failed to make my mouth water. I might not have liked the guy, but I wasn't blind. He was pretty much a walking, talking advertisement for sex and bad decisions.

There was a reason *People* magazine had given him the title of Sexiest Man Alive.

Any girl with the internet could find his stats. He stood six three, at two hundred and ten pounds post-rehab, with dark blond hair and fuck-me-now brown eyes. Those stats didn't mention how tiny he made me feel as he towered over me. Nor did they reveal the way his back tattoos rippled with his movements as he walked across the deck, or that his ass could make sweatpants cool again.

Nope, those were facts you could find only in my head. I knew way too much when it came to Nixon Winters because I was the one tasked with cleaning up his messes, including anticipating the ones he hadn't gotten into yet.

"You're not usually up for another couple hours, so it's early for you," I finally said.

"You sound disappointed." He turned and leaned against the railing, lifting his coffee mug to those carved, sinful lips.

"Nope, not at all," I lied, ripping my gaze from his and focusing extra hard on the words "lunch appointment" in my planner as my brain chanted *abs, abs, abs*. Given the amount of time he'd spent dragging me to the gym this week, it was easy to see why he was so cut.

Focus, Zoe.

"And why the hell are you dressed for church on a Friday?"

"I'm sorry?" I glanced at my classic, navy linen sheath and matching sweater.

Ahh, and so it begins. Another day of Nixon pushing every button I had. I guess it was better than him trying to get in my pants, but I wasn't exactly his type. Nixon liked tall, model-thin lemmings who never asked questions in the morning. I wasn't any of those things, which was exactly why Ben had charged me with this assignment.

The payoff would be well worth it.

"You heard me." He tilted his head and gave me an appraising once-over.

"I'm dressed for work, not church. Because I'm *working*. You may have blown off your producer every day this week, but I can't exactly do the same when it comes to Ben. Hush Note doesn't just run on its own, you know."

The skin between his eyes wrinkled. "So, you have to dress like Jackie Kennedy at eight in the morning while working from home?"

God, I hated him. Hated that smug look on his stupidly attractive face.

"First, that's not an insult, and second, what would you prefer I wear to work? Something to match you?" I gestured from his toes to his torso.

"I'm cool with you going shirtless. I mean, you're not exactly my type, but—"

"God, just go back to bed!" I snapped. *Shit.*

He chuckled, knowing he'd gotten to me, and my stomach tightened.

I never won with him.

"So really, what do you do out here every morning?" he asked.

"I check over my day, and yours." Because how else would I know to let in the cute little blonde masseuse he'd scheduled for a ten p.m. massage?

"In a paper planner? You may as well break out the stone and chisel," he challenged and took another sip. "And besides, it's already in your phone. How many planners does one woman need?"

I scoffed. "The calendar on my phone is accessible to everyone at Berkshire Management. So even Been-here-two-

days Tommy can log in and move things around. But this baby?"
I pointed to my leatherbound love. "I'm the only one in control
of it, so I know the why's and when's of an appointment being
moved."

He looked at me like I'd lost my mind.

"What?" I raised my brows at him. "When the service and
Wi-Fi go out, I'll be the one who makes my meetings. Watch and
see." There was nothing wrong with organization, especially
when I spent all day working with creatives who had none.

If anything, I was making up his deficit.

"Riiight." He sipped his coffee. "So now that you've been
torturing me for a week, why don't you go ahead and tell me
why you drew the short straw."

I blinked. "The short straw?" Every assistant at Berkshire
had begged for this job.

"You hate me." He rubbed his hand over his light beard.
He'd stopped shaving three days ago.

"I do not."

"Liar. You can't stand to be around me, any more than I can
you, so why sign on to be my nanny? You into S&M? Figure a
little pain is good for the body, Shannon?"

I bristled at his use of my last name. That was the crap Ben
did because he thought it kept his relationships with underlings
impersonal, making it easier to fire people. Which he did. A lot. I
was the first of Ben's assistants to have lasted an entire year, and
definitely the only one to reach four years.

"Well, *Winters*, my sexual preferences include anyone who
isn't you, and the rest is none of your business. But since you
asked, I was the best option, and I'm dedicated to the band, so
here I am." My sexual preferences hadn't mattered in the last
four years since joining Berkshire Management. It wasn't like I
had a lot of time for a relationship, and I'd never been into one-
night hookups, not that he'd understand.

His eyes narrowed. "You're seriously telling me that you're

putting yourself through all this because you're *dedicated* to the band?"

"What would the other reason possibly be?" I stood and gathered my things. So much for having a calm start to my morning. Did he have to throw every single moment into disarray?

"You want something."

I stilled.

"Nailed it." He smirked.

"Fine." I set my things down on the table and crossed my arms. "I have a deal with Ben. Happy?"

"Intrigued, maybe, but not happy. You and happy don't exactly go together. That's like throwing SAT prep into the homecoming dance. Then again, I bet you believe I never took the SATs, right? Because you think I'm an *irresponsible, egotistical ass who will fuck up the first time he's left alone for five minutes*." Those intense, show-stopping brown eyes hardened. "Just because it's a big penthouse doesn't mean I can't hear your nightly check-in's with Ben."

Heat flooded my cheeks, but I lifted my chin. At least he hadn't pressed me for details…yet. I'd watched Nixon chew other assistants up and spit them out with a smile over the last four years, and I was not about to add my name to the list—not when I was this close. "You got a thirteen-fifty on the SATs, which got you accepted to the University of Washington."

He tensed.

"How the hell would you know that?" He set his mug down on the railing so hard I was surprised it didn't shatter.

"It's my *job* to know that, Nixon, and I'm damned good at it. I also know that you were accepted to Carnegie Mellon, Vanderbilt, and USC for music, but you didn't go to any of them. Why is that?" I'd always wondered.

"Not everyone can afford those schools." His jaw ticked.

"They can when they're offered a full ride like you were," I bit back.

He glared at me.

"Want to know what I think?"

"Sure, since it's not like I can stop you from telling me anyway." A muscle in his jaw ticked again.

"I think something—someone—kept you here." The morning breeze was brisk, but the look in Nixon's eyes turned downright glacial. "And honestly, that's none of my business. But don't, for a single moment, operate under the assumption that I think you're stupid, because I know better, and you should too. Now, I'm going to go call your producer and stall him yet again, because ignoring someone's phone call is the kindergarten equivalent of hiding behind your own hand and swearing no one can see you. News flash, Nixon. We all see you."

I scooped up my planner and phone, turned to walk back into the apartment, then ruined my grand exit by forgetting my coffee. *Damn.* When I squared my shoulders and retrieved the cup from the table, he arched an eyebrow at me. *Busted.*

"I'm just saying, maybe we should go for casual Fridays before you run the LOFT completely out of dresses."

Cue snappy subject change.

I pressed my lips together to keep from sputtering as I turned my back on him and headed into the penthouse. "This dress is from Nordstrom," I said over my shoulder, "and this is as casual as I'm going to get." I pointed at my bare feet. "And while yes, you are an irresponsible, egotistical ass, I didn't say you couldn't be left alone for five minutes without fucking up."

"You didn't?" he called after me.

"Nope. I gave you ten." I closed the sliding glass door on his infuriating ass and got my day started. With any luck, the next six months would be the last I'd have to spend with Nixon Winters.

———

THE REST OF THAT WEEK, he did his best to show me exactly how much trouble he could get into when left alone for those ten precious minutes.

In the time it took me to go to the bathroom, he left the building entirely. I found him at a driving range forty minutes later, slaughtering golf balls with the worst swing known to man. When he'd looked genuinely surprised to see me, I simply crossed my arms and waited for him to finish. What? Like I wouldn't have his phone tracked? I wasn't a rookie, and I sure as hell wasn't about to fail when I was this close to making it.

I'd be able to hold my head up in my little town the next time I went home.

Today, I'd taken a call with Ben on the deck, and four minutes later, found myself racing for the car, tracking Nixon's cell phone through traffic to a yoga studio.

"I'm going to throttle him," I muttered, shoving the heavy glass door open a little harder than necessary and walking straight into a small, crowded reception room with a dozen people in exercise clothes.

"Just a moment, and we'll begin our session," a calm voice called from the back of the room.

I rose on my tiptoes, sweeping my gaze from left to right, but I felt a tap on my shoulder before I hit the midpoint.

"Glad to see you could join us," Nixon said, flashing a smirk from under his ball cap. At least he hadn't been recognized yet.

"Seriously? This isn't on the schedule. And you couldn't wait for me to get off the phone?" I turned to face him, thankful we were in a corner.

"Not everything has to be scheduled, Shannon. There's this little thing called spontaneity." He folded his arms over his chest, pulling the fabric of his T-shirt tight against his biceps.

"Then be spontaneous when I'm not on the phone!"

"Friends, we're ready for you now," the voice called out over the crowd, and people began moving toward the back of the room.

"Guess it's time." Nixon leaned over and picked up two rolled yoga mats, holding one out toward me. "Figured you might be unprepared."

"It's hard to be prepared when you don't tell me what you're doing," I muttered, glancing at the light blue mat. "Wait, I'm not doing yoga. I'm in a freaking pants suit!"

"Better than a dress." He shrugged, moving around me and heading toward the reception desk. The rest of the class had already filed into the studio.

"I'll just wait for you out here." I clutched the long strap of my messenger bag, already mentally planning what I could get done during his session.

"And when I sneak out the back door?" he asked over his shoulder.

I blew out a long, frustrated breath. "Fine. I'll watch from inside."

"Put her session on me," Nixon told the receptionist as he walked by, then paused to hold the door open to the studio. "Let's go, Shannon. You're making us late."

"*I'm* making us? Ugh. Thanks." I took the mat he offered and walked into the studio. It was bright, with pale hardwood floors and lined with mirrors. The rest of the class had already taken their positions, leaving the back row open. I found a spot against the wall and set my bag down as Nixon kicked off his shoes and spread out his mat.

I sat against the wall and did my best not to notice the way his athletic pants draped over the curve of his ass but failed miserably until the instructor stepped into my line of sight.

"Come now, there's room right here," she said with a glowing smile, gesturing to the space next to Nixon.

"Oh, no, I'm just watching." I offered her a smile of my own and reached into my bag for my planner.

"There are no spectators here," she said joyfully. "Only participants. Tell me, do you want to be a participant in this world? Or are you going through life as a spectator?"

My jaw dropped an inch.

"Yeah, Shannon. Are you really just existing to watch other people?" Nixon asked with mock concern, his eyes dancing.

My eyes narrowed slightly on Nixon before turning back to the instructor. "Fine. I'll participate," I told her, slipping off my heels.

"Good. Your attire might limit your motions, so just modify as you feel comfortable," she said in a soothing tone that grated on my every nerve. "Welcome to Baa-Maste." She walked away, taking her position at the head of the class.

"Weirdest name ever, but okay," I muttered, unbuttoning my suit coat and draping it over my bag. At least my silk blouse was sleeveless and my pants had a little Lycra for stretch.

Nixon laughed softly, ducking his head so I couldn't see his expression under his ball cap. "Bet you're wishing you'd gone a little more casual, huh?"

"Shut up." I unrolled my mat and sat, modeling myself after Nixon's pose—cross-legged with my palms facing up on my knees.

"Welcome to Baa-Maste," the instructor said. "Our friends Juniper, Juno, Jules, and Jose are joining us momentarily. Please remember that they may leave gifts, but there's often no odor."

"What the hell?" I whispered at Nixon.

He laughed quietly, his shoulders shaking.

A door opened on the right-hand wall, and four baby goats bounced in, followed closely by a handler. Two of them rammed heads.

"Don't worry, that's just how they play!" the handler said with a wide smile.

"Oh my god." My eyes flew to Nixon's. "Goats? You brought me to goat yoga?"

"Baa-maste, Shannon," he replied with a wink.

"Unbelievable." I'd just bought this suit.

"When in doubt, trust the goats," the instructor said, her voice monotone.

She led us through a breathing exercise, which I did with one eye open. There was zero chance I was getting blindsided, even if they were the cutest little goats I'd ever seen. They even had tiny little shoes.

"Try to relax, Shannon. Trust the goats," Nixon whispered.

"Bite me," I responded, moving into child's pose on my knees and stretching my arms out in front of me.

"Better watch it, you're coming unraveled over there," he said, looking my way. "Is that a hot pink bra strap? You little rebel."

"Get a good look, because this is the only time you'll see my underwear," I retorted as a goat climbed onto my back. Okay, that wasn't too bad. Kind of fun, actually...until I felt a yank at my scalp. "Stop eating my hair!" I flailed, tugging the now-slimy strands free and receiving a bleat of protest.

"Yes, they do like to eat hair," the instructor said, like it was the cutest thing in the world. "And don't worry if they leave a gift on your back. It happens all the time."

They *pooped* on people?

Nixon flat-out laughed.

"If a goat poops on me, you're buying me a new suit."

"It would be worth it just to see your face."

"You really do love getting under my skin, don't you?"

"It's the highlight of my day," he replied as we rose to table-top, bracing our weight on hands and knees. His gaze flickered back to my ass, then snapped forward as the hair-hungry goat approached his head. "Hey, little dude."

Little dude took the hat straight off Nixon's head.

I sputtered a laugh as Nixon reached to steal it back, but the goat was too quick, leaving Nixon flat on his face. He regained his pose quickly as we moved into cat, arching our backs.

"I think that goat just peed," he whispered, nodding toward the wall where a goat meandered away from a puddle.

"And now it's eating the paper towels," I noted as we were given the instructions for tiger pose.

"Do you have questions there in the back?" the instructor asked.

"Nope, we're all good here," Nixon replied.

"Okay, then please pay attention to your breathing, not your fellow classmates," she lectured as the goat sauntered by, munching on a paper towel.

"She told you," I whispered at Nixon.

"Better watch your planner," Nixon said with a smirk, kicking his back leg up but unable to catch it for the pose.

"That's not even funny." My gaze snapped to my messenger bag, which was still zipped shut. Then I battled my pants and won, kicking my right leg back and gripping my ankle with my left hand.

"Hot. Damn. Who would have thought someone so rigid could be so…flexible," he noted, lifting his eyebrows.

"I'll have you know I'm incredibly bendy," I said as straight-faced as possible, my lips quirking up at the end.

"Apparently." The appreciation in his eyes flushed my cheeks.

"Now breathe deeply, moving the air into your core with intention," the instructor said. "Exhale the negativity, and inhale the positive energy of our little friends."

Another goat climbed onto my back. "Oh no, I'm not that good at—" Its weight threw me off balance and sent me careening into Nixon.

His arm wrapped around my ribcage as he tucked me against his chest, cushioning me from the impact as we fell to the floor, the goat bounding away to harass the next available student.

"You okay?" Nixon asked, his mouth against my ear, sending a shiver down my spine.

"Yep," I squeaked, managing a nod. At least I would be as soon as I could put an inch or two between us. His hand was splayed protectively under my breasts, holding me tight, and my entire body heated. The man somehow did the impossible and managed to smell delectable in a sea of goats. "Thanks, I'm good."

"Please be mindful and present," the instructor sang, her voice no longer so soothing as she arched her eyebrows at us.

"Oh, I'm present," Nixon muttered as he released me. "A little too present."

I scurried back to my mat as we entered wheel pose, which was basically the same as the backbends I'd done as a kid. My shirt came untucked, sliding over my belly, but I hit the pose.

"Better watch that shirt, Shannon," Nixon teased. "Pretty soon, I'll be seeing a lot more than just your strap."

I scoffed, but the silk slipped even higher, resting above my belly button as a goat walked perilously close to my messenger bag. "Don't even think about it!"

He pranced, jumping slightly.

"Guess it's about to be digital only," Nixon joked.

"If you two can't be mindful of your classmates, I'm going to have to ask you to leave," the instructor said, coming up behind us.

"We'll be good," I promised her, the blouse falling to pool at the undersides of my bra. Nixon was right, the entire class was about to get an eyeful, but I wasn't giving him the pleasure of breaking the pose.

"Speak for yourself," Nixon chided as she walked away, his focus shifting to my very exposed midsection.

The goat bleated, jumping and prancing as he came our way.

"See, aren't you glad I—" The goat backed up a step and

then charged, headbutting Nixon in the face with an audible *thunk*.

"Oh!" I winced as Nixon collapsed, falling out of his arch and smacking flat on his back.

"You have got to be kidding me." He laid there for a second, rubbing his forehead as the goat pranced to the next row.

I laughed hard and loud, almost dropping myself.

"Are you okay there in the back row?" There was zero peace in the instructor's voice this time.

"Yep," Nixon answered, climbing to his feet and walking onto my mat. "You win this round. I'm sneaking out the front door. Want to come with? Or follow via tracker?"

"Come with," I answered.

Before I could drop to the mat, Nixon gripped my waist with one hand and spread the other over my back, lifting me to my feet. The blood rushed from my head as my blouse slid in a rustle of silk, stopping at his hands as it fell back into place.

There were a few gasps in the class as more than one person recognized him.

"Let's go before the goats turn on us," he said quickly.

I nodded with a laugh as my equilibrium returned, but the slide of his hands on my skin as he pulled away made me light-headed again.

"You two—"

"Don't worry, we're leaving," Nixon announced as we rolled our mats.

I slipped on my heels, grabbed my coat, and threw my bag over my shoulder while Nixon put his shoes on. As we left, the instructor crossed her arms and shook her head at us.

"Baa-Maste," I said to her with a grin, joining my hands and bowing my head slightly.

I laughed as Nixon gripped my elbow and pulled me out of the studio.

———

THE NEXT DAY, he'd made it into the crowd of adoring fans just outside his building by the time I caught him. He spent a half hour signing autographs and taking pictures with a primarily female audience, and his smile never faltered, even as the swarm thickened. They were mad about him, which bode well for record sales, but there was a part of me that wished they'd give him a little more space. The ropes that marked the path clear from the street to the door were hardly enough to keep them from reaching for him.

It was worse than living in a fish tank. Thanks to social media, fans felt like they *knew* him—like they deserved access. It was a double-edged sword.

"How was Palau?" one co-ed asked as he signed her T-shirt just below her shoulder. I had to give Nixon a little credit—she'd offered him a few inches lower.

"Gorgeous. Peaceful. Perfect." He grinned at her with a wink, and the brunette damn near melted as I snapped the picture for her.

I was the only one in the crowd besides Nixon who knew he hadn't been to Palau. That was just another picture on an Instagram account he was barely involved in.

"Hungry?" he asked me as he finished making the rounds.

"Sure. You want to go out or order in?" I was already flipping through the apps on my phone, looking for his favorite restaurants. When he didn't answer, I looked up and caught him staring at the pub across the street with a painful gleam of longing in his eyes. *Oh no.* "Want me to grab some carryout?"

His mouth tensed, and when yet another fan called out his name, his smile faltered.

"Come on." I put my hand in the middle of his back to urge him inside. "I'll order for delivery. Fish and chips?" That was his favorite.

He nodded, uncharacteristically quiet as I led him back up the elevator.

"You sure you don't need a meeting?" I asked.

"For the tenth time, it wasn't a twelve-step program," he growled. "And if you think I'm going to stand up in front of a bunch of strangers and air my shit, you don't know me half as well as you think you do."

Okay. No meetings.

Instead, he spent an hour on the phone with his therapist from the rehab center.

———

TWO DAYS LATER, I left him playing *Madden* on the X-Box while I grabbed a quick shower. I'd confiscated his wallet, car keys, phone, and even tipped the bellman to alert me the second Nixon tried to leave the building without me, so I felt relatively safe during the nine minutes it took to wash the day off me.

My hair dripped as I wrapped a thick terry robe around my body. The loud, pumping music coming from the living room made me groan. What the hell was he up to now?

I threw open the bathroom door, then marched through the guest suite and into the hallway that led to the living room. It was lined with pictures of the band mid-show. Some were almost a decade old, and others were from this last year. I pulled the edges of my robe a little closer as I strode into the living room.

"What the he—" My jaw dropped.

Nixon sat lounged on his couch, his arms stretched across the back and his thighs spread wide as two young *ladies* in underwear ground on each other in front of him.

This was exactly the kind of scene I would have expected to stumble in on a few months ago, so I wasn't sure why I was remotely shocked...but I was.

"Want to join in?" Nixon called over his shoulder, barely sparing me a glance.

"Think I'll pass." I shook my head but didn't turn around. There were parts of my job that I absolutely loved—this was not one of them. I picked up the remote, pressed a button, and the music died.

"Hey!" the girls complained.

"Come on, Shannon, you gotta let a guy have a *little* fun," Nixon threw at me with a smirk. "Or did you think I was going to tone it down just because you're in the guest room?"

"I honestly don't give a shit who you *have fun* with," I snapped as my stomach turned over. To be fair, I'd walked in on him in far more compromising situations. Nixon's biggest addiction after the alcohol was sex. The drugs had always come after that. "But I do need to see some IDs, ladies." That was one scandal that wasn't happening on my watch.

One girl—the blonde—grabbed her purse while the other one scoffed.

"Nine minutes," I said to Nixon. "I'm impressed."

"Only took three." He shrugged with a grin. "Didn't even have to leave the building. Just pointed through the glass doors and nodded."

Great, because that was going to do a ton for discouraging the fans to stake out his door.

"Here's—" The girl fumbled her wallet and dropped the purse. "Crap," she muttered as the contents spilled on my bare feet. Condoms, lip gloss, some cough drops that looked like they'd been purchased during the last presidency…and one small skull-shaped bottle of vodka.

Shit.

Nixon rose to his feet, his eyes narrowing on the bottle.

This was bad. This was so, so, *so* bad. Any other liquor would have been better.

"Sorry," she muttered, shoving everything but the vodka

back into her bag. That, she held between her fingers until her friend snatched it, offering it to Nixon like a tithe.

No, no, no.

"It's Crystal Head," the girl explained, like we were idiots. "We read that article in *Rolling Stone*, and you said it's your favorite."

That was enough. "Okay, I think you ladies had better—"

"Get the fuck out," Nixon barked as he stormed into the kitchen. "Now."

Relief swept through every cell in my body as I ushered the girls back into their clothing and out the door. What the hell would I have done if he'd reached for the bottle? Smacked it out of his hands? Wrestled him to the ground? The truth was, if he wanted to drink, there was little I could do to stop him. He could have slipped away to a bar—instead of the driving range—at any point this week, but he hadn't.

I put the girls in the elevator, then closed the door behind me after I came back inside the penthouse. A warm, tight feeling filled my chest, and I put my hand over my heart. I was *proud* of Nixon.

"Fuck this," he spat, ripping his hands over his hair. "And could you put on some clothes?"

So much for that warm, fuzzy feeling.

What the hell? I was wearing more clothing than those two had been. "Can you keep your dick in your pants long enough for me to get dressed, or should I expect *Girls Gone Wild*, Volume Two when I get back out here?"

"You jealous or something?" He strode past me and took one of his bajillion guitars from a stand near the coffee table.

"Hardly." Would I have wanted to know what it was like to sleep with him? Maybe. Okay, definitely. But wanting to know and actually sleeping with the man were two different things. I valued my career and my body more than that.

"Nice fucking robe." He stalked off, heading toward his in-home studio.

"It's Casual Friday, remember?" I called after him.

He spent the rest of the afternoon in his studio, and I caught up on work at the dining room table. Dinner was silent and tense, and I'd never been happier to hear him say he was headed to bed early, because that meant I could too.

Except, I didn't sleep. My mind wouldn't quiet. It was too busy thinking of every scenario Nixon could get himself into, and how I could possibly keep him from risking his sobriety.

At two a.m., my phone lit up with yet another email, and I cursed. I really needed to turn the notifications off on that thing. The world wasn't going to burn down while I caught a few hours of sleep, but I wasn't about to let some other assistant at Berkshire get the jump on me either. Besides, I was up anyway, so I headed toward the kitchen, reading through yet another endorsement offer for the band.

Not that I should have bothered. The band didn't do brand placement. Ben only forwarded these to me so I could craft a thoughtful rejection, which he would then send.

My phone in my face, I opened the cabinet closest to the refrigerator and pulled down a box of tea, then turned and put it on the island...and screamed at the figure sitting across from me at the kitchen's bar.

3

NIXON

"WHAT THE HELL ARE YOU DOING?" Zoe shrieked from across the kitchen island.

"Sitting in my kitchen. What the fuck does it look like I'm doing?" I fired back, her scream still ringing in my ears. Damn, the woman had some lungs.

"Who sits in their kitchen, in the dark, at two o'clock in the morning?" She slammed her phone down on the counter. "You scared the shit out of me!"

"Am I supposed to apologize?" I gripped my glass of water between my hands, wishing it was something stronger, like that bottle of Crystal Head those girls had taken with them.

"Yes! No. I'm honestly not sure." She flicked on the light, and I blinked rapidly at the assault on my eyes. At least she'd gone with the softer, under cabinet ones instead of the overhead. "You have every right to sit wherever you want in your home at whatever time you want to do it. I just wasn't expecting you... here...at two in the morning."

Any retort I would have fired back died on my tongue. Her plaid shorts barely reached her mid-thigh, exposing her shapely, toned legs, and her pink ribbed tank top didn't leave much to the imagination.

Had she always had such incredible breasts? Where the hell had she kept them hidden for the last four years? They were high and firm, the curves straining the material between the peaks.

"Were you having trouble sleeping?" she asked, turning away to fill the teakettle.

My grip tightened on the glass. *Stop looking at her ass. She's off-limits. Everyone is off-limits.*

"Nixon?"

"Uh. Yeah." I wouldn't have called it *trouble*. It was far past that.

"Is that normal?" She finished filling the kettle, then put it on the stove.

"For me, it is." Sleep was something that didn't happen for me anymore, and without the alcohol as an aide, I spent a shit ton of nights right where I was now, running from my own memories. But on nights like tonight, when I hit decline on *her* call, it was worse. *Fourth time this week.*

She'd already threatened to show up here, at which point I'd stopped listening to that voicemail…all voicemails.

"Want to talk about it?" She leaned back against the counter and faced me.

"No." I wanted to drink about it, but that wasn't going to happen. Another face danced across my mind—big blue eyes, curly blond hair, and a smile that had gotten her anything she'd ever wanted from me. Anything except the one thing she'd actually needed. I closed my eyes like it would dull the pain, but it never did.

I didn't deserve relief anyway.

"Okay. Well, how about some tea?" she offered.

"Tea?" What was I? An eighty-year-old woman?

"My dad used to make me tea when I was little and couldn't sleep." She picked up the box she'd dropped on the counter. "Chamomile, valerian root, and lavender. It's always worked for me." She tilted her head and looked off in the distance, a wistful smile transforming her face in a way that made my chest tighten. "Or maybe it was just knowing that he was there that relaxed me." She shrugged, then tucked a piece of hair behind her ear nervously when she caught me watching her. "I guess it's kind of my comfort food...except it's comfort tea. Anyway, do you have anything like that? A comfort food? I can make it for you."

There was something about seeing her all sleep-rumpled and soft that made me answer honestly.

"A few shots of vodka usually does the trick." I rolled the glass of water between my hands.

"Oh." Her eyes flared momentarily with surprise, then softened in understanding. "Okay, well, when you were a kid, what worked? Warm milk? A bedtime story?"

"As a kid, no one gave a shit if I was sleeping as long as I was quiet." I snapped my jaw shut. Why the hell had I said that?

"Oh."

I guessed that was her word of choice this evening...morning, whatever it was.

"Not everyone grows up with a picket fence and a dad who makes tea." Shit, I really needed to shut up.

Her lips parted, but before she could respond, the kettle whistled. She took it off the burner, then filled two mugs with steaming water, followed by a tea bag each. Then she carefully carried them to the island.

"I like mine with honey," she said. "Would you like to try it?" She looked at me without pity or judgment for the way I'd snapped at her. She seemed...patient.

"Sure. I mean, yes. Please. That would be great. It's in—"

She was already opening the correct cabinet. Not that I should have been surprised. The woman knew more about my life than I did most of the time, but I knew almost nothing about her personal life.

"Tell me about it…what it's like to grow up with a dad who makes tea." If nothing else, maybe she'd bore me into a state of sleep.

"It was…normal, I guess. But everyone thinks their childhood is normal when they're in it, right?" She took the tea bags out of the mugs.

"I guess." I hadn't. I'd known by the time I was seven that something was very fucked up in my corner of the world. "What are your parents like?"

She smiled as she stirred honey into both cups. "My parents are both teachers. Dad handles high school English and Mom tackles kindergarten. Everyone in our little town jokes that the kids start with Mom and end with Dad." She pushed my cup toward me, and I took it, exchanging it for the tepid water. "My older brother is a hell-raiser." She laughed softly, shaking her head.

"What?" The cup warmed my hands, and I gave it a second to cool off.

"I was just thinking that label's relative. Jeremiah has *nothing* on you. I bet you'd blow my little town apart at the seams." She grinned, then took a sip of her tea.

"And that would be a good thing?" I leaned forward.

"Since this is purely theoretical, it would be a fun thing to watch." She shrugged. "Small towns are a whole different world. You grew up in Tacoma, right?"

I drank my tea, ignoring her question. It wasn't half bad. "Tell me more about this whole different world."

She relaxed with each story she told, and in the half hour it took to drink that tea, Zoe Shannon transformed from an uptight, scheduled pain-in-the-ass, to a funny, intriguing woman I might have genuinely liked in another life.

A life where I wasn't a self-medicating asshole incapable of conquering my own selfishness. But I was said asshole, and guys like me didn't go for girls like her because those girls knew we weren't nearly good enough to bring home to dads who made tea.

And for a small sip of a second, I kind of wished I was the guy who was.

———

MY LEGS SCREAMED as Buckcherry pounded through my headphones.

I pushed my body past the point of exhaustion as my feet hammered out a steady rhythm on the treadmill

One good thing rehab had given me—besides a shot at sobriety—was a chance to get back into running again. My mind emptied when I ran, as if my feet literally carried me away from the shit that swirled inside my head. There was no past. No mistakes to atone for. No commitments I couldn't handle. No album I couldn't manage to write. There was no future beyond the next hundred yards, and my only competition was myself.

At mile number five, my body gave out.

I killed the treadmill, then stretched as I looked out over the bustling streets below congested with early-morning commuters. There was so much life out there. So many opportunities and ways to dull the ceaseless roaring in my head waited right outside my door.

Which was exactly why I was too chickenshit to leave my fucking building unless I was headed to work out.

"With the degree of struggle you're feeling, I really would recommend coming back to live at one of our sober living houses for a month or so. You never dealt with the root of this problem, and until you do, you can't really heal." That's what my therapist had said yesterday afternoon before I promptly switched off speakerphone when I'd walked into the living room and found

Zoe reading. Pacing during my therapy calls was going to get me into trouble, but at least Shannon was under an NDA.

What the fuck was I supposed to do? Crawl into one of those sober houses and hide? Cancel the tour dates? Fuck up Jonas and Quinn's lives more than I already had simply because I couldn't get my shit together?

I couldn't sleep, but I'd made my peace with that years ago —couldn't silence his voice in my head and couldn't black out to keep from hearing *hers*. But I also couldn't stay up here forever. Eventually, I was going to have to handle civilization.

Fuck, I wanted a drink. I wanted ten. I wanted to walk out of this building and straight into the bar across the street. It wasn't just the taste—oh no. I craved the oblivion. It was September already. I just needed another month, and it would all ease up. Just another month.

October was always easier.

But we had a show in two and a half weeks, and if I wasn't strong enough to leave this damned building, how was I going to make it through an entire show without giving in to the buffet of shit readily available at a festival?

A quick glance at my cell phone would tell me that everyone had the answer.

Quinn's text told me to come to Montana.

Jonas told me to come to Boston.

My producer told me to get my ass in the studio and write.

The only person not currently bossing my ass around like a child was the one woman I expected it from. Zoe might lecture me about my general assholery, but she let me take the lead when it came to what I needed.

I killed the Bluetooth and took out my earbuds when the song changed and "Sorry" filled the room through my phone's speaker.

"Hey, you done?" Zoe asked from the doorway of my home gym.

Speak of the devil.

"No, I'm still running." Sarcasm dripped from my voice as I turned to face her. "Obviously." Damn, she was fun to rile up. I hit pause on my phone, killing the music.

"I like that song."

"Most girls do. Pretty sappy, if you ask me."

She rolled her eyes. "It's a love letter. It's supposed to be sappy."

"It's a ridiculously public apology for how shitty it is to maintain a relationship in the music industry."

"Well, there's nothing more romantic than pouring your heart out in public, and if you don't get that, I can't help you."

I crossed my arms over my chest, and her eyes followed, raking down my naked torso. Her lips parted as her attention lingered on the ink stretching across my lower abs that read *Apathy is Death.* I personally liked the wings on my chest, but hey, if that was the one that did it for her, that was fine by me, because *holy shit,* she was looking. And not just looking in the clinical sense she usually did either.

There was heat in those green eyes.

My dick stirred. If she kept looking, it was going to get really fucking awkward around here. "I can get you a poster, if you want."

She startled, and her cheeks flushed a sexy shade of pink as she shook her head. "Sorry!" She squeezed her eyes shut.

Sexy shade of pink? Shit, I was seriously going to have to get some. I didn't care about the "don't replace one addiction with another" bullshit. Not when I was looking at Zoe-freak-ing-Shannon like she could be lunch.

"You look good," she blurted with a forced smile. "I mean, you put on, what…ten pounds in rehab?"

"Fifteen in the past two months." Turned out my body was down with the whole less-drugs-and-alcohol and more-food-and-exercise thing. I hadn't realized just how emaciated I'd become until I'd stepped on a scale. Weightlifting helped too.

"You look healthy," she gushed. "That's all I meant." She rocked back on her heels and clasped her hands in front of her navy-blue dress. "Healthy boy. Healthy, healthy, healthy."

I pressed my lips in a line to keep from laughing at how flustered she was. "Right, and now that we've settled that, what did you need?"

"Oh. Harvey called. He said you haven't returned his last two calls." She arched an eyebrow.

Uptight Zoe has returned.

"Funny, I don't have any voicemails from him." I shrugged.

"Because your voicemail is full." She crossed her arms. Too bad that dress's neckline wasn't just an inch lower. I would have killed to see just a little cleavage.

"Huh." Hell yes, it was full. If I wanted to talk to someone, I picked up.

"And he mentioned something about three or four texts?" She tilted her head and narrowed her eyes.

"I'll be sure to look." I wouldn't.

"You're such a liar." She blew out a frustrated breath. "Just tell me what you want me to say to him. How many songs have you started? How long do you think you'll need for three?"

"Zero, and I don't know."

"You're killing me, Nixon."

"There's nothing inside my head you'd want on the page. Not right now." Music had always been my outlet, my escape. It was where I channeled the emotions too messy to voice and too crippling to willingly recognize. But everything in my soul was too much right now, and I was too tight to let it free. It was like trying to force the Mississippi River through a keyhole, and I didn't have alcohol to ease the way.

She studied me carefully, and whatever she saw was enough to drain some of her tension. "Have you considered that writing about what you're going through might help? I heard what your therapist said—"

"Have you considered that I might not want the world to sing along to what I'm going through?" I challenged as the sweat chilled on my skin. "That maybe there are pieces of my pain you can't profit off?"

"Me?" She drew back like I'd hit her. "I would never—"

"Sure you would," I snapped. "You all do. You, Ben, Harvey, Ethan…everyone in this industry makes money when Jonas falls in love and Quinn goes back to the guy she left behind. Usually I'm cool with it. I've made a lot of damn money ripping my heart open and bleeding out for the audience. But this part of me isn't for sale." I marched toward her, but she didn't budge from the doorway. "Get out of my way."

"No." She raised her chin and stared me down.

"I'm sorry?" I had more than a foot on her, and she still looked undaunted.

"I said, no. I'm not moving. We're having a discussion." She shifted her weight, popping her hip like she was digging in for the fight. "You run away from everyone but me, Nixon Winters."

"What the hell do you want from me?" I snapped.

"Right now? I'd settle for you understanding one fact."

"And that would be?" I glared down at her.

"I don't give a shit if you give Harvey the song. If you need to write something to work through everything that's eating you from the inside, then go lock yourself in the studio, write it, then burn it for all I care." She looked up at me unflinchingly, with nothing but honesty radiating from her eyes.

"You're serious," I said softly.

"As a heart attack. I chose this business for the same reason you did—because I love music. I love the way it can change my emotions, and the way it can give voice to things I can't seem to say. I love when a song becomes the soundtrack to a moment in my life, and then hearing it takes me right back. I love the feeling that courses through my body when you're on stage, playing a solo that speaks through the music instead of the words. It skips right over my brain with a direct hit to my heart." She tapped right above her neckline.

My chest tightened—swelled—but I couldn't look away. Her emotional honesty was magnetic, humbling, and turned me on faster than any half-naked groupie in my dressing room ever could.

"So, don't you dare stand there and accuse me of wanting to profit off everything you're going through, when I only care about you surviving this. Don't you dare think, for one minute, that you love the music more than I do, just because I can't carry a tune. The only difference between you and me is that you were born with a once-in-a-generation talent to make music, and I was born with the brains to make sure that music gets heard."

Damn.

My gaze dropped to her lips. I wanted to back her against the wall and sink into her mouth to see if all that passion had an outlet. Hell, I wanted to *be* the outlet. My fingers curled at the idea of sinking them into her hair, and my pulse kicked up a notch like I'd started running again. There was a palpable hum of energy between us.

This was dangerous.

Sex was a need I fulfilled. It was an itch to scratch, a thirst to quench, or a way to pass the time while feeling really damned good. It was another source of the oblivion I was always chasing. But the person I was having it with never mattered.

I'd never wanted someone more than I wanted the act.

Until now.

"Do you understand?" she questioned, her eyes bright with purpose. God, they really were gorgeous.

"I understand."

"Good. Now go shower. You're all sweaty."

"You like it."

She scoffed and spun on her heels to stride down the hall, not swaying her hips like most women did around me, because she honestly didn't care if I found her attractive or not.

Which only served to make her more attractive.

Shit.

I headed straight for the shower. We had to get out of this apartment, and not just because I needed to know I could look at booze and not drink it. Sure, that was part of it. I couldn't be sure of my power to resist until I was tempted, right? The city was too much, and I knew it. We needed to get somewhere far enough from civilization to keep me from fucking up but close enough to build my resiliency.

Mostly, we had to get somewhere I could find enough space to kill whatever this…chemistry was between us. The close confines of the past two and a half weeks were going straight to my dick, and I didn't fuck the women on staff. I wasn't supposed to be fucking anyone right now, according to the rehab protocols. No new dependencies—including people.

The idea came as I was drying off after my shower.

It was perfect. More than enough room to get some distance but enough opportunity to ease me back into the real world…if that could be considered the real world. But it was better than hiding up here in the penthouse.

I made all the arrangements with a single phone call, then packed two suitcases…and one guitar—my first acoustic. Just in case.

After I carried it all downstairs, I walked out onto the deck to see Zoe pacing back and forth, actively arguing with someone on her phone. Her feet were bare.

"You can't rush it, and don't even start with me about deadlines. You can push it and get shit, or you can wait and get gold. Either way, if you don't ease up off his neck, you're going to suffocate him." She saw me and stilled. "They're the highest-grossing rock band in the world, and have been for the last two years, Harvey. Trust me, the anticipation of a new album is only going to work in their favor." She held my gaze as she battled with him.

Harvey. She was having it out with Harvey because I wouldn't pick up my phone. She was taking his hits for me. *Shit*, my chest was tight and heavy again. I didn't want to like her, and I definitely didn't want whatever this melty feeling was in the pit of my stomach.

"Go ahead and call Ben. He's going to say the same thing. You need to give Nixon some space, or I'm going to accidentally throw his phone in the dishwasher." She hung up.

My eyebrows rose. On a smoking-hot scale of one to ten, that was an eleven. Yeah, we had to go. Now. Right now.

"Pack your shit," I said.

Her jaw dropped. "Wait…what?"

"Pack. Your. Shit." A corner of my mouth lifted in an irrepressible smile.

"You're seriously going to fire me after I just went toe-to-toe with one of the best producers in the world for you?" Her voice pitched to a near shriek, but a gust of wind blew her hair across her face, and she started sputtering.

"Who said anything about you being fired?"

She swiped her hair to the side, revealing a pair of narrowed eyes.

"I'm over Seattle. I'm leaving, and you have to follow me wherever I go, right? Or things don't work out with whatever deal you have with Ben." Oh, this was fun.

"Right," she said slowly as her eyes narrowed.

"Good. Then get packed, Zoe Shannon, because you're taking me home." I grinned as I walked back into the apartment. "Not only that, but I've managed to make all the arrangements without you, and it only took eight minutes." I glanced at the clock on the wall. "The car will be here in half an hour to take us to the airport."

"We're going to Tacoma?" she called out as she came after me, her feet soft on the floor.

"Tacoma?" I turned back so abruptly she almost ran into me, but I caught her shoulders. They were small but strong, just like the rest of her. "We're not going to my hometown. We're going to *yours*."

Her face drained of color.

4

ZOE

HE WASN'T KIDDING. The entire flight and even part of the drive in from Gunnison, Colorado, I thought he'd start laughing that I fell for his horrid joke and demand to go back to Seattle.

But no, he was serious. It was now a little after five p.m., and we'd just passed the sign that read LEGACY, COLORADO, ALT. 9,689 FT. We were as proud of our altitude as we were of the mountains that made it possible. I took a deep breath and savored the slight burn in my lungs that came from the lack of oxygen. God, I'd missed home.

"You're going to have to tell me where to turn," he said from behind the wheel of the rental car—a black Range Rover that had magically been waiting at the airport. It was the first time I'd ever seen him drive himself...well, anywhere.

"I thought you said you booked a house?" Pure sugar saturated my tone.

"I know where we're staying. It's called the McClaren Ranch."

My eyes widened. The McClaren Ranch was one of the only estates that hadn't burned when a wildfire decimated our little town ten years ago. The place had to be a hundred years old, and it was *huge*.

"Well, are you going to say anything?" He glanced over at me.

I quickly jerked my gaze away. "Watch where you're going or you'll fall off the mountain."

"There are buildings on both sides of the street." He rolled his eyes.

"Whatever. And you don't have to turn to get to the McClaren place. You go straight up—"

"We're stopping at your parents." He braked for the only red light in town.

My stomach lurched.

"We're *what*?" This wasn't happening. This was all a really bad dream I'd wake up from, right? We'd still be in Seattle, and I would not be faced with introducing Nixon-freaking-Winters to my *mother*.

"I already called ahead, and they're at home." He grinned. "Told them I was delivering a package, but if you're not going to help, then I'll find it myself." He picked up his phone, flipped through his texts, and plugged something into the GPS.

Good God, the man was actually *excited*. "When did you have time to call my parents? How did you even get the number?"

He looked at me like I was an idiot. "Called Ben when you stopped into the bathroom at the airport. He gave me the number. I called your parents. It takes you a ridiculously long time to pee." The light turned green, and he drove on.

"You can't…" I sputtered as we passed The Chatterbox, my favorite diner, and came up on Sweet Cheeks, my favorite bakery. Everything here was my favorite. It was my home, and he was invading it with his…rock-starness.

"I can't what? This should be the turn, right?" He glanced at the GPS.

"You can't just barge into my private life without so much as asking!" Especially when certain ex-parts of my private life had very much mocked my career ambitions.

"That's fucking hilarious." He laughed, his shoulders shaking under his black T-shirt. The muscles of his forearms rippled beneath all that ink as he straightened the wheel. "You moved into *my house* without asking me. Isn't that my private life?"

He slowed, then stopped, allowing Mrs. Henderson to cross the road with her corgi.

"It's not the same," I hissed, fighting the urge to slump in my seat. The minute she spotted me, everyone within ten miles would know I was home. At least she favored the Christian station, so she wouldn't know I wasn't the hottest news in town —Nixon was.

I'd been gone eight years, and my only accomplishments were getting my ideas rejected by Ben and fetching his coffee. Eighteen-year-old me would have been horrified. According to past me, I was supposed to be scouting bands and cutting deals for the next big thing. Instead, I was Nixon Winters' live-in nanny. Disillusionment didn't begin to describe the soul-sucking grunt work that was the music industry, and I'd come into it with a college degree and a recommendation from one of Ben's closest friends, who'd happened to be my professor.

"Do they have a spa here or anything? Because you seriously need to unwind." He crept up Mulberry Avenue at a very respectable twenty-five miles per hour. At least I didn't have to worry about him terrorizing the general public with his driving skills.

"We have a hair salon that doubles as a mani-pedi place, but if you want a spa, you came to the wrong town. I'm sure we could tip her extra if you need a little waxing. Have to say, I kind of like the idea of you writhing in a little post-rip pain."

"And people think *I'm* a sadist. Sheesh." He turned onto Honeysuckle Lane, and my heart leaped. How long had it been since I'd been home? Christmas?

Admit it, you can't wait to see them.

"It's the white house with the green shutters," I said, pointing down the block.

Nixon pulled the SUV into the driveway, killed the engine, and peered up at my parents' house. It wasn't a four-million-dollar penthouse, but the three-bedroom craftsman was...everything. It was home.

"You grew up here?" he asked, his brow puckering as we got out of the car, then stood on the sidewalk that led to the front porch.

"Yep." I loved this place and everyone in it.

"But...it looks new. Everything around here looks new, actually." He glanced down the street.

"We had a fire about a decade ago." My heart clenched, just like it did every time I thought about it. "It took out the whole town. Mom and Dad rebuilt from the foundation up with the same floor plan. It's kind of creepy because it's the same...but it's not, which is awesome at the same time. My parents..." God, how did I explain my parents to Nixon?

He studied me quietly. "Look, I'm not a complete dick, and I know there's a line here. So, if you don't want to go inside, or if you want me to wait in the car while you do, I understand."

I blinked, but there was no teasing glint in his eyes. The guy was serious. And even if I was terrified of what this impromptu visit might do to my little town, I really, *really* wanted to see my family.

"You wanted to come, so now you're stuck. Let's go." I walked up the front steps, then paused. Was I really about to introduce Nixon to my mother and father?

He looked good. I wasn't lying earlier when I said he'd put on some healthy weight. His T-shirt was plain, so nothing to worry about there, and it wasn't like I could do anything about the sleeves of ink going up his arms. I wouldn't even if I could. They were part of what made him…him. When I got to his face, I found him watching me.

"Relax. Moms like me. I'm very popular in the forty to sixty demographic." He winked.

I ignored what that wink did to my stomach, rolled my eyes, then opened the screen door and knocked on the solid wood one. Giving my parents a heart attack by walking in wasn't on this afternoon's agenda. My heart pounded during the half minute or so it took for the door to open.

"Oh my *god*!" Mom's jaw dropped, and her arms opened.

"Hey, Mom!" I was immediately engulfed in her hug. She squeezed with the perfect amount of pressure and smelled like home.

"Thomas, Zoe's here!" she called as she yanked me back to arm's length for inspection. "You look wonderful!" Her mouth pursed in concern. "Have you been eating enough? It looks like you've lost a little weight."

"I'm fine," I assured her as I looked back over my shoulder for Nixon.

"Mom, this is Nixon. Nixon, this is my mom, Alice Shannon."

"It's nice to meet you, Mrs. Shannon." He gave her the public smile.

"Well, get on over here!" Mom stepped out onto the porch and hugged Nixon, pinning his arms against his sides.

His eyes flew wide and locked with mine. I flat-out laughed.

"This is just…wonderful!" Mom stepped back and gave Nixon the same inspection. "Well, aren't you handsome?" Mom looked back over her shoulder at me and raised her eyebrows.

"No, Mom—" I started.

"Did I hear you say something about— Zoe!" Dad exclaimed, barreling through the door and sweeping me into another hug. "Oh, Zoe." He sighed and rocked me slightly, resting his chin on my head. Dad had the kind of hugs that simultaneously made me feel protected and invincible.

This right here was worth it. No matter what Nixon saw while he was here, or who he managed to scandalize, this moment was worth it.

"How long are you here for?" he asked, pulling back and glancing between Nixon and me.

"Uh…I'm not sure, actually. Dad, this is Nixon. Nixon, this is my dad, Thomas Shannon." I repeated the introduction.

Dad's perceptive gaze narrowed on me slightly, but his smile was warm as he shook Nixon's hand. "Well, come on in."

I tried to see my house through Nixon's eyes. It was modest and clean, with a thick wooden bannister up the stairs at the entrance and dark hardwood floors. The furniture was traditional and the clutter scarce. The only pictures on the wall were the family photos Mom had either taken since the fire or had backed up online. Except that gem of me in the third grade with two missing teeth and unruly hair. That one had been in a fire safe with the rest of the school pictures, and hence survived.

Man, I wish that one had burned.

"You were a cute kid," Nixon noted as we passed it.

"Shut up," I muttered, leading him into the kitchen.

During the rebuild, Mom and Dad had made the kitchen open-concept, and the massive island that separated it from the living room was currently covered in dinner preparation.

"Jeremiah should be here any minute. You'll stay for dinner," Mom said. It was not a question. "We have more than enough."

"Of course," I responded, then motioned for Nixon to take a stool at the island.

"Is there anything I can do to help?" He sat, then shifted his hand from the counter to his lap and back again.

A corner of my mouth lifted. I'd never seen him in a situation where he wasn't a hundred percent sure of his footing.

Mom softened. "You just sit there and prepare to answer about fourteen million questions. Zoe, get the potato peeler."

"On it." Second drawer down and there it was.

The kitchen door opened and shut, bringing in the crisp fall breeze. Jeremiah's eyes bugged out when he saw me.

"Zoe!" He crossed the kitchen with my nephew in his arms, and I got double-hugged. "Levi, do you know who this is?"

"Aunt Zoe!" the three-year-old responded with a toothy grin.

"That's right!" I clapped. "Hi, Levi!" God, I'd missed his chubby cheeks.

"Guess those weekly FaceTime calls are paying off." Jeremiah smiled down at me.

"Nice beard." It was the same shade of red as our hair.

"Naomi likes it." He shrugged. "She's running late, but she's going to freak when she sees you." He let me go, then froze as he looked over my shoulder toward the island.

"Jeremiah, this is—"

"Holy shit, you're Nixon Winters!"

And so it begins.

"Holy shit!" Levi exclaimed, clapping his little hands.

"Levi!" Mom chided.

"Nixon!" I accused.

"I didn't even say it!" Nixon countered, putting his hands up.

"Bad influence," I muttered, then introduced Nixon to Jeremiah. My older brother had that starstruck look for all of thirty seconds before he let Levi down to go play in the living room.

"Okay, no offense, Zoe, but what the hell are you wearing?" Jeremiah asked.

"It's a dress. This is a work trip, and I'm working." I shot a look at Nixon, wondering if he'd put him up to it.

Nixon grinned and folded his arms across his chest. How was this even my life right now?

"She looks *lovely*." Mom glared at Jeremiah. "But, Zoe, you must be uncomfortable, and I wouldn't want you to get anything on it."

"I've been trying to get her out of it all day," Nixon agreed.

Every head snapped toward him, and my mouth fell open.

He read the temperature of the room in a heartbeat and grimaced. "Not that way. I swear. We are strictly professional."

Dad cleared his throat and stood across the island from Nixon.

"Well, that's nice. Zoe, why don't you run up to your room and change? You still have an entire dresser of clothes here," Mom suggested.

I nodded in agreement, and as I walked by the island, Nixon grabbed my wrist, his eyes flaring slightly. "I'll be right back," I assured him, leaning in to keep our conversation private.

"Your dad's about to grill me. I can tell," he whispered.

I gave his hand a little pat. "You've survived press conferences with major news outlets. I think you can handle my dad. Besides, you were the one who wanted to come here. Time to pay the piper." A flash of a smile later, I raced up to my room and got changed.

When I came back down, Dad was mid-interrogation, asking why Nixon felt the need to share his entire life on social media.

"It's not about how I feel," Nixon answered as he saw me. His shoulders dipped in relief, and then his eyes flared slightly as he looked me over. My jeans were old, worn, and hung a little lower on my hips than they had when I bought them years ago. I'd pushed the sleeves up on my fitted black shirt and unbuttoned the top two buttons over my gray cami. It was the most casually dressed I'd ever been around Nixon, which wasn't exactly helping me remember this was a business trip.

Nixon was not my friend and most certainly not my anything else.

"But you kids still broadcast your whole lives," Dad continued.

I took mercy on Nixon and explained that not only did he loathe every platform, he didn't even post on it himself, taking care to relate both the positives and negatives of social media and the importance of marketing. The conversation shifted to what I did for the band as we all chipped in to get dinner going, and by the time we were ready to sit down, Dad was almost finished grilling Nixon.

"And your family?" he asked.

I stopped scooping the potatoes into the bowl.

Nixon's jaw ticked once as he took the spatula from my hand and finished the job. "Not much to tell. Parents divorced when I was young. Dad got remarried. He died in a car accident a few years back."

That was the standard answer given in every media interview, and it stopped my father's inquisition as he gave his condolences.

"So, why exactly are you here?" Jeremiah asked again as he reached for the glasses in the cabinet. "Did you come in for the Fall Festival? Because it's this weekend. Wait, is Hush Note playing?"

"No, Hush Note is not playing at the Fall Festival." I shook my head at my brother. Until this morning, Nixon hadn't even known Legacy existed.

"Too bad, because that means we're stuck with—"

Thud.

Jeremiah winced, and Mom sent a sympathetic smile my way.

Guess *that* hadn't changed since I'd left.

"I thought Zoe needed a break." Nixon rolled right through the awkward pause. "So, I rented out the McClaren Ranch and brought her home for a little R and R."

"Together?" Jeremiah's eyebrows rose.

"She's on babysitting duty while I write a few songs for the next album." Nixon shrugged as he helped Mom carry dishes to the table. "We're kind of a package deal for the next few months."

That was me, all right. Glorified babysitter.

"And now we have our very own rock star here in Legacy. Surreal." Jeremiah shook his head as he opened the refrigerator. "Fat Tire, sweet! Dad, Nixon, you want a beer?"

"No!" I shouted.

"No, thank you," Nixon replied.

Everyone stilled.

"I'm driving, but thanks," Nixon said easily, but that smile was his fake, fan-and-media one.

"Okay, then," Jeremiah replied.

The door blew open and Naomi rushed in, still wearing her scrubs from the clinic. She gasped when she saw me, then let out a yelp when Nixon stepped into the kitchen. "Oh, sweet mother of all that is holy. Nixon Winters."

"Hi there." He turned that trademark smirk on her, and I almost pitied my sister-in-law. That thing was pretty damn lethal.

She stared at Nixon so hard she walked right into the kitchen island.

"Easy now." Jeremiah laughed. "She's got your picture taped up in her locker at work."

"I do *not*," she hissed at her husband.

"She does." Mom gave Naomi a pat on the shoulder as she passed by. "Now, Nixon dear, do me a favor and carry the mashed potatoes to the table."

"Yes, ma'am." Nixon looked at me with mischief in his eyes, then leaned in to whisper, "I'm popular with that demographic too."

"That's my demographic, idiot."

"I know." He grinned.

My cheeks flushed with heat.

"Just get the potatoes." I rolled my eyes, but I smiled the whole time.

THE MCCLAREN RANCH was some of the best acreage around Legacy and boasted a spectacular view of the mountains from the wraparound porch, where I currently sat. The cows were long gone, so ranch was a loose term, but the property still contained a massive house, a large barn, and a machine shed.

It had been on the market for years before Lisa McClaren gave up and turned it into a fully furnished vacation rental. She was one of the ones who never came back after the fire.

I tugged the edges of my blanket closer, then curled my feet under me and sipped my coffee in the rocking chair, looking out over the Rockies. God, I loved being home. There was a settling feeling to it, like my feet found rock after walking on the sand for far too long.

"Damn, it's cold!" Nixon exclaimed as he came around the corner in a short-sleeved shirt, rubbing his arms. His hair had that purposely messy look I knew took other guys product and effort to achieve, but not Nixon. The guy looked photo-ready straight out of bed.

Half his photo shoots *had* been straight out of bed, actually.

"September at nine thousand feet isn't exactly September in Seattle," I reminded him, ripping my eyes from the sight of his lean hips in those jeans. "We'll stop by the store and get you a jacket."

Jesus, I was no better than Naomi when I ogled him like that, and I couldn't even blame her. She did exactly what I wanted to and made no apology for it.

I could have looked at Nixon for days and never tired of it. Sure, I might have spontaneously combusted from sexual frustration, but it would have been worth it to finally see each of those tattoos up close and personal.

"Let's do that after breakfast," he noted. "What, no planner?"

"No plans." And, to be honest, I wasn't really sure what to do with myself.

"That's the best way to live. Relax a little. Sleep in. Binge-watch a TV series."

"I don't watch TV." There was always something that needed to be done, read, or planned.

"Well, you do now. If I have to stay sober, you have to learn how to relax, and this seems like a pretty good time to do it. This place is something else." He leaned against the porch railing. "I thought you said the entire town burned down, but this place feels pretty old."

"It's one of the only properties that didn't burn," I said, taking in the thick, heavy beams and stonework. "The fire, the flashfloods that followed that spring...nothing ever touched this place."

"Huh." He looked out over the pasture to the steep rise of the mountains. We'd gotten in late last night, so he'd missed the full effect. He studied it like an artist, his eyes skipping from detail to detail, lingering as though he needed to memorize it before moving on. "It's stunning."

"It's home," I stated simply.

He turned and looked at me with such awe on his face I couldn't help but smile, even as my heart stuttered. This wasn't the Nixon I was used to, the one I was well-armored against. I had no defenses when it came to this softer, more accessible side of him, and worse, I wanted to keep that look on his face. He needed this break way more than I did. I wanted to show him life outside the three-ring circus of the music industry, even though I knew it was my job to shove a guitar into his hands and point him to pen and paper.

"Show me," he said, his voice low and gravelly.

"What?" I stopped rocking. Had he read my mind?

"Show me your home." He shoved his hands into his pockets.

I worried my bottom lip with my teeth and mentally ran through the list of ways he could get into trouble here. There weren't actually that many, especially on a Saturday morning.

"Come on, Shannon. What could possibly go wrong?"

If he kept looking at me with that little smolder of his, a whole hell of a lot could go wrong, and we wouldn't even have to leave the ranch. Not that he had any interest in me. I wasn't that stupid. Nixon liked his girls tall, lean, and entanglement free, and I was none of those things. I also wasn't looking to throw my career and self-respect away in pursuit of a few orgasms.

"How do you feel about pancakes?" I asked slowly.

He grinned.

Forget Nixon, I was the one in trouble.

5

NIXON

"HERE YOU GO, SWEETIE," a waitress with pink hair said as she slid my orange juice across the counter.

"Thank you," I responded absentmindedly, staring at the orange flyer tacked to the diner's bulletin board, advertising this weekend's Fall Festival.

I'd never lived somewhere that threw a giant party at the changing of the seasons, or maybe I'd been too wrapped up in other things to notice...or too drunk to care. Either way, welcoming fall was definitely something I was down for. Fall was when everything got a little easier.

The longer I stayed sober, the more I realized how much I'd missed. There were countless nights I couldn't remember and blotches of time that were blurred or just flat in my memory.

Hell, every summer for the past nine years felt like a TV show I'd napped through, only picking up bits and pieces and wondering if any of it had really happened or if it was all in my head.

I fucking hated summer.

"Nix, will you teach me to play guitar?" Her sweet voice sliced through me without warning, paralyzing my muscles as I fought the memory's grip.

Her eyes had been big, blue, and so full of hope that what breath I could drag into my lungs felt like inhaling shards of glass.

"Sure, I will," I'd responded.

"Thank you!" She'd practically jumped up and down with excitement.

But I hadn't taught her.

I'd left a week later and then broke every promise I'd ever made to her.

"Nixon?"

"Nixon." Zoe's voice broke through, and I blinked rapidly. Her hands were warm on my face, and her eyes wide with concern. "Are you okay?"

"Yeah. Fine," I lied. I was never going to be *fine*. I sure as hell didn't deserve to be.

"Are you sure?" Her thumbs stroked over my cheeks.

I swallowed the rock in my throat and pulled away from her soothing touch. "Yeah."

She wasn't convinced, but she lowered her hands to her lap and pivoted on her stool to face the diner counter, watching me from the corner of her eye.

I shaped the brim of my ball cap and buried my face in the menu. *Drink. Erase it. Run as fast and as far as you can.*

Damn, would that instinct ever *not* blare at three hundred decibels in my head? Probably not. But I'd gone eight weeks without giving in, and I had no intention of today being the day, so I did what I had to and shoved it to the furthest corner of my mind.

After we consumed the largest stacks of pancakes known to man and I won the battle over the bill, Zoe led us out to Main

Street. This town wasn't just small, it was tiny, but I liked it. There were no blaring horns or screaming fans, so it was a hell of a lot calmer than Seattle, but quiet had always been my brain's worst enemy. It let the thoughts in, the memories, the never-ending abyss of guilt.

"You did it!" Zoe beamed at me as we walked toward the car, her cheeks pink from the chill.

"Ate breakfast? Is that the new standard? Or does the lack of oxygen up here make it especially challenging?" We passed the store where I'd purchased my jacket a couple hours earlier and crossed the street.

She rolled her eyes. "You ate an entire meal out in public, which is a first since you got back." She tilted her head at me. "But what happened in there?"

"What are you talking about?"

She gave me a hefty helping of side-eye. "You know what."

"I don't." *Nope. Not going there.*

"You zoned out." She halted, and I let out a long, frustrated sigh as I stopped a few feet ahead.

I counted to three, then I turned to face her. She didn't look quite so *Ms. Shannon* today. Maybe it was the jeans or the messy bun, or just being in her hometown, but she was missing that little layer of uptight, organized frost that usually served as a perfect barrier between us.

She arched an eyebrow.

"Let it go," I warned.

She tilted her head and debated.

"Let. It. Go." My voice dropped.

Her gaze cooled to glacial, and she walked right by me. *There she is.*

I cursed myself under my breath and followed her. Every person we passed waved or said hello to her by name, and she responded in kind. We'd never been somewhere together where she'd been the recognized one, which was yet another change of our dynamic. I kept my hat low and avoided eye contact. It was easy to escape recognition when no one expected you to show up in the middle of small-town Colorado.

The drive back to the ranch was tense and silent, but at least she wasn't pestering me for answers I wasn't going to give her. Even turning on the radio didn't help lift the mood. It only served to remind me I had three songs to write and nothing I wanted to write about.

We walked into the house, and I headed straight for the great room, stopping short when I realized I hadn't brought a single video game or mind-numbing distraction with me. *Shit.* There had to be a DVD player or something, because sitting around thinking was only going to get me into trouble.

"You know what I think?" Zoe snapped, ripping off her jacket. She threw it on the back of the couch, then stood between the arm and the wall, blocking my exit.

"No, but I'm pretty sure you're going to tell me." I left mine on to keep as many layers between us as possible, but I wasn't sure if it was for her protection or mine.

"I think your problem is that too many people have *let it go*." She folded her arms under the V-neck of her tee, and I yanked my eyes from the sight of her breasts rising toward her neckline, nearly swallowing my tongue.

I promise to never make fun of her dresses again if you just get a fucking grip. Holy shit, I was seriously bargaining with myself.

"I'm right, aren't I?" she asked.

"You have no idea what you're talking about." And yet she was perilously close to the mark.

"Oh, really? Because, from what I've seen, you go off the rails every summer, lose complete control by mid-July, then manage to somewhat pull your shit together in the fall. Except every year, it's a little worse, and you can't quite get back to center." There was zero condemnation in her voice, just pure, straight fact, and maybe a hint of compassion that only managed to irritate me even more.

"Your point is?" I glanced to both sides of her, looking for the best escape route.

"Have you ever talked to anyone about what happened?"

I stilled, yanking my gaze back to hers. *How the fuck did she know?* No one knew. Not even Jonas, Quinn—

"I mean, something *must* have happened for you to lose it every summer the way you do, right?" The skin between her eyes crinkled.

If I hadn't been consumed with relief, and she hadn't looked so damned concerned, I would have canned her ass.

No one was allowed to get that close. Ever. Not even the people I paid to smooth over the top layer of my psyche.

"When you space out like you did back in the diner, where do you go?" Her voice softened.

"Let it go." How many times did I have to say it? Fuck this, I was out of here. Even if I had to climb over the fucking couch, I wasn't staying in this room with her.

"Okay, well, if you're not talking to me, and you're not talking to your therapist from rehab"—she put her hands up —"remember, I was in the room when you took that call, then please tell me you're talking to *someone*." The plea in her eyes made my chest ache.

"Why do you care?" I snapped. But it was her job to care, wasn't it? It was always *someone's* job to care. Someone had to watch me, care for me, clean up whatever mess I'd made, and generally be the adult in my life. It was easy to care when you were being paid to.

"Why do I care?" She flinched. "Because I've watched you systematically self-destruct for the last four years, and I don't want to see it happen again! You're working so hard to stay clean, and if you don't talk about whatever drives this—whatever flips your switch every summer—you'll never be free of it."

Free of it? There was no getting *free* of it.

"What the hell makes you think I deserve to be free of it?" I asked, my voice dropping to a whisper. "You know jack and shit about me, Zoe. Not where it really matters."

She sucked in a breath like I'd wounded her, and I was halfway to her before I even realized I was moving. For every step I took forward, she moved back one, until she was flush against the exposed rock of the decorative wall.

"Fine, then talk to your therapist, a friend…anyone," she countered softly. "You've got to let someone in."

The hell I do.

My palms met the wall on either side of her head. "And you've got to stop thinking you can save me. Spoiler alert—you can't. Your only job here is to manage the fallout when I inevitably fuck up." The day, or night, would come eventually. It always did.

"I don't believe that." She lifted her chin, and the honesty in her eyes twisted my stomach. Only undamaged people were that certain of their ability to save the ruined ones.

"Then you're a fool." I leaned in close, and my gaze dropped to her lips. *Not for you, Nixon.* It didn't matter that she was kind, naïve, and unflinchingly sincere when it came to her emotions— I'd still end up shattering her because I was none of those things. "Stop trying to dig around in my head. You won't like what you find. And, quite frankly, all you'll accomplish is pissing me off." I pushed off the wall, grabbed my guitar from the stand next to the couch, and headed toward the porch before I did something we'd both regret.

———

"So, what exactly does someone do at a Fall Festival?" I asked as we walked under the giant orange banner that had been strung across Main Street between lampposts. The road had been shut down just past their lone stoplight, and though there were a few booths lining the sidewalks, the majority of the foot traffic was headed toward the park where Main Street ended.

"You play games, buy cakes, vote on the best-carved pumpkins," Zoe answered as she shoved her hands into the pockets of her jacket.

It was more than six words, which made it the longest sentence she'd spoken to me in the last five days, beating out the previous record of *what do you want for dinner?*

In that time, I'd managed to write two shitty choruses and an equally abysmal verse to three different, yet all horrible, songs. Having Zoe pissed at me wasn't doing much for my creative flow, but I couldn't blame my block on her either.

That was entirely on me.

I longed for vodka—not a shot, the whole fucking bottle. Instead of acting on it, I scanned over the gathering. "Is it always this packed?" The entire population of Legacy had to be here.

"Usually. You didn't have to come."

"I wanted to." I shrugged. Actually, I'd wanted to see her smile and hoped that getting her out around other people might accomplish that since she sure as hell wasn't smiling at me. It pricked my pride a little to admit, but now that we were here, I wasn't sure I wanted her smiling at anyone else, though, which put me in a predicament.

You have zero right to feel territorial.

Turned out, there was some truth behind the whole "you don't know what you've got until it's gone" thing, because I wanted the smiling, funny, softer Zoe back.

She heaped a dose of side-eye at me. "Right. Because this is your idea of fun. Spending a Friday night at a small-town festival, where the highlight of your evening will be spiced apple cider?"

I noticed the spark in her eyes and grinned. "I happen to like cider and small towns. This one is growing on me." Literally, if I didn't quit it with the pancakes. "It gives me insight into why you're so…" *Naïve. Good-hearted. Genuine.*

She arched a brow in obvious challenge.

"You." *Good one.*

She rolled her eyes as we crossed into the park. Booths lined various lantern-lit pathways that all led to a small amphitheater where a band was finishing up their set.

"You didn't mention live music." I tugged my skull cap down further over my ears to ward off the chill. It got cold here fast once the sun went down behind those mountains. A baseball cap would have been better to keep a little anonymity, but I wasn't willing to lose my ears over it. Besides, I wasn't exactly covering the tats that ran up the back of my neck, and those weren't common around here from what I'd seen.

She looked toward the stage and froze.

"Shannon?"

Nothing. She didn't even blink.

"Zoe."

Her head whipped toward mine.

"Who's the band?" I took my best guess at what was freaking her out.

"No one." She shook her head and marched off toward a tent marked Cakes and Stakes.

"Zoe!" I caught up to her quickly and lightly gripped her elbow. "What the hell?" I couldn't remember the last time I'd had to chase a woman anywhere, let alone one who worked for me. Then again, I also couldn't remember the last woman who'd been worth running after the way Zoe was.

"It's my ex," she muttered, so low I had to lean down and ask her to repeat the answer. "*My ex.*"

My brow knit as I glanced between the three scrawny figures on stage and Zoe. "Which one?" What kind of guy was her type? The drummer with the long hair? The bass guitarist with the goofy grin? The lead singer with the arrogant little smirk as he attempted—and failed—to tune his guitar?

"Does it matter?" she ground out between mashed teeth.

"The lead singer."

"You suck." She ripped her elbow out of my grasp and strode toward the tent.

"Really?" I took another look at the guy, then ran after Zoe. "That Joe Jonas-looking fucker is your ex? He can't even tune his guitar. And since when are you into musicians?" That would have been nice to know at *any point* in our history.

"Shut up and pick a cake," she snapped as we entered the massive tent and were met with rows upon rows of displayed cakes, with at least a couple dozen people snaking their way down the aisles.

"Zoe!" An older woman engulfed Zoe in a hug. "I heard you were back in town!"

"It's just for..." Zoe trailed off because she had no idea how long we'd be here.

Knowing me, I'd probably be bored with the place in a week or two—hopefully long enough to spit out enough songs to keep Harvey off my ass.

"We're just glad to have you!" The woman pulled back and sent me a curious smile.

"Mrs. Kendrick, this is Nixon Winters." Zoe's shoulders tensed.

"Nixon"—Mrs. Kendrick extended her hand, and I shook it —"I'm so glad our little Zoe brought you home for a nice long visit. We've all been worried that she'd work herself single, but you're just as cute as a button."

I grinned as Zoe turned at least five shades of pink.

"No, Mrs. Kendrick, we're not—"

Wrapping my arm around Zoe's small waist, I tugged her close. "We're not sure how long our visit will be, but I'm enjoying every minute of it." *Thoroughly.* She fit against me exactly how I'd pictured, tucking neatly under my arm.

Well. Damn.

Mrs. Kendrick gave us that gushy look I usually despised, and I smiled even bigger. "Well, you're a gorgeous couple. Now here, take a pen and get to bidding."

"Where is Mrs. Whitcomb's?" Zoe asked quietly.

Mrs. Kendrick glanced around as if Zoe'd asked for the nuclear launch codes. "Table six, and she's up a good fifty... maybe more by now." Her lips thinned.

"Gotcha."

We took off down the first aisle, and Mrs. Kendrick greeted the next group.

"I can't believe you." Zoe shoved me off. "Now people are going to think we're together."

"I quit giving a fuck what people thought about me a long time ago, Shannon. You should try it, sometime."

She shot me a glare, then bent over the table halfway down the aisle and scribbled on a sheet taped to the plastic table. *Fuck. Me.* Her ass really was a masterpiece, and those jeans cupped her curves so deliciously I nearly sank my teeth into my fist.

"Tell me about the douchey ex." *And tell me why he got to touch you.*

"Why do you care?" She slipped the paper into the desig-nated shoebox, then straightened.

"Because you lied."

"I what?"

I leaned down so our foreheads nearly touched. "You. Lied."

"I don't recall us ever having a discussion about the people we've slept with." She arched a brow but didn't go for the low blow of mentioning my list.

"I do recall you saying that you *don't do musicians*." What I couldn't recall was the number of women I'd slept with. My stomach rolled slightly, and for the first time, that fact…bothered me.

"I said I don't do *rock stars*, and, honey, Peter Whitcomb might have a nice set of hands, but he's no rock star."

Whitcomb. The same as the cake lady? How small was this town?

"According to *Rolling Stone*, I have magic hands." I wiggled my fingers and gave her my best smolder.

That did it. The ice thawed as she fought her smile and lost, finally shaking her head. "That might be the cheesiest thing you've ever said. Now pick a cake, and let's bid. It all goes to charity."

The band started outside the tent, and yep—that low E was flat as hell. I hoped, for Zoe's sake, he'd been better with his hands on her than on that poor guitar.

Then a cat died—or he started singing, it could have been either. The song changed around row two, but not for the better. I'd never thought much about the thickness of tent exteriors, but I would have paid to relocate to a concrete bunker.

She cringed as he missed a high note, playing it off as she examined a cake.

"This one?" I suggested around row three, motioning toward a chocolate one.

"Nope. That's Mrs. Armstrong's cake, and Mr. Armstrong always bids for hers. See? She's sitting right at fifty-five dollars, which is how many years they've been married."

"How would you know that?" I studied her soft expression, and that ache flared again, right in the middle of my chest.

"Small town," she answered with a shrug, like that explained it all.

Fifty-five years, and he still bids on her cakes. What was it like to love like that? To spend fifty-five years with one person and never grow bored? To let someone in so completely that they knew everything about you?

We rounded the row and started into the fourth aisle, then the
fifth.

"Tell me about the ex," I repeated, placing a bid on a random
cake that hadn't gotten any yet. When I lifted my head, I found
her watching me, like she was trying to figure me out.
"Come on."

"Nothing to say." We made it to table six. "We dated for a
couple of years, and then he decided Laura Fletcher looked
better in her cheerleading skirt than I did in jeans." She stopped
in front of a nice, chocolate, tiered, professional-looking cake.
"Would have been nice if he'd told me *before* prom, instead of
letting me find them in the back of his truck, but whatever. Water
under a bridge and all that."

My muscles locked. "He cheated on you *at* prom? Who the
fuck does that?"

"Shh!" Her eyes flew wide and darted toward the middle-
aged couple bidding behind us.

"Don't *shh* me. I'm not Douchebag Dan up there."

"Peter," she corrected me. "And I haven't talked to him since
we graduated. I'm sure he's grown up by now. Shit. Mrs. Whitcomb's cake is already up to two hundred and fifty. She's going
to win, just like she does every year." Her face fell, and she
walked off, her shoulders slumped.

Just chalk that up to yet another small-town thing I didn't
understand. At least in the music industry, no one got pissed
about easily bought cakes. But Whitcomb was the same last
name as her ex, right?

"If you want the cake, I'll buy you the cake." I followed Zoe
to the ninth table, where she stared at another tiered cake, but
this one was golden vanilla, edged with fudge and strawberries.
The sheet next to the cake read *A. Shannon.*

Alice Shannon. Zoe's Mom.

Okay, cakes were something I didn't get, but rivalry? I sure
as fuck understood that.

"Bid." I motioned to the sheet.

"I can't," she muttered. "Mom would kill me. She always says that if the last bid is by a Shannon, she won't speak to us until Christmas."

"Harsh."

"That's Mom for you." She blew her breath out slowly with a rumble through her lips. "There's always next year."

Someone called her name, and Zoe was engulfed in another group of hugs, this time from women her own age. Thank God she had friends—I'd been on the brink of actually worrying about her. I'd taken at least a dozen calls from Quinn and Jonas in the last few days, but Zoe's phone had been silent, other than her family and Ben. Even little Type A's like Zoe needed friends.

I was introduced, and a quick flare of their eyes told me they knew exactly who I was but neither of them mentioned it, which made me like them. Then they ignored me completely and asked Zoe about how she was, which made me like them even more.

"Go ahead," I urged her when they asked about cider. "I'll be there in a second."

Zoe's forehead crinkled. "Are you sure?"

"There's zero alcohol at this family-filled festival, and now that someone has finished strangling an animal on stage, I think I just might make it. You can trust me for five minutes. Go hang with your friends. I'm going to place a couple bids. I'm in the mood for Devil's food."

"Of course you are." Her eyes narrowed slightly, but she finally nodded. "It's the booth right next door. Just walk out of the tent and you can't miss it."

"I think I'll be able to find it," I drawled slowly.

She rolled her eyes but just about vibrated with excitement as she took off with her girlfriends.

I ignored the stares that followed me as I took myself back to the tables and three more bids. Once that was done, I bought a cupcake from the table of bake sale items and wandered out of the tent.

The high school choir sang from the stage as the crowd varied between watching the show and meandering toward other booths. Thank God, Zoe's ex wasn't the main event. Jesus, how long had it been since Hush Note had been anyone's opening act? Seven years? Eight? We'd been selling out stadiums for the past few years—long enough for me to take what had been years of struggle for granted.

I glanced over at Zoe with her friends, marveling at her carefree smile, and the ache in my chest sharpened. For all the time I'd spent with her, I didn't know her nearly as well as I should have.

I ripped my eyes away from Zoe, and then really took in the crowd. Couples swayed on the night-chilled grass as rambunctious toddlers ran happy circles around them. Guys in letterman jackets puffed out their chests for the girls they'd mucked up the courage to talk to. An older couple looked after their grandchildren. There were countless little moments happening in the park, and I tried to catalog them all, to file them away with the scent of apple cider and the taste of lemon cake and raspberry buttercream in my brain to be accessed when I was writing.

From the corner of my eye, I saw Zoe approach without her friends and started toward her, but her ex got there first. Whatever he'd said had her mouth hanging open, but she hadn't tossed either of those cups of cider in his face, so he had that going for him.

It was probably my duty to warn the guy her temper was pretty vicious.

"You didn't even make it to LA?" he scoffed, and my hackles rose.

Zoe winced. It was slight, but it was there.

I stilled. This fucker wasn't allowed to make her flinch like that.

"Nope. The management firm I work for has a branch in Seattle, so I stayed there," she said calmly, keeping her cool just like she always did.

"And how many bands do you manage, now? Let me guess —none." He smirked, pointedly looking at her left hand. "And no husband either. So, no career, no family. No wonder you avoid the shop every time you're home. I wouldn't want to see me either. I told you you'd fail."

I fucking lost it.

6

ZOE

GUESS PETER HADN'T GROWN up after all. He looked exactly the same—dark hair, hazel eyes, slightly crooked nose. The same but tired, and about thirty pounds on the Dad-bod side. At one time, my world had revolved around this guy, and now I wasn't even attracted to him.

I was, however, completely mortified by his on-point assessment of my life.

"The fact that I don't eat ice cream when I'm in town has nothing to with you," I assured him, my hands clenching the no-longer-steaming cups of apple cider. It felt like half the town was watching our little reunion.

"Hey, baby."

Oh God, no.

I turned slightly toward Nixon's voice and found him smiling down at me. Great, now he'd have more than enough ammunition for the next six months of his let's-piss-Zoe-off game. Wait. Did he just call me *baby*?

Before I could form a phrase, his hand splayed possessively over my hip, and he tugged me against him, the fingers of his other hand tunneling through my hair. It was only sheer dumb luck that kept me from spilling the cider.

What the—

He kissed me.

Nixon Winters was *kissing* me with those impossibly soft lips. It was wrong—I knew that somewhere—but it felt so deliciously good I couldn't bring myself to care.

He swiped his tongue across my lower lip, and I gasped.

He took complete control, sliding into my mouth like he already owned it, laying claim to every line and curve with nimble strokes and swirls of his tongue. *Holy shit,* he kissed like he played guitar—like nothing else mattered on the planet, and in that moment, nothing else *did.* He wiped away the rest of the world and altered the universe so it centered around us.

It blew every kiss I'd ever had out of the water, and I surrendered to it, kissing him back, chasing the taste of lemons and raspberry that clung to his lips. His grip tightened, pulling me closer, angling my head so he could take me deeper, then groaning softly when I flicked my tongue against the roof of his mouth. Then he sucked my tongue all the way in, and I melted.

I wanted to rake my hands through his hair, to tug on the strands and hold him prisoner so I could live in this one moment where he desired me. My hands ached to slide my fingers under his jacket and shirt to trace the lines of his abs, and I wasn't going to stop where his jeans began. Longing filled me, demanding to touch, to taste, to feel every single part of Nixon, but my hands were already full for a reason I couldn't seem to remember.

"Zoe," he growled against my mouth.

My knees weakened, my entire body humming with energy, and his grip shifted to my ass, gently lifting me from my feet with one arm, but it felt more supportive than passionate—as if he'd recognized exactly what he'd done to me. A soft whimper escaped my lips as I felt him hardening against my stomach from what I'd done to *him.*

He slowed and drew my lower lip between his teeth, gently raking the flesh before letting it slip free, ending the kiss with his mouth but somehow continuing it with his eyes as he looked down at me.

"Sorry, I couldn't wait another second." His voice was low and rough as his gaze darted to my lips again, like he was already planning a return trip.

"I'm glad you didn't." I meant it.

He slowly steadied me on my feet, and I blinked as the rest of the world came into focus. *Oh God.* Nixon had just kissed me in front of the entire town, and I'd liked it. "Liked" wasn't even the right word. I'd been consumed by it —by him.

What was he thinking?

Scratch that. What was *I* thinking? I was supposed to be keeping him sober, not kissing him, let alone jumping him in the park.

And *what* was that sound?

I stepped away from Nixon, but he simply moved to my side, keeping his hand at my waist as the other adjusted the angle of the cup I was holding—and spilling, hence the sound. I'd sloshed out at least half of our cider onto the grass.

"This one's yours," I muttered.

"Thanks, Zo." He pressed a kiss to my temple and took the cup from my hand. "Who's your friend?"

My face whipped forward.

Peter stood in front of us with his mouth gaping open, and it clicked. The kiss. The *baby.* The adoring look. It was all for Peter's sake. How much of our conversation had Nixon heard? Was I supposed to be thankful for Nixon's intervention or pissed it hadn't been real? Because I was both.

"Peter Whitcomb." He stuck his hand out in a rush. "You're not who I think you are...are you?"

"Peter." Nixon shifted his cup and shook Peter's hand before reclaiming my waist. "Depends on who you think I am."

Peter's gaze shifted between Nixon and me a few times, his eyes narrowing. "You're Nixon Winters."

"Yes." Nixon offered him the media smile and tugged me closer to his side.

"And you're with..." Peter looked outright befuddled as he stared at me.

My spine stiffened. *Oh, fuck it.*

I settled against Nixon, sliding my hand under his jacket and up his back as I sipped my cider, letting Peter draw his own conclusion.

"Well...yeah." Nixon raised his eyebrows. "Why else would I be here?"

Peter's eyes widened to nearly impossible proportions.

"There you are!" Laura appeared from the crowd, grabbing Peter's arm and hugging it. "You sounded great, sweetie." She flashed a fake smile at me and tilted her head. "Hey, Zoe... nice to see you."

"Laura." It was most definitely *not* nice to see her, but it was a far cry from the agony I'd felt when I'd bumped into her during a visit my freshman year. Sometimes small towns were just too small. "How's the family?"

Nixon's gaze darted to mine, darkening with question as he squeezed my waist once.

I nodded slightly, lifting my cup.

"We have two kids now. Girls. You know, married life." She shrugged and sang it in that completely passive aggressive tone she'd apparently kept since high school.

"She would if she'd ever agree to marry me," Nixon said with a sigh. "I swear I ask her at least once a week, but she keeps holding out."

I nearly spit out my cider.

Nixon patted my back. "You okay, baby?"

I nodded, barely managing to swallow.

"Sweetie, Nixon here is the lead guitarist for Hush Note," Peter told his wife.

She looked Nixon up and down like he wasn't wearing any clothes, and my blood pressure spiked. "I knew I recognized you from somewhere. It's harder with that hat on."

"Did you hear me play?" Peter blurted, his eyes lighting up.

"I did." Nixon nodded slowly, then finished off his cider.

"And?" Peter prodded.

My hand tensed on Nixon's back, and my stomach dropped. He'd never been known for candy-coating his opinion on anything, especially music.

"And...it was...something," he offered. "Babe, why don't we go—"

"You two are impossible to find," Jeremiah announced as he came up on my left. "Which is ironic since you'd think Nixon would stand out like a sore thumb." He glanced between the four of us but didn't say a word about the way Nixon and I stood wrapped around each other. Instead, he leveled a flat stare on Peter.

If this had been a board game, we would have reached a whole other level of awkward.

"Hey, Laura." A brunette I had a vague memory of waved from about ten feet away. "We need you up front to do the donations update."

"Of course." She gave us all a beaming smile, ending with Nixon. "Gotta run."

She hurried off, leaving me standing with someone I loved, someone I used to love, and someone who was pretending to love me.

"This is why I don't go to reunions," I whispered at Nixon in a hiss.

"Imagine how much fun I would be at your reunion," he whispered back, adding a wink.

"Right, so if you ever need a backup guitarist—" Peter started.

Kill me now.

"He's sure as hell not calling you." Jeremiah laughed.

"Why? Because his girlfriend makes the decisions for the band?" Peter snapped back, rolling his eyes.

"Actually, she does," Nixon stated, like it was an assessment of the weather.

My cheeks heated as everyone's focus shifted to me.

"She's the assistant manager," Nixon added with a shrug.

I was the assistant *to* the manager, but right now didn't seem like the best time to argue semantics. "Let's go find my parents," I said softly to Nixon.

"Bullshit." Peter's voice held every note of disbelief possible to fit in two syllables.

"She is," Nixon argued without raising his tone.

"You work for Hush Note?" Peter shook his head. "No way."

"It's not like it's a secret." My unflinching eyes met Peter's wide ones.

"We keep it quiet," Jeremiah admitted to me. "Figure if you wanted anyone to know, you'd post it on the social media you don't have."

"Wait, you don't have social media?" Nixon's mouth dropped.

"Not the time." I lifted my brows.

"Just wait until we have our next argument about the require-ment that *I* have one." The corner of his lips lifted in a smirk.

"It's not remotely the same, and you know it." The only people who wanted to keep up on my life were in my family.

"It's not?"

"It's not," I confirmed. "I'd have all of six followers, and all of them live right here in Legacy. Besides, I'm too busy making sure someone else's social media is well-managed and just a little less colorful than his real life."

"I'd follow you." He leaned down slightly, wicked delight dancing through his brown eyes. "Twitter. Instagram. Even Facebook. I'd love to know what your Hogwarts House and Disney Princess mash-up quiz says."

I scoffed but couldn't halt the smile spreading across my face. "Guess you'll never know."

He flicked his tongue over his lower lip and studied me. "The first is easy. You're a Ravenclaw with that incredibly sexy brain of yours. And your hair is all Ariel, but you spend your days trapped with a beast, so I might have to go with Belle."

"You're ridiculous." I tilted my face up toward his.

"I'm right." He lowered his just a fraction, his attention shifting to my mouth.

"Now it makes sense," Peter said, popping the little bubble Nixon and I had found ourselves in again.

"What does?" Jeremiah asked.

"Is he how you got the job?" Peter challenged, nodding toward Nixon.

"No." Nausea washed over me.

Nixon's muscles turned to stone under my fingertips, and his weight shifted, reminding me of a jungle cat preparing to strike.

"Yeah, okay. You've been out of college, what? Four years?" Peter smirked, which was oddly disgusting considering how sexy the same expression was on Nixon's face.

"You'd better not be implying what I think you are," Jeremiah growled.

"And all four years she's worked for us." Nixon's hand flexed at my waist. I locked my elbow over his fingers like that would provide some modicum of barrier to any impending explosion. There were hundreds of cell phones in this crowd. "I'm going to say this once. If you're implying that she got to where she is by sleeping with me, let me assure you, that's not the case. I met her *after* she was hired, and I didn't have the balls to make a move on her until recently because, as you can see, Zoe is clearly out of my league."

Peter swallowed.

The nausea evaporated, but my chest swelled at Nixon's words, even if they were only for Peter's benefit.

The microphone shrieked into the speakers, causing a crowd-wide cringe.

"Oh, sorry about that!" Laura apologized from the stage of the amphitheater. "Hi, everyone! I'm Laura Whitcomb, but you already knew that." She flashed a smile, and the crowd chuckled.

"You're way hotter," Nixon whispered in my ear.

"Stop," I whispered back.

"Thank you all for coming out for the seventy-ninth annual Fall Festival!" She clapped, and the crowd followed suit. "Now, there's two hours left to get your cake bids in, and the Legacy Fire Department has assured me they have more hot dogs on the way, but I just wanted to tell you we've already doubled last year's donations!"

This time, I joined in with the applause. There were so many good causes being represented tonight.

"We don't have any more entertainment scheduled for tonight before the auction results, but I happen to know that Nixon Winters of Hush Note is in the crowd. Isn't that amazing?"

Cheers sounded all around us.

"Oh shit," I whispered, my shoulders deflating. "Nixon, I'm so sorry."

A muscle in his jaw ticked. Nixon was normally cool with being publicly outed as long as it was on his terms, but these weren't his terms, and this situation was far from normal.

"What do you say we ask him to play something just for us?" Laura lifted her hands.

The cheers around us only intensified.

"She didn't," I hissed. I couldn't even remember the last time Nixon had performed sober…or solo. I turned to Nixon. "I will take care of this. Stay with Jeremiah."

Without waiting for his answer, I stepped out of his arms and slid through the crowd. The chill bit at me without Nixon's warmth, but my anger was hot enough to burn the hair right off Laura's head.

I marched up the steps at the side of the stage and crooked my finger at her.

"Oh! Zoe Shannon is here to give us his answer!" She abandoned the mic and walked toward me with a self-satisfied little smile I wanted to swipe right off her face. "Well?"

"You can go fuck yourself," I said with a smile of my own.

Laura blinked at me. "What?"

"You heard what I said. You didn't even ask him, and you think he's going to, what? Pull a guitar out of thin air and perform because you said so?"

"He can play Peter's guitar," she answered with a shrug. "And come on. It would make tonight unforgettable."

My eyes narrowed. "Because you're chairing the festival committee."

"Co-chair with Peter's mom. So what? You brought a rock star home." She lifted her eyebrows.

"The answer is no. I understand that you're not familiar with the word, so listen again. *No.* And I'm not even going to put him in the position of saying it. I'm saying it for him." With every scenario I'd run through regarding Nixon finding himself in the spotlight in my tiny town, I'd never expected the actual spotlight.

"Are you serious?" Laura challenged.

"As a heart—"

"Shannon." His voice hit me straight in the heart. We were back to the last name, putting us firmly on professional footing. I'd failed him.

I turned to find Nixon standing two steps below me, making us eye level. My family waited right behind him. "I told her no."

"I heard." His jaw clenched.

"I'm so sorry," I whispered.

He softened with a sigh. "There's no reason for you to be. I dragged you here, remember?"

"Yes," I admitted. "But that doesn't mean you have to play."

"But we'd love it!" Laura added, popping up behind me. "I mean, if Zoe won't *let* you, the town will understand, but no one like you has ever been here—"

"Shut up, Laura," I snapped over my shoulder.

Nixon laughed. "Look who's losing her temper now."

"If she thinks you're going to fall for such blatant manipulation, she obviously doesn't know you. Which she doesn't." I bit that last part back at her.

She backed away, her palms up slightly.

"I wouldn't do it for her, anyway." His gaze intensified, turning molten. "But I'll do it for you."

I felt my defenses melt like an ice cube dropped into warm water. "Nixon," I whispered.

"It's okay. You'll never hear the end of it when you come home, and that's not fair to you." He unzipped his jacket, and I moved down a step, holding it closed.

"It's not fair to you either. You don't have Quinn or Jonas or your guitar…"

Or the alcohol.

"I'll be fine. I *am* fine. Let me do this for you. Consider it my penance for barging into your private life." A corner of his lips lifted, and his gaze turned to steel.

I knew that look. He'd made his decision. With a nod, I stepped back, helping him with his jacket. By the time he removed the skull cap and ruffled his hair, he wasn't the Nixon I'd spent the last two weeks with.

He was the rock star.

I handed his things to Jeremiah and turned to see Laura pick up Peter's guitar from the side of the stage and offer it to Nixon.

He looked straight at me.

Right.

"Thank you," I said to her, taking the guitar from her hands and giving it to Nixon, cutting her off completely.

"Let me know if you need anything!" she called over my shoulder, but Nixon was already busy tuning the guitar.

"You good?" I asked over my shoulder, unwilling to turn my back on Laura.

"I'm good." Nixon had the strap over his shoulder and was plugging the aux cord into the guitar.

"Sorry, he doesn't speak to venue staff." I offered her a professional smile, then walked off the stage to stand at the edge of the front row with my family.

"Did she really put him on the spot like that?" Mom asked, her brow puckered with worry.

"She did," I answered as Nixon took the microphone.

"Your wife is a piece of work," Mom said to Peter, who'd moved to stand at my right.

"Why? I'm sure he gets asked all the time," Peter remarked, crossing his arms.

My breath caught at the sight of Nixon up there. He didn't just take a stage, he devoured it with the kind of presence only he had. Quinn was the beat of a show, she drove it forward. Jonas brought the heart. Nixon...he was the energy, the palpable hum of excitement. It seemed to emanate from him like a magnetic field, drawing everyone a little closer.

That wicked smile of his broke across his face as he stepped into the spotlight, and the crowd cheered. It was the smallest crowd he'd played to in years, and yet none of them knew how momentous this was. They were the first he'd gotten in front of since rehab.

"Hi there." He pushed up the sleeves of his Henley, revealing the tattoos running down his arms.

Another cheer sounded.

"So usually, I have a couple other people up here with me, but it's just me tonight." He turned toward me, his gaze catching Peter's. "Peter, I hope you don't mind that your wife offered up your guitar."

"It's fine with me!" Peter called back.

The crowd laughed.

"It's in better hands," I muttered.

Mom pinned me with a glare.

Dad laughed.

"Quinn and Jonas—they're the other two-thirds of Hush Note, for those of you who don't know who I am or why someone put a guitar in my hands—we always talk about doing a concert series in smaller, more intimate venues, but I never considered branching out on a solo tour."

I held my breath, thinking of every song in his arsenal he could whip out right now.

His gaze locked onto mine. "But for Zoe, I'll make an exception. Just for the next three minutes and seventeen seconds."

Another murmur of laughter rolled through the crowd, but still, he looked right at me.

"I think there's something to be said for Zoe Shannon—"

My stomach pitched as the crowd cheered. They didn't know him like I did—know he could go either way—sweet or sarcastic—in this moment.

"Something to be said for the hearts who dream big. You see, a wise woman once said that it takes two kinds of people in the industry to bring the music to life. Those with the talent to make it, and those with the brains to make sure that music gets heard. I'll amend that wise statement to add, it takes talent, brains, and a nearly obsessive level of drive to get the music heard, and Zoe has all three. Tonight is a perfect example, since I wouldn't be up on this stage if she wasn't involved in Hush Note."

Another round of cheers rose from my little town. As backward as his reasoning was for being here, that was the truth. There was a bona fide rock star on my little town's stage because I'd worked my ass off to get and stay where I was.

He grinned, and, God help me, my heart jolted.

Don't fall. Don't fall. Don't fall.

"So tonight, this one is for you, Zoe." He winked, then finger-picked the opening chord to "Courage of Fools," a widely overlooked song off their first album.

They hadn't released it as a single. Hadn't made a video or promoted it. In fact, it had barely made the album, according to the people who had been there, but it was my favorite.

And Nixon had written it.

Usually, it was sung a key lower, in Jonas's register, but tonight, Nixon played it just as he'd written it—for his voice.

My lips parted as he started to sing. I was familiar enough with his voice to pick it out of a crowd—he always sang backup for Jonas, and even took lead on a song or two, but never this one. Never this way.

He'd slowed the usually upbeat melody, turning it into a poignant ballad about falling in love with someone you knew you'd never keep but couldn't help but fight for anyway.

It was the ultimate song for the dreamers, and I was probably the only person in the audience who knew it hadn't been written for a woman but for the music industry.

For what he'd hoped it would be when they signed their first contract.

And as he sang the last line, I felt it in every beat of my heart.

He picked out the last notes, and the crowd roared in applause—if a crowd this small was capable of roaring.

From the corner of my eye, I saw Peter clapping, and it hit

me. I'd been waiting to feel accomplished—to feel like I made it so I could prove him wrong—but I already had.

"I graduated top of my class," I said, getting his attention.

"What?" He gave me that same dismissive look he always had, but this time I didn't try to make myself more interesting to keep his attention, like I had all through high school.

"I graduated top of my class, which earned me an interview at Berkshire Management. My boss took me on with one caveat —that I follow through on my plans for law school on my own time, and I did. I specialize in entertainment law and passed the bar two months ago, not just in Washington but in California too."

Peter blinked, his brow furrowing.

"I love my life, and I have nothing to prove to you." I turned my attention to Nixon and met him as he came off stage, slipping the guitar strap over his head. "Amazing," I told him.

"A little bird told me you liked that song." The smile he gave me turned my insides to a puddle of mush.

"That was great!" Peter said, stepping forward to take his guitar.

"Tuned her up for you. Thanks for letting me borrow her." He handed the guitar over.

"That E is stubborn," Peter grumbled.

"Not when you warm her up right." Nixon lifted a brow.

Peter paled.

"And we're leaving!" I announced, taking Nixon's hand and pulling him away.

"Not yet," he protested with a glimmer in his eyes. "I bought cakes."

I rolled my eyes. "You *bid* on cakes. It's impossible to buy them outright."

"You'll see." He swiped his tongue over his lower lip, and I fought the urge to taste it myself. That kiss hadn't been the real thing. It had been a calculated maneuver on his part to save me from myself.

An hour and a half later, bundled up against the cold, my mother's hand flew to her mouth as the highest cake bid was announced.

Nixon had bid ten thousand dollars for Mom's cake.

My face slackened as I stared at him, feeling another crack in my defenses cleave into a canyon.

"Suck it, Mrs. Whitcomb," he muttered with a smirk, right before my mother hugged him, then lectured him, then hugged him again.

I knew this side of Nixon wouldn't stay at the surface for long, that it was only visible because he was fresh out of rehab. Because he was sober. Because there weren't paparazzi and models and half-naked groupies in his dressing room. I knew it was temporary, but instead of scaring me, it only made me feel like this glimpse of what he could be was private…precious.

And God help me, I wanted it to be permanent.

I wanted him to be real.

7

NIXON

"What the hell is wrong with you?" I muttered, striking through the last two chord progressions I'd written and ripping the page from the notebook. There was nothing remarkable about them, which meant they landed in the heap of similarly crumpled papers in the trash can at my feet.

I set the pencil down on the table, then strummed an A minor seven, bringing it to an E as I looked out the massive window that showcased the landscape of the Rockies. I couldn't imagine a more picturesque setting to write a song. The skies were bluer than anywhere I'd ever been, and the mountains were painted in gold with autumn aspen leaves. This place was enough to inspire symphonies, and yet here I was, struggling to get out a few simple songs.

Another breathtaking view walked into my line of sight, and my heartbeat kicked up a notch. Zoe set a piece of chocolate cake down next to me, offered me a ghost of a smile, and retreated toward the kitchen. She knew the cardinal rule of my writing time: never talk to me while writing.

To my unexplainable disappointment, she honored it, but then again, she always followed the rules.

My eyes followed the curve of her ass as she walked away.

Rules had always been more like guidelines to me.

I'd kissed her yesterday. It wasn't something I'd planned, but I couldn't bring myself to regret it either. Fuck, she'd tasted good —like cider but sweeter—and I'd fallen into her like an all-night bender, with complete abandon and zero thoughts to the consequences.

My fingers moved over the strings as I replayed that kiss in my head. The shock that had been obvious in the set of her lips had evaporated as she'd kissed me back, and our chemistry... I'd never felt anything that intense from something so innocent in my life.

I wanted to feel it again.

My hands moved, physically manifesting the melody that drifted through my mind. The music came first—it always did. The lyrics would follow, putting words to the emotion, but without the music they were nothing, just pretty poetry. It was the notes, the lows that swelled in tone and then pitch that brought the listener to their feet...or their knees, all depending on my mood.

I scribbled down the chord progression and tablature, then tinkered with it a bit as my stomach grumbled. Right, I'd skipped lunch.

Which was probably why Zoe had brought me cake.

I set my guitar down on her padded stand, then dug into the cake. Zoe's mom was one hell of a baker. The chocolate melted against my tongue, and before I forked in a second bite, I was on the hunt for milk.

I had the refrigerator door open when Zoe walked in, and I forgot all about what I was looking for.

"Hey," she said, setting an empty glass on the counter. "Everything going okay in there?"

"Yeah," I answered, shutting the stainless-steel door.

We stared at each other across the expanse of the island, and the air between us shifted, growing thicker with every second we held the contact. She was so damned beautiful. So kissable. So beyond my reach for so many different reasons I couldn't even start to number them.

Staff. She's on the staff. I repeated the mantra three times, trying to remember why it was I couldn't act on my craving for her.

"So…" She tilted her head.

"So." We'd danced around each other all morning, but there was no avoiding the impending conversation. I opened my mouth, then shut it. This was supposed to be easy, right? Then why was it so hard to say the words—to cut myself off from something I hadn't even realized I wanted, but now…

"So, I think it goes without saying that what happened last night can't happen again," she stated, like she was going over today's agenda.

"Right," I said slowly.

"I mean, it was just for Peter's sake, anyway." She tucked her hair behind her ears.

"Right," I repeated. That's how it had started, but how it had finished was something entirely different, and we both knew it… at least, I thought we both had.

"And it's not like there's any chance that we would actually…" She lifted her eyebrows.

"Right." Why the fuck did I say that? I didn't even know what she was going to finish that sentence with, and I'd agreed?

It's for the best. Let it go. That was the mature response.

"So, we're okay?" She tugged her lower lip between her teeth.

"Right." I nodded. No wonder I couldn't write a song. I had a one-word vocabulary at the moment.

"Good talk." She gave me a thumbs-up but stopped short of rolling her eyes at me.

"It's fine. We're fine. It was just a kiss." I gripped the edge of the counter.

"Absolutely," she agreed. "It's not like we slept together." She cringed. "Not that we would…or that you'd even be interested. I know I'm not—" She slammed her eyes shut, pressed her lips into a tight line, and rubbed her forehead. "I'm just going to stop talking."

Interested? That word didn't begin to cover the fantasies I'd had about her, but saying that was going to get us both into a shit ton of trouble, so I kept my mouth shut, exercising some of that self-control my therapist was always harping on me about.

"Let's just forget it happened." She sighed.

"Okay." There was exactly zero chance of that happening. None.

Her eyes widened for a flash, but she quickly shook her head and straightened her spine. "Fine. Look, the San Francisco show is next week, and I just need to know where we're going to be."

"In San Francisco." The thought of it being this awkward between us for the remainder of our time together was enough to have me reaching for a glass. *Milk*, I remembered. I'd come in for milk.

"No shit," she retorted. "I'm asking where I need to make travel arrangements from. Are we still going to be here?" She tucked her hair behind her ears again, even though it hadn't fallen forward.

I bet that hair would feel like silk sliding over my stomach.

"I booked the ranch out through February," I said as I poured myself a glass of milk. I'd have to cut the dairy in the next few days for the show—it always clogged up my voice.

"Are you serious?"

"Yep." I put the milk away and turned to face Zoe, who looked like I'd just told her aliens were landing in the back-yard. "I need to get these songs written, and I like it here. So far, I'd say ninety-eight percent of the population is pretty great. There are no fans at my door, no groupies pouring tequila onto their breasts and declaring 'body shots,' and no party invitations that I have to come up with excuses to turn down. It's pretty much sober-living heaven since I don't even know where the liquor store is." Not that I couldn't look it up on my phone.

"Ninety-eight percent?" she challenged, lifting an eyebrow.

"I'd say I've probably met about a hundred people between the diner, the grocery store, shopping, and the Fall Festival." I shrugged. "So, there's just your douchebag ex and his socially obsessed wife, who, I might add, was the *only* person in this entire town to post a video online of me singing last night." The fact that it was only one person posting blew me away. If I'd pulled that shit in Seattle, it would have been caught and shared by at least half that audience.

Just another reason I liked it here.

She cringed. "I was hoping you might not see that."

"At least I look good." A smirk lifted my lips.

"And sound good," she noted with a little smile. "In all the years I've worked for the band, I've never heard you play an acoustic set, let alone an acoustic guitar, and yet that's the only one you brought with us." She walked past me, opening the fridge and taking out the apple juice to refill her own glass.

"We've never been an acoustic set band." It was always something I'd wanted to try but had never brought up.

"Doesn't mean you can't be." She lifted the glass to her lips and drank. "The video is getting around. I might even call it viral."

"Is it?" I wanted to be that glass.

Our eyes locked again. Regardless of our conversation, the

tension between us hadn't dissipated—it had tightened like a bow string right before you nocked an arrow.

She broke first, studying her glass. "Right. So, I'll make the arrangements for San Francisco. I'm assuming you want to charter a private flight out of Gunnison?"

"That sounds fine." Usually, we'd take Quinn's plane, but since we were scattered across the United States now, that wouldn't work out. "But I don't want to stay the night."

Her brow furrowed. "Ethan sent over the schedule already, and sound check is pretty early."

I gritted my teeth. The longer we were surrounded by my vices, the more likely I was to indulge in them. "Fine, then we can stay the night before, but I want out of there as soon as possible."

"I'll make it happen."

I nodded, knowing she would. Then I headed back to my guitar in hope I hadn't lost what inspiration had struck earlier, but all I could think about was the gig.

The booze. The girls. The drugs. The fucked-up decisions… they all went hand in hand with the shows. It was always the same. My emotions rose, the memories flared, and I took a shot to steady my nerves—that's how it started.

"Always" needed to become "used to," and next week, we'd know if that was possible.

———

Two NIGHTS LATER, I cursed as I fumbled through the kitchen cabinets, holding my phone up as a flashlight so I didn't wake Zoe.

Yesterday, she'd bought that same tea she'd given me in Seattle. I knew it was around here somewhere, and since I'd pinned all my hopes for getting back to sleep on that little box, I needed to find it. The teakettle was already full and heating on the burner behind me.

The dream tonight had felt real. They always did to some degree, but tonight I'd woken up covered in sweat, my neck arched, and my muscles straining against a villain who only existed in my memories.

Let me help. That's what she'd said in real life. She'd found a bag of frozen peas and wrapped it in a dishtowel, then held it against my cheek. In my dream, she'd been on the floor, her curls matted and red, staring at me through lifeless eyes.

Fuck, I wanted a drink. I wanted anything that would block out the dream and help shove the memories back in the little locked box I tried my best to keep them in.

But I couldn't take the drink, because I wouldn't stop at one. I couldn't refill the Xanax prescription or the Ambien. The only thing I could do was make some goddamned tea, and I couldn't even find the box.

I knocked something out of the cabinet, and it fell to the granite beneath, shattering.

"Fuck!"

Sure enough, a moment later, the hall light came on, then the kitchen light blared overhead, harsh and brutally bright.

"What are you doing?" Zoe asked, her cheeks pink with sleep.

"Stay there," I barked over my shoulder. "I broke something, and I don't want you to get cut." There was sugar all over the counter, and little shards of crystal lay scattered from the granite to the floor.

The teakettle started to whistle.

"You stay there," Zoe ordered, walking around the island to take the water off the stove. "You're the one who's barefoot...and shirtless. At least I have on slippers."

"A shirt isn't going to help this situation, and I'm not just going to stand here while you clean up my mess." I brushed the sugar and glass into my open palm as she grabbed the broom and dustpan.

"That's exactly what you're going to do." She swept around my feet, and as soon as I had a path, I dumped the contents of my hand into the trash can.

"Shit." She hissed.

I turned to see her on the floor, cradling her hand. My stomach twisted at the thin line of blood just below her thumb. "Zoe. Damn it." I came up behind her and scooped her up beneath her arms, turning so I could sit her on the island. "I told you not to clean up my mess."

"That's literally my job," she snapped. "And it's not bad. See?"

"What I see is you bleeding because I couldn't find the damned tea. Just…stay there. And this time, I mean it." I pointed at her, like that would help, then grabbed the first aid kit from where I'd seen it in the downstairs bathroom.

"It's not that bad," she repeated as I came back. "Just needs a Band-Aid."

I put the kit on the counter and snapped open the lid, then glanced at the blood that welled along the cut. "Let me help."

Let me help. It was her voice I heard now, reminding me that when she'd been the one to need it, I hadn't been there. The blood on Zoe's hand was the same shade as the curly hair in my dream. My chest tightened as I fought the urge to let the box fly open, fought the urge to stand in that kitchen and scream at the injustice of a world that allowed someone like me to live, but not—

"Nixon?" Zoe prompted softly.

I blinked, bringing her face into focus, using the startling green of her eyes to ground me.

"It's okay," she whispered. "I don't like blood either." She plucked a bandage from the container, cleaned the cut with an alcohol pad, then dressed it herself. Calm. Efficient. Steady.

Everything I wasn't.

"Good as new." She flashed a smile, but when she moved to jump from the counter, I gripped her warm hips over the thin shorts of her pajamas.

"Stay put." I finished cleaning up the glass, and only when I was certain there was nothing left that could cut her, I nodded. "Okay. It's good."

She slid off the island, then grabbed the box of tea from the cabinet next to the one I'd been ransacking. Without asking if that's the one I had been looking for, she prepared two cups and set them on the counter, then brought the honey over.

"Does it hurt?" I asked as the tea steeped, motioning to her hand.

"No." She shook her head, her hair sweeping softly over her bare shoulders.

"I'm so sorry." That tank top was going to be the death of me if I stared too long, so I focused on the cups in front of us.

"Better me than you," she said with a little laugh, hopping back up to sit on the island.

"Don't say that," I snapped. Our gazes collided.

"It's true." Her eyebrows rose.

"It's bullshit."

"I'm not the one who has to play a show in four days. You need your hand for that." She shrugged.

"You shouldn't have to pay for my mistake!" That's always how it worked, wasn't it? I fucked up. Someone else paid the price. But not Zoe. She was where I drew the line—where my "always" became "used to."

"Nixon," she whispered, softening as she slid her hand toward mine on the counter, but stopped just shy of touching it. "It's just a little cut. Tiny. No stitches. No blood loss."

"For now," I muttered.

"You act like you're some kind of wrecking ball. You're not." Her finger brushed mine.

"Says the woman who currently has to babysit me." I scoffed. "Not sure if you've noticed, but I'm not exactly easy on the people around me." *Including you.*

"What I've noticed are a lot of people trying their best to get close, and the ones who do fight to stay." She squeezed the honey into our teas, and I removed the bags and stirred.

"I'm sorry I woke you up," I said after my first swallow.

"I don't mind. My boss sleeps late." She flashed a teasing smile.

"When he sleeps," I admitted.

"Have you slept tonight?" she asked, holding her cup between sips.

I nodded.

"What woke you up?"

I set the tea on the counter. "I have nightmares." I shouldn't have told her, but there it was.

"I'm sorry. Are they memories or fears?" Her pinky hooked over mine.

I froze at the question—not the touch.

"It's okay. You don't have to tell me. I just wish I could help you."

My focus shifted from our linked fingers to the smooth, creamy skin of her thigh, and I wondered if it was as soft as it looked. "You said something about me not being interested," I said, dragging my gaze up her body to meet hers, well aware of my subject change.

Her brow puckered in confusion.

"A couple days ago, when we had the incredibly awkward conversation about that kiss," I reminded her.

"Oh." Her lips remained parted. "Sorry, I was trying to say that I understood."

"I didn't contradict you because it would open a door." I shifted so I stood in front of her. "And usually I don't give a shit about what someone thinks, but with you, it's different."

"I don't understand." She leaned forward slightly, bracing her palms on the counter.

"We said the kiss wouldn't happen again," I reminded her, moving closer. Her knees brushed against my stomach, and the contact tensed my abs.

"Right. I remember that." Her gaze flickered downward but jerked back to my face.

"I agreed with you because it shouldn't." My eyes focused on her lips. "Because you work for me. Because we're living together for the next few months. Because I'm not supposed to embark on any relationships fresh out of rehab, and you don't strike me as the one-night stand type of girl."

"I'm not," she blurted.

"I know." My face felt so tight it almost hurt to smile. "Those are my reasons. It has nothing to do with not being interested. Trust me." I let her see it—the hunger I felt for her—as I stepped forward.

"But we're not going to let it happen again, right?" Her knees parted and her breath hitched.

"Right," I agreed. "Because we both know it would end badly."

"Why are you telling me this?" Her words were at odds with her thighs, which split, leaving me enough room to stand between them.

"Because I keep enough secrets, and we're together too much to not be perfectly honest about this." I gripped her hips and tugged her to the edge of the counter, until she was flush against me from the juncture of her thighs to her breasts.

Too far, my brain warned me. I was taking this too far. But she felt so damned good against me. Warm, and soft, and lush.

Her fingers skimmed my shoulders, then came to rest behind my neck. "But we're not going to let it happen again."

"We're not," I agreed, lowering my mouth so it hovered a breath above hers. "I just didn't want you to think it was because

I didn't want you, because I do." Energy hummed through my body, and my lips ached with the need to kiss her.

"You do?" she questioned, her voice pitching higher.

"I do. And if you were anyone else, I'd have you naked already." My hands flexed on her hips. I couldn't even remember the last time I'd denied myself someone I wanted—or the last time someone hadn't wanted me back, and if the speed with which her breaths hit my lips was anything to go by, Zoe felt exactly the same way I did. "But you're not anyone else."

"Right." Her fingers slid into my hair, and it took everything in my power not to groan and give in to the situation I'd put us in.

"Just wanted to clear that up." I leaned in.

She pushed off my chest and scrambled back across the island, then spun and jumped to the floor. "Glad we got it sorted out. Night!" She practically ran from the kitchen.

My dick throbbed as I hung my head, struggling to steady my breathing. It had been a stupid move, an easy way to change the subject, but that wasn't the only reason I'd told her. Maybe I was sick of feeling like I was the only one tortured here.

Maybe the best thing for us both would be for me to find a willing woman at the show in a few days, so at least I wasn't strung out on my need for Zoe.

Problem was, I didn't want some random hookup.

I wanted the only woman on the planet I couldn't have.

8

ZOE

Nixon had been on edge since we landed in San Francisco. He was tapping his foot, rolling a pick over his knuckles, or jiggling his knee—he certainly wasn't sitting still.

"Is he doing okay?" Quinn asked quietly as Nixon, Jonas, and Ethan strolled down the hall ahead of us at the hotel. "He seems a little…"

"Off?" I suggested.

"Wound up," she offered. "But yeah, off works too."

"He's not usually this bad." Dinner had been just the five of us in a private room, since both Quinn's and Jonas's kids had started school a few weeks earlier, but Nixon hadn't been able to relax. "He's been restless since we left…" *Home*, I almost said, but we really hadn't been at home. We'd been in Colorado for the last two weeks. "The house," I finished lamely. "We haven't been in public much. This is really the first time he's been around everything that could set him back."

"I wish he'd let us cancel it." She sighed. "I get the optics of it, and why he's so adamant that we not, but it's really not worth the risk to his sobriety."

Ahead of us, I saw Nixon's tattooed knuckles as he rubbed the back of his neck.

"Is it?" Quinn asked, pausing in the middle of the hallway.

"Is what?" I stopped to face her, noting the worry in her eyes.

"Is this risking it? We called ahead and made sure there was no alcohol at dinner and there were no surprise gifts in his suite—your suite—whatever you guys call it." She tucked her thumbs in her pockets and rocked back on her heels. "But I don't know if it's enough."

"I think every day is another risk to his sobriety," I answered as truthfully as I could, keeping my voice down even though the band had reserved not only this floor but the two beneath us. "Is being here harder? Yep. Does he keep secluded? Yeah. Does he avoid temptation? Absolutely. But don't, for one minute, think that he couldn't sneak off to the bar or the liquor store if he wanted to."

She nodded, looking over my shoulder. "I just don't want to be his reason for failing."

"I think you guys are a major part of his reason for staying sober."

Her forehead wrinkled. "Is he being a complete dick to you?"

I scoffed. "He's Nixon."

"That says it all." She winced.

"No, he's fine, really," I assured her.

She arched a perfectly groomed eyebrow.

"I'm serious." I grinned. "He's…" There weren't any words to describe him. He was infuriating one moment and bone-meltingly sweet in the next. Ice cold, then flipped to scorching hot. He was just Nixon.

"How many girls have there been?" she asked, her voice dropping to a whisper. "Anything we need to worry about?"

I swallowed. Hard.

"Shit, I shouldn't be digging into you like this, but if we get him on the phone, it's only for a few minutes, and he's not exactly an open book with us right now. I just want to know that he's not trading one vice for another, you know?"

"Hey, are you two coming?" Jonas called down the hall.

"Give us a second!" Quinn waved him off. "I swear to God, they harass me about not having any female friends when we tour but won't let me talk to another woman for a few minutes without butting in," she muttered. "So, normal level of women in his life? More?"

"Um. That's…" I cringed. The number of people who could call Quinn a friend was small to say the least, and I wasn't in a hurry to piss her off. "That's a question for him to answer." I was there to keep Nixon sober, not report the details of his life. "But I would say that you don't have anything to worry about."

She tilted her head, studying me for a nerve-wracking moment. "Huh. I knew I liked you for a reason." She shrugged, then we started walking again, heading toward the end of the wing where the rooms were.

The guys were gathered outside the door to the suite Nixon and I shared. He shot me a curious look before jumping back into the conversation with Jonas and Ethan.

"I hope he's slowed down a little. I swear to God, he was at risk for chafing," Quinn remarked.

My eyes popped wide, but I schooled my features quickly. Nixon's exploits were so well known that women usually lined up backstage like Baskin Robbins, hoping he'd pick their flavor for the night. *Reason number four hundred and six that kiss can't happen again.*

"Chafing what?" Nixon asked, obviously having heard.

"Your dick," she answered with a smile.

Nixon's gaze flew to mine.

"Don't look at me." I dug into my purse and took out the

room key. Nixon stepped to the side, so our shoulders brushed as I approached the door.

"I asked her if you were man-whoring," Quinn explained.

"And what did Ms. Shannon say?" Nixon's voice dipped to a purr.

God, even his voice turned me on. My stomach tightened at his tone, but I managed to get the door unlocked. If he only knew how close I'd been to kissing him in the kitchen last week, perhaps he'd be a little more careful throwing around his sex appeal.

Maybe I needed to stay out of the kitchen and away from his mouth, period. Every day, it got a little harder to ignore the hum between us, and giving in wasn't something I could afford. If I went down that path with Nixon...well, Peter wouldn't be the only one making false assumptions about how I climbed the company ladder.

"She said that your sex life was private," Quinn answered. "Which I respect, but I also know how...hmm...how do I say this. How *public* your liaisons can be?"

The guys chuckled, and I winced, pushing open the door.

"I haven't slept with anyone since before rehab. Not that it's any of your business," Nixon answered smoothly. "Now, my babysitter and I would like to get a few hours of sleep before sound check."

"Eleven a.m.," Ethan reminded us.

"I'm sure Shannon has it in both her planners." Nixon followed me into the room, the door shutting heavily behind him.

"And three alarms set," I responded sweetly, slipping my purse over my head and dropping it onto the massive dining room table. The suite had two bedrooms and an open-concept living and dining area, so it wasn't like we were sharing the same room or anything, but it still felt more intimate than the house in Colorado or even his apartment in Seattle. There weren't as many places to run. I kicked off my heels and sighed in pure pleasure when my bare feet met the polished hardwood.

"Ooh, getting all casual on me?" Nixon asked with a grin.

I looked down at my black sheath dress and single strand of pearls. "Hey, not all of us go out for business dinners in…whatever that is." I motioned to his outfit.

He glanced down at his vintage Doors tee and jeans that rode low enough on his hips I got a quick flash of skin when he shrugged. "This is what we call dinner-with-friends attire."

"Because you were having dinner with friends," I said. "While I adore Quinn and like Jonas and Ethan, it's business for me."

I felt that smoldering gaze like a flame as he ran it up and down my frame. "Well, hopefully now that we're in our room, you'll go grab your Casual Friday pajamas, because I'm not continuing our *Westworld* marathon with you dressed like you might be called at any moment to race off and host a cocktail party." He lifted his brows.

"Fine. I'll change." I rolled my eyes.

"I'll order room service. I'm feeling snacky." He was already headed for the phone. "How do french fries and ice cream sound to you?"

"Like I'm going to gain ten pounds," I called over my shoulder as I walked into my room. I reached behind my neck, then grumbled. This dress was such a pain in the ass.

"Real men dig the curves," he called back.

"Since when?" I asked as I walked back in. "Last time I checked, all the women you sleep with are thin enough to wear designer-sample sizes."

"What?" He paused with the phone halfway to his ear.

"You like thin women. It's okay to have a type. I'm just saying that you do *not*, in fact, dig curves unless they're on your guitar." I turned around, giving him my back. "Would you please unzip me? I can't reach."

His footsteps drew near, and then he swept my hair to the side. "You always smell like coconuts."

"It's my shampoo."

His fingers skimmed the length of my neck. "I like your curves."

"Nixon," I whispered, shaking my head. He liked to break the tension with shameless flirting. I understood that was part of who he was, but I was reaching my threshold. Every morning, I wondered if today would be the day I broke and finally jumped him—the day I threw away my chances at being taken seriously in this industry.

His hand was warm on the exposed skin of my back as he steadied the fabric, and then he unzipped my dress, moving so slowly it felt sensual and intimate—like an act between lovers, not roommates.

"Your skin is flawless," he whispered once the zipper reached the bottom.

"Yours is like a living canvas," I replied, my chin grazing my shoulder. "Covered in art and stories." There was a ghost of a caress at the dip in my spine, and I felt more than heard him retreat.

"So that's a yes to the ice cream?" He cleared his throat.

"Sure. Just as long as it's—"

"Not strawberry, I know. By the way, I like the green. It matches your eyes." He dialed room service, and I escaped into my room.

I glanced at my dress in the mirror. If he thought this was green, he needed to get his eyes checked. It only took a second to slip out of the dress and hang it up, but as I passed by the mirror, my cheeks heated.

My underwear was green. Both the lace bra and the matching thong.

I hurried into a set of pajamas but left my bra on under the "I heart Colorado" tank top. When I came out, Nixon already had our current binge-watching show cued up. No devices, no planners, no work whatsoever during TV time—those were his rules. Had to admit, they were growing on me. It was nice to turn my brain off for those hours.

"I'm jumping in the shower," he said. "Will you sign for room service when it comes?" He yanked his shirt over his head, and my mouth went dry, just like it did every time I got a good look at his torso.

"Yep." I swore he did that on purpose, like he'd moved from the annoy-Zoe-for-fun game into the torture-Zoe-with-sexual-frustration edition, but I kept a smile on my face as he disappeared into his room. A minute later, I heard the shower start up.

I flipped through my messages while he was in the shower, then answered the door when room service rang.

But it wasn't room service.

Ben's eyebrows hit the ceiling as he looked down at me. "When I said loosen up around the office, I didn't mean pj's."

"It's ten o'clock, and I'm in my hotel room." I rolled my eyes. "Did you need something?" Reason number five hundred and nineteen I couldn't act on my craving for Nixon—I never knew who would show up at Nixon's door...like my actual boss.

He nodded, then walked in the room without being invited. "Sorry. I would have come by earlier, but I was checking out a new band. Tiger Kiss, or something else equally awful. Decent vocalist, though." His gaze swept over the room, taking in every detail.

"Nixon's in the shower." My tank top and flannel pants didn't seem nearly professional enough next to his tailored suit. *I should have stayed in my dress.*

"Good. Alcohol?" His gaze narrowed.

"None."

"Drugs?"

"Zero." This whole trip was starting to feel like less of a show and more like a report card for Nixon.

"Excellent. Women?"

"This question is getting old. My job is to keep Nixon sober, not monitor his love life. He deserves a little privacy." Besides, the only person he was kissing was…well, me, and Ben was the last person on Earth I was going to discuss that with.

Ben arched a brow at me but continued. "Is he writing?"

"Some. Nothing that he wants to share yet, but he sits down to write every day." I'd begun scheduling my work around his just so I could listen from the next room.

"He's going to blow the deadline." Ben's posture stiffened.

"Like I told Harvey—move the deadline. You have to give him some time."

"How much time?" He glanced at his Apple watch as a text rolled in, and for the first time in my career, I didn't want to know what it was about.

"I can't even begin to guess." I didn't want to know the details of Ben's life, or how I could make it easier. I didn't want to lessen his burdens or prove my worth by stepping in for his bands when he was called away. The last few weeks with Nixon had shown me I didn't just want my own bands to manage, I was ready for them too.

"You can't speed things along?" His jaw popped.

"You so much as try to rush Nixon and he's going to go twice as slow just to show you he can. You know that. Quinn and Jonas are fine with the delay, so we back our *clients*, right?" I folded my arms across my chest. "That's who we advocate for, go the extra mile for. Our clients."

Ben blinked, then studied me. "Are you sleeping with him?"

"I'm sorry?" My mouth gaped for a moment. He'd never questioned my ethics, but I'd never given him a reason to either.

"Are. You. Sleeping. With. Nixon? Because I'd hardly consider that—"

"Be careful what you say next, Ben," Nixon said casually from his doorway. Thank God he hadn't come out shirtless after Ben had crossed that line, or he would have jumped to the conclusion anyway. "Because the only way to finish that sentence without me losing my shit is by adding the words, *any of my business.*"

Ben sighed, then glanced between the two of us, as if he were measuring something I couldn't see. "Fine. But keep your dick in your pants with this one," he said to Nixon. "She's not some intern, and we all know what happened the last time you—"

"Fuck off." Nixon's eyes narrowed to slits, and his posture stiffened. "No one gave a shit who I was fucking when I was drunk, whether it was on the bus, in my dressing room, or in the lobby of a hotel. You didn't care if it was a different woman or even two every night."

I flinched, and my stomach turned over, flooding me with nausea at the thought.

"So again, unless I'm propositioning you for some action, Ben, it's none of your business who I take to bed, and I don't swing that way, so spoiler alert: it's never your business. I'm fine. I'm sober. Unless there's a contract we need to go over, get the fuck out so I can get some sleep."

Ben appraised the situation and then nodded. "Fine. I'll see you both tomorrow." He let himself out, the door shutting loudly behind him.

"You didn't tell him I kissed you." Nixon leaned back against the wall.

"No." I shook my head.

"You didn't tell Quinn either."

"Of course not."

"Why not?" He turned those narrowed eyes on me, and my nausea grew tenfold. "Embarrassed?"

"That I kissed you? No. That I crossed a professional line I swore I never would? Absolutely. And what happens between us isn't fodder for gossip, or anyone's business but ours," I snapped.

"Professional lines…because this is just business, right, Shannon? You're just doing your job so you get whatever Ben promised in that little deal of yours." He let his head fall back against the wall. "You're only here because I need a babysitter, and I only let you stay so I don't shit all over my friends' lives."

Something in my chest crumpled, and it *hurt*.

There was another knock at the door, and I took the easy way out and opened it, then signed for the snacks as the attendant laid the spread out on the dining room table. Once he was gone, Nixon pushed off the wall, regret flashing through those dark eyes.

Regret over what? That he'd lost his temper? Or that he'd kissed me in the first place?

"I got you salted caramel," he said softly, pushing the dish of ice cream my way.

"I liked you better when I knew you were an asshole," I replied. "At least I expected it then."

His eyes whipped toward mine.

Guess it was a statement on how far we'd come that I'd say something like that to him, but what he'd said felt like more of an accurate measurement.

"I'm going to bed." I grabbed my phone from the table and walked off.

"What about *Westworld*?" he called after me.

"I've had enough drama for the night."

If this was the night *before* the show, I couldn't wait to see what he was like after it.

———

"GET THAT OUT, NOW!" I yelled at one of the roadies, pointing to the bottle of Crystal Skull in Nixon's dressing room.

Thank God Nixon was with Jonas right now. He'd been ice-cold this morning. Every move he made was distant, professional, and completely dismissive. I'd gone from being someone he binge-watched shows with and played guitar for to the hired help.

But I'd always been the hired help, hadn't I?

The roadies cleared out the alcohol, and I made a quick sweep of the dressing room to be sure there weren't any more presents lurking in corners or drawers. Once I was certain the room was clean, I put out two shot glasses and set the little bottle of amber liquid between them on the coffee table in front of the little love seat.

Then I smoothed my hands over the line of my pencil skirt and checked in the mirror to make sure the buttons on my blouse were still lined up all the way to my throat. The outfit would have been entirely too hot for the weather, but the sleeves were sheer. I'd ordered it last week, and a stab of disappointment had pricked at me this morning when Nixon hadn't even glanced my way.

He's not supposed to glance your way, you idiot. But I wanted him to.

The door burst open, and Nixon stalked in, his jaw tight.

"He's all yours, Zoe." Jonas gave me a sympathetic wince before shutting the door, leaving me alone with Nixon.

He paced along the line of guitars that waited on their stands. All eight were electric, and he'd tuned six of them to specific songs this morning, then retuned them, only to do it all again.

I'd never seen him so tense before a show.

"No leather?" I asked, noticing the way his jeans hung on his ass. If I were a pair of jeans, I would want to be Nixon's, that was for sure.

"I've gained a little since our last tour. Nothing fit," he muttered, studying the neck on his Fender. "Has anyone been in here?"

"I'll get your measurements and order you some new ones. And no, just me and the roadie I called in to haul something out." I settled back against the counter that ran the length of the room.

Nixon turned and lifted his eyebrows in question, which was the first time he'd looked me in the eyes since last night.

"You don't want to know." I shook my head. "No one has touched the guitars."

"Hmm."

The silence stretched painfully between us, and I couldn't help but wonder if he was playing last night's argument through his head the way I was.

"No one would look at me the same if they knew about that kiss," I said softly. I couldn't stand the freeze-out anymore, not now that I knew who he was under all that mocking, bitter armor he loved to wear.

"What would they see?" he retorted. "A flesh-and-blood woman with needs? Trust me, I'd get far more shit from my friends and my manager for corrupting the squeaky-clean Zoe Shannon than you would for coloring outside the lines for the first time in your entire life."

"That is *not* true."

There was a knock on the door, which earned a hard glare from Nixon, and I moved quickly to answer it.

"Hey, Zoe," Ethan said, then looked past my shoulder to watch Nixon pace the line of his guitars again. "Damn. Jonas said he was restless, but…" He shook his head.

"Yeah." Nixon wasn't restless. Nixon was a caged lion prowling at the bars of his cell, waiting to be fed or freed.

"How much of his pregame ritual is he keeping the same?" Ethan asked quietly.

"How about you stop talking *about* me and talk *to* me, Ethan," Nixon said, crossing his arms and straining the seams on his T-shirt.

Ethan sighed. "I've got options out here if you need to work off that"—he fumbled for a word—"energy before the show." He nodded toward the hallway.

I pressed back against the wall as Nixon filled the space in the doorway, looking out of his dressing room. His jaw ticked once—twice—as he took in whatever options Ethan was offering.

"I know post-show is more your thing, but I wasn't sure if…" Ethan glanced at me, and his cheeks flushed.

"She's not a kid, Ethan, and she's been around enough shows to know what happens." Nixon braced one hand on the door and the other on the frame as he leaned out a little farther.

There was more than one feminine gasp of delight, and I didn't need to look to know exactly what kind of lineup was out there.

Nixon looked down at me and arched a brow in clear challenge. "What do you think, Shannon? Blonde? Brunette?" His gaze shifted to the heavy waves of auburn hair that stopped just above my breasts. "Redhead?"

I swallowed, refusing to look away as he dragged his eyes back to lock on mine.

He wasn't mine.

I wasn't his.

He was free to do whatever he wanted with whomever he wanted to do it with, and we both knew it. I had zero right to the jealousy that was currently lifting my chin, daring him. None. But if he brought one of those women back here, I was going to rip her arms off and beat her with them before I turned on *him*. I didn't care how irrational that made me.

Whatever this fragile truce between us was wouldn't survive me seeing his hands on another woman.

Oh no. No, no, no.

My heart pitched sideways.

I was falling for him.

Stupid, foolish girl.

"Nix?" Ethan prompted.

"I'm good," Nixon answered, turning toward Ethan, but before I could let loose the breath currently frozen in my chest, he smirked. "We'll see how I feel after the show."

Fucking asshole.

"Sounds like a plan," Ethan responded. "See you in ten."

Nixon shut the door and didn't so much as look at me as he strode to the middle of the dressing room, but then he stopped right in front of the table. "What the hell is that?"

I made my feet move, even though my knees weren't with the program. "Apple juice."

"I can see that."

I managed to pour the juice into the shot glasses without spilling a drop, despite the fine tremble in my fingers. Now I was the jumpy one. How had I let myself get so close to him? Let my feelings get tangled up in a man who clearly had no interest in them?

"I was trying to think of simple ways to keep your routine the same," I said softly, picking up the shot glasses. "And I know it's not vodka, or tequila, or the various other things you used to use to take the edge off, but I thought maybe we'd trick your nerves with some good old muscle memory." I offered one of the shot glasses to him.

"You're replacing my vodka with apple juice." His forehead crinkled.

"Yes." I nodded once.

He took the glass from my fingers with a small chuckle. "You are something else, Zoe."

Zoe. Not Shannon.

"Here's to my favorite words at the moment. *Used to.*" He raised his glass to mine, and we both slammed our drinks back. "Showtime."

I took his glass, then set them both down as he slung the strap of his favorite Les Paul over his shoulder, then tugged until the guitar ran up his spine.

"You know me pretty well, don't you?" he asked as we headed for the door. The stagehands were already on the other side, waiting to take his guitars to the wings.

"I'm getting there," I admitted as we walked into the hallway, pausing so the guys could pass single file into the room, each returning with one of Nixon's prized possessions.

"Good," Nixon said with a smirk. Then he leaned down, letting his lips brush the shell of my ear. "Then I'll trust you to pick one of those girls behind me for later."

My spine stiffened.

He laughed as he lifted his head. "Aren't you going to wish me luck, Shannon?"

Shannon. The pieces clicked into place. We were in public. Here, he wasn't the Nixon I shared cider with, or the one who bought my mom's cake. Here, I was his manager's assistant, and he was every bit the rock star a hundred thousand people had filled a stadium to see. Now who was embarrassed? At least I had a reason. My career was on the line. What was at stake for him if someone caught him being human? His reputation as a card-carrying member of the asshole club? Was this just another way to get under my skin?

"I really hate you sometimes," I whispered.

His eyes flared with delight. "Is that any way to talk to your favorite client?" He walked backward a few steps, then flashed a smile at the women who'd remained outside his dressing room with the hopes he'd change his mind. "See you later, ladies."

Right before he turned around, he winked at me. Then he threw his arm around Jonas's shoulders and they met Quinn outside her door and headed for the stage.

I fucking hated him and his ability to switch from hot to cold, like it was nothing more than a faucet setting. I loathed how badly I wanted his warmth back, but the lines were clear. He was a client. I was his manager's assistant. But…what if I wasn't?

What if I was already managing another account? What if I was just another girl? Would he still want me the way he'd said he did? Or was it all a game to him? The possibility was too painful to contemplate.

And if it wasn't a game to Nixon, if he really did want me, then I was the one inflicting his wounds with my inability to bend my own rules or risk my reputation.

No risk. No reward.

I gnawed on my lower lip as Nixon walked away. Maybe the right question to ask wasn't what I would risk. If Nixon had been real with me that night in the kitchen, at the festival, every time he was considerate or protective—if that was the real him, then what *wouldn't* I risk to be with him?

I wanted him, and not just physically. I wanted the complicated man under all that ink, the one who bid on my mother's cake and admitted he had nightmares. The one who battled his demons every day and still had the guts to walk right into their lair when it was time to show up for his friends and perform. The one who trusted me, defended me, and pushed my neat little boundaries.

If I had a shot with *that* man, I'd risk more than my reputation—I'd put my heart on the line. No regrets. No safety net. No guarantee.

If it wasn't a game…and with Nixon, who knew?

"Hi, um, excuse me?" a brunette who was easily a foot taller than me asked. "You work with Nixon Winters?"

"Yep." And speak of the devil, he looked back at me over his shoulder. Or maybe it was her. Hell if I knew when it came to him. That was the problem.

"Oh wow. Is there any way I could—"

"No." I walked off down the hall, following the path Nixon had just taken.

I might have had some very complicated feelings for the asshat, but I wasn't serving him up on a platter either. If he wanted another woman, he could damn well get one himself.

Then we'd both have to live with the consequences.

9

NIXON

THE CROWD ROARED, filling my bloodstream with my favorite drug—straight-up worship—as I hit the last note in the encore. The stage went black long enough for us to exit stage left as the lights in the stadium came up.

"That was good." Jonas slammed his hand against my back. "Better than good."

"Phenomenal," Quinn added, coming up on my right.

"Yeah it was," I agreed as energy pumped through me. I'd forgotten how it felt to get high off the crowd without the alcohol in my system. Back in the early years, it had just been that first shot to steady my nerves before we took the stage, but recently I'd taken to bringing out a drink instead of a water bottle.

Just another used to, I promised myself.

God, this felt good.

"I liked the way you switched it up in that second set," Jonas said to Quinn.

"Thanks, I wanted to try something a little different," she replied, sliding her sticks into her back pocket.

"It worked. And damn, Nix, you nailed that riff in 'Silver Streets.' I haven't heard you play it like that since..." He cocked his head to the side.

"Since we recorded it," I guessed. That song was impossible to play perfectly without a clear head. The notes were too fast, the timing too critical, and usually I'd been too drunk.

"Hey, are you guys sticking around?" Quinn asked as we passed by her dressing room. "I want to check in with Graham real fast."

"Yeah. I want to hear Kira's voice too. Meet out here when you're ready?" he offered.

"Sounds good. Nix?" She paused, her hand on the door handle.

"I guess I can call Graham and Kira too," I said, straight-faced.

"Shut up." Quinn rolled her eyes. "See you guys in a few." She disappeared into her dressing room, and Jonas and I continued down the hall until we reached his.

Then it was just me. There was so much electricity humming through me I was surprised the lights weren't flickering. That was a post-show buzz I expected, one I used to work off with sex, but—

"Hey, you guys were mind-blowing tonight!" A guy with green highlights rushed at me with dilated eyes and a bottle of Jack. It took me a second, but I recognized him—the lead singer of the opener.

"Thanks." I adjusted my strap and kept moving, keeping my eyes firmly off the destruction he held so casually in his grip. A couple months ago, I would have snatched it out of his hands and taken a few swigs before handing it back.

Fuck, I could taste it on my tongue right now.

"So, we're all headed out, do you want to come?" he asked,

using the bottle to motion toward his band, who were all gathered outside my dressing room.

Hell yes, I wanted to go. I wanted to down a fifth of vodka—or whatever reached my lips first—and smother the emotions that ran amok inside me. Wanted the sweet oblivion that came with a blackout and the dreamless sleep of the wasted. One night. Just one night.

My dressing room door opened, and Zoe walked out, wearing a smile that hit me like a punch to the gut. Fuck the rest of it, I wanted *her.* I pushed out the memory of saying *client* like it was a dirty word last night and focused on her eyes.

Zoe. Zoe. Zoe. She might be pissed at me, but she wouldn't let me go with them. Wouldn't stand by and watch me fuck up the last ten and a half weeks of sobriety.

"I'm going to take a rain check," I said to Green Hair, vowing to look his name up later.

"You sure?" His face fell with disappointment as we reached my door. Three of the girls hanging off their members looked at me with wide, hopeful eyes, but I didn't want them either.

The buzzing in my head roared to be released, but I managed to nod.

"Damn. Well, if you change your mind, we're heading out in about twenty minutes," he said. I saw him shake his head from the corner of my eye, but I was focused elsewhere.

"You sounded like you were having fun out there," Zoe said as I walked past her into my dressing room. I cracked open the nearest bottle of water and chugged the whole thing. Performing sucked the water right out of me. How the hell had I done it drunk?

"I was," I assured her, dragging my cases from the wall.

Right on time, the stagehands knocked, then filled my cases one by one, tucking my girls in for the night. "They're coming back to Colorado with us," I told Zoe as I closed each one of them personally. "It just about gave me hives thinking of someone else bringing them here."

"Not a problem." She jotted down something in her planner as she sat back on the counter, crossing her legs.

How could someone so buttoned up be so incredibly sexy? Even her heels were hot.

I finished with the cases, then started to strip out of my sweat-drenched clothes. Zoe looked up, raising her eyebrows. "I'll…um…wait outside."

"No." Outside was too far. Outside meant I had to make another choice of going to get her once I was done or leaving with that other band, and with the energy coursing through me, that was a very bad option to have.

"All right." She pivoted on the counter slightly, turning her back to me. "You feeling okay?"

"I feel like a ball of billion-watt electricity held together by bones, with some skin stretched over it," I admitted, stripping off the last of my clothes and shoving my legs into the clean ones. A shower could wait. Everything had to wait.

"Oh."

I could almost hear the cogs in her mind turning from here.

"Well, do you want me to follow through on your last request?" she asked with a hint of snark in her voice.

"My last request?" I tugged a shirt over my head, trying to recall what it was. Bringing my guitars back to Colorado?

"You know, that I…" She sighed. "That I pick a girl."

I paused with one sock on. That's right, I'd been an ass and given her shit just before I'd taken the stage, which, oddly enough, had worked almost as well as alcohol to take my mind off the nerves. And it wasn't like I didn't have a reason to be just as pissed at her as she was with me.

She was embarrassed that *she'd* crossed a line? Hell, I was the one who'd kissed her, then caged her in on the kitchen island, confessing how badly I wanted her. I was the one in knots because I couldn't decide if I was thankful she guarded my privacy with such ferocity or livid she only saw me as a *client.*

"Well?" she prompted.

I finished putting on my socks and shoved my feet into my favorite Converse. "No, I don't want you to get me a girl." Unless that girl was her, in which case I was more than on board.

She glanced over her shoulder, then turned fully when she realized I wasn't naked. "Then why would you be such an ass and ask me that in the first place?"

I ignored the question completely. I wasn't getting into this with her right now. Not when there was a very real chance I'd cross that *professional line* she loved so much. This shit between us was too raw, too powerful, and way too tempting.

"I need you to get me out of here. Call the pilots, we're going straight to the airport." I looked her dead in the eye and let her see the trembling in my hands, the monster of addiction that lived just under my surface.

Her entire presence softened, transforming her from Shannon to Zoe. "Okay. I'll call." She took out her phone and made the arrangements as I guzzled another bottle of water. "When do you want to leave?"

"Right now."

————

WE'D BEEN airborne for forty minutes and I still couldn't get myself level.

"Anything else I can get you?" the flight attendant asked with a professional smile as she delivered our drinks.

"Privacy," I snapped. People had been in my face since ten o'clock this morning and I just wanted to be left the hell alone. I felt like I was dancing on a tightrope between two high-rises in the rain, risking my life to perform for everyone below, and it wasn't just on stage.

"No, thank you, Kelly," Zoe replied. "I think we might just need a little space for the duration of the flight."

"Of course. If you need anything, just press that button." With those instructions, I was finally, blissfully alone.

Guess my standards for privacy had changed with Zoe around.

I leaned back against the soft leather of the couch and swirled the ice in my glass, watching the cubes spin round and round, wishing it was something a little stronger than orange soda.

"You didn't have to be a dick." Zoe put down her laptop and unbuckled her seat belt from the single seat across from me.

"That's just who I am. You think you'd be used to it by now."

"That's not true. You're still pissed at me for last night...or what I said before the show, since it's all interconnected."

"That's just a part of what's going on in my head, Zoe," I admitted, rolling my shoulders. My skin felt too tight.

She closed the small space between us and took the seat next to me, kicking off her heels and curling her bare feet under her. "Want to talk about it?"

"No." If I wanted to talk about it, I would have.

"I'm not embarrassed about kissing you." She relaxed, resting her cheek against the back of the couch.

"Just at how people would look at you if they knew." I looked away before those eyes of hers could unravel me. The strings on my self-control were already frayed. I'd actually run away from my own band, sending lame texts to Quinn and Jonas on our way to the airport.

"You know how Peter assumed I'd gotten my job because I was sleeping with you?"

"Peter is an asshole, and you're not sleeping with me." I leaned forward, bracing my elbows on my knees.

"But if I did—"

My gaze snapped to hers.

"And if people knew, everyone would assume that's exactly how I advanced." She kept her voice soft, and I heard the honesty in what she was saying.

"But it's not the truth."

"Come on, Nixon, we both know that in this business, perception is truth." Her lips turned up in a sad smile. "You might get crap for slumming it with the assistant, or breaking your promise not to sleep with the women on staff, but no one would ever doubt your right to a piece of that stage."

My brow furrowed. "So, it's really about your career and not that you just see me as part of your job?"

Her eyes widened. "You're not..." She swallowed. "You're not just the job. Not to me. If people like Jonas, Quinn, Ben, or Ethan saw the way I'd kissed you back? Or if they knew how badly I wanted you, it would do some serious harm to my professional credibility. I'd rather be known as the buttoned-up, organization freak who can't color outside the lines but nails her job, than the girl who nailed the rock star to climb the ladder."

"You want me, huh?" Shit, that was knowledge that could only do more harm than good, especially when she put reasoning like that behind her logic.

"Of course that's the one thing you latch on to." She rolled her eyes.

My stomach sank. "That night in the park...did I screw it up for you?" Had that single moment undone her reputation? Just the thought of it added a heaping serving of anxiety to my already overloaded system.

"No." She shook her head. "No one cares what happens in Legacy. If there was only one video of you singing, I highly doubt anyone has one of us kissing."

By that logic, no one would care about what happened on this plane either, or at the house in Colorado, or anywhere we couldn't be seen. My focus dropped to her lips, my memory all too happy to play back that kiss in my mind. She wanted me. This was just as hard on her as it was for me. That shouldn't have made me feel better, but it did.

"Since that was only a part of it, what else is on your mind?" she asked.

She'd been honest. It was only fair that I was too. "I can't figure out if I miss the buzz of the alcohol, the release of the post-show adrenaline, or the blackout that usually followed," I said quietly.

"Maybe all three."

"Maybe." Round and round, I swirled the ice, pausing only to drink.

"Is there anything I can do?" Her voice was so soft.

"You already did it." I tried to force a smile, but it wouldn't come. "You got me out of there. Another few minutes and I might have taken the green-haired kid up on his offer to go party."

"I'm glad you didn't."

"Me too." I would have been plastered by now, knee-deep in bad decisions with zero fucks given.

"His name is Ryan De Rosa, and he's the lead singer for Blue Lotus. They were the first opener. Sound is a little raw, but the bass player's dad is a friend of Ben's." She braced her palm on the seat between us. "I think Ben might take them on."

"Would you?" I swirled the ice faster and faster.

"No. I don't think they have a unique enough sound to make a dent in the market. They might develop one, but they're not there yet."

"I only heard one of their songs, but I wasn't exactly blown away." One shot, that was all most of us got in the industry. One night where some exec wandered into a bar. One song before they tuned us out. One chance.

"Exactly. It's not enough to be good, you have to stand out."

She shook her head slightly. "I kept telling Peter he—" She pursed her lips.

"What?" I put my glass in the cup rest and turned to face her.

"I told him that he had to offer something no one else could if he wanted to get picked up." Her eyebrows knit, as if she were reliving the moment. "I spent my senior year filling out college applications. He spent it sending in demos. I knew he didn't have it," she whispered, her face falling, "but I couldn't tell him that. I had instincts but no experience, and you can't look at someone you love and crap all over their dream."

"You don't look at someone you love and then fuck the cheerleader," I countered.

"I guess it worked out for them. It doesn't hurt anymore, but we'd been together for years, and when you're that young, it's hard to see how much more to life there really is."

"He said you'd fail?" I asked, remembering his words from the night of the festival.

She nodded. "I got into college. He didn't."

"He knew he couldn't hold you back, so he found someone he could." Maybe it was the pent-up energy still coiled inside me, but I couldn't stop my stomach from tensing in frustration. Was it jealousy?

"Maybe." She shrugged. "Either way, he's partially right. I haven't made it yet. But I will."

I scoffed. "Zoe, you're smart as hell, fuckably gorgeous, and currently flying back to your little hometown on a private jet. I think you've made it." I downed the rest of my soda, leaving the ice cubes to melt.

"It's not my jet," she countered with a chuckle.

"Semantics." I abandoned my glass in the cup holder of the coffee table and my fingers started drumming on the seat beside me. I was going to have to come up with a new way to channel the post-show high or I'd never stay sober.

"Do you still feel like a ball of electricity?" Zoe asked, sitting up slightly as she watched my fingers.

I nodded. "It's always been like this for me. Jonas and Quinn get the post-show high too, but for me, it's different." How could I possibly explain this to her? "What's your favorite drug? Don't look at me like that, I don't mean illegal ones. I know you better than that."

"Caffeine."

That was something I could work with. "Okay. You need caffeine to function because you've taught your body to expect it. Right?"

"Right."

"So, you need it, but then something like tonight,. it's like being fed espresso shots by a hundred thousand people over the course of two hours, and they're draining that energy out of you, sure, but not at the same rate they're putting it in. Maybe you've burned off fifty thousand of those shots when you walk off the stage, but there's still fifty thousand more coursing through your bloodstream, giving you the jitters, searching for an outlet."

"You get overstimulated," she said quietly. "The alcohol helped you manage the sensory overload."

I nodded. "It feels…" There weren't enough words, but then again, I'd never tried to describe it before, so I stopped trying. "Like this."

I showed her instead, spearing my fingers through her silken hair and bringing my mouth to hers in a hard kiss. Fuck the professional lines. There was no one here but her and me. The only lines between us were the ones we chose.

Her lips parted, and I plunged into her mouth, taking it with deep, sweeping strokes. She tasted like ginger ale and the sweetness I now recognized as Zoe, and I tilted us both to seal that perfect angle of our lips.

God, this was exactly what I'd needed. The first time I'd

kissed her, I'd gone in playfully. It had been symbolic to start with, then quickly sparked to more.

This felt like pouring jet fuel on a bonfire.

Her hands gripped my shoulders as she gave it back just as hard as I was dishing it out. There was too much space between us, too much clothing, too many reasons we weren't supposed to be doing this. Handling the first problem was easy. I left the other two to sort themselves out later.

I palmed her hip and tugged her toward me. She slid over my lap, then groaned in frustration when her skirt didn't accommodate her. I grinned against her mouth as she yanked her skirt up so she could settle a knee on either side of my hips.

I stopped grinning when she sank onto my lap. Then I was the one groaning, tightening my grip in her hair to hold her mouth to mine as I kissed her breathless, losing myself in the process. This wasn't just chemistry—this was nuclear, something capable of powering the world or destroying it.

She rolled her hips over mine, grinding against my dick, and I ripped my mouth from hers, sucking in a breath through my teeth before setting my lips to the column of her neck.

"God, Nixon." Her fingernails bit into my shoulders as her head rolled back.

"How do you feel right now, Zoe?" I asked, then ran my tongue over the patch of skin between her jaw and ear. Given where she was sitting, she already knew *exactly* how I was feeling.

"Good."

I bit gently on her earlobe, letting my teeth scrape along the sensitive skin. "Just good?"

She rocked against me. "Better than good." Her lips dipped to my jaw, and then she pressed openmouthed kisses to my throat.

Holy shit. The hum in my blood channeled into pure, unfiltered need. "A little buzzed?" I asked, desperately trying to remember what I was supposed to be showing her.

"Buzzed. Hot. Achy. Restless." She punctuated each word with a kiss until she'd made her way back to my mouth.

"Like you have a pretty good idea what to do about it, but getting to that release is going to make you cross some lines you've promised yourself not to cross?" My hands shifted to her ass and I squeezed lightly, groaning at the feel of her.

"Is this a game to you?" she asked softly, looking me in the eyes and gripping each of my wrists in her hands.

"What?" A game? I stopped in my tracks.

"Me. This. Whatever's between us. Is it a game? Just something to get under my skin?" She swiped her tongue over her lower lip as a flash of something that looked a lot like fear streaked through her eyes, her breaths as unsteady as mine.

"No. This isn't a game." I held her gaze so she knew I meant it. There was far too much at stake here for any miscommunication. "Nothing about you is a game to me."

She exhaled a sigh of relief, then smiled slowly as she took one of my hands from her ass and placed it on her breast.

"Fuck." My mouth watered at the weight that more than filled my hand.

"Then forget the lines and touch me." She arched into my palm, her lips kiss-swollen, her eyes glazed, and her hair disheveled from my fingers.

I nearly swallowed my tongue.

Then I pulled her back to my mouth, kissing her deep and hard as I shaped her breast, running my thumb over her nipple. Seeing the green lace of her bra as I unzipped her last night had just about undone me, and, given the texture beneath the silk of her blouse, my bet was on lace again tonight.

Her fingers tangled in my hair as the kiss spun out of control. Who the fuck was I kidding? Everything about this was out of control—just the way I liked it. I flicked open the middle button of her blouse and slid my hand inside.

Lace.

She gasped as I worked her nipple through the fabric, her breath coming in pants against my lips. I checked to make sure the door to the cabin was still shut, then flicked open the next button and shifted her blouse so it opened right where I needed.

Lifting her slightly with one hand, I sucked the peak of her breast into my mouth, then teased her nipple between my teeth, playing with the lace to increase the friction.

Her grip tightened in my hair, so I flicked her with my tongue, then moved her blouse so I could give the other breast equal attention. Her responsive little whimpers had me harder than stone, and the way her hips moved was simultaneously torture and bliss.

"Nixon, you're killing me."

I lifted my head as my hand slid from her knee to her bare thigh. "You're so damned soft." It wasn't like I didn't know she had a killer body—I'd been around her twenty-four seven for the last month, but she didn't exactly share that body with the same frequency I did.

Used to.

It wasn't just the fulfillment of a fantasy to touch her. It was a privilege—one I knew she'd end at any second, because Zoe wasn't the one who lost control in this relationship. That was my role.

Our eyes locked and held as I moved up her thigh. One sign from her that this was too far, and I'd back off, but she swept her tongue over her lower lip and nodded.

I slipped under her skirt, which had bunched just a few inches shy of the juncture of her thighs, and still she held my gaze, nothing but desire in those green depths. Fuck me, she was wearing lace here too.

My girl had a thing for matching underwear.

I nearly flinched at my own thoughts—Zoe wasn't my *anything*, but then I felt just how wet she was for me, and I decided she might not be mine, but I was sure as hell hers in this moment.

"Zoe," I groaned, running my fingers beneath the fabric of her— Holy shit, that was a thong? No wonder her ass looked seamless in this skirt.

She rested her forehead against mine, then moaned my name softly when I skimmed my fingertips over her clit.

I wanted to hear her scream it.

But we were on an airplane with three crew members just beyond a wall so thin it may as well have been a curtain.

Every muscle in my body locked. What the hell was I doing? I'd wanted to show her what the need crawling beneath my skin felt like and gone for the easiest example, and now I had us so worked up I was a zip and fabric shuffle away from being inside her.

You're using her.

Just like she was a random hookup backstage or on the tour bus, when she was so much more.

"Nix?" Her brow knit in concern. "You okay?"

God, she was worried about *me*.

"You deserve better than this," I ground out.

"How about you let me decide what I deserve." She kissed me, swirling her tongue around mine. It took all of two seconds for me to respond and assume control of the kiss, but then she swayed, moving against my fingers, and I lost it.

"Zoe—"

"Please," she whispered. "I'm on fire."

Hell yeah, she was. She was so hot and liquid against my fingers I knew I'd slide home in a single thrust, but I wasn't going there. I'd cut off my own dick before I used her like that, no matter how badly I wanted her. I wasn't even sure *want* was the right word anymore. She'd become a need, like air, or water, or music.

But I could ease her.

"Come here." I cupped the back of her neck and brought her mouth to mine as I circled her clit with my fingers.

I swallowed every moan, every sigh, every gasp as I built her pleasure higher and higher, and when her hips writhed over mine, I strummed her clit fast and light until her thighs locked, then trembled. She was so close I could almost taste it in her kiss.

I deepened the pressure and pushed her right over the edge, capturing every sound from her mouth with mine as she rode out her orgasm.

It would have been so easy to kick her into a second—she was that responsive—but I eased her down instead, ignoring the demands of my impatient body.

When she lifted her head, her cheeks were flushed, her eyes wide, her breaths ragged—just like mine. I'd never seen a more beautiful woman in my life, never wanted one more than I wanted her in that moment.

"Nixon," she whispered, her hands trailing down my chest.

Oh God. My control was whisper-thin and disintegrating with every inch she traveled. I felt that touch in every cell in my body.

Not here. Not like this.

I captured her wrists, then flipped us so her back was against the couch, pinning her hands above her head. Instead of demanding to be freed, she gripped my hips with her thighs and lifted her mouth to mine.

I lunged backward, barely managing to stay on my feet. Then I practically ran to the back of the jet and flung myself into the bathroom, closing and locking the door behind me. The counter was solid under my palms as I balanced my weight, my chest heaving as I recited every single reason I couldn't go back out there.

She was on staff.

She had her own valid issues about what would happen if we did this and it got out.

We'd already agreed not to do the very thing we'd already done.

She deserved better than to be fucked on what was pretty much an aerial tour bus.

She deserved better than me, period.

I refused to use her like I had the innumerable women who'd come before.

"Nixon?" she asked through the door.

Just the sound of her voice was enough to send a shot of longing down my spine. *Get a fucking grip.*

"Yep." I lifted my head and saw someone I barely recognized —not just in the healthier lines of my face but in the stark fear that lingered in my eyes.

Zoe Shannon scared the shit out of me.

"Were you thinking about coming out?"

My fingers gripped the counter so hard my knuckles turned white under the ink that marked them. The door was all that separated me from the heaven of her body, from treating her like one of those girls outside my dressing room.

"Nope."

"Oh. Okay."

The fact I was actually hiding in the bathroom from the sexiest woman on the planet only made me grit my teeth even harder.

"Now is when you choose to grow a conscience?" I muttered at the guy in the mirror. The timing was shitty, but nevertheless, here we were.

I stayed in that bathroom until the captain requested we take our seats for landing. Then I found myself wishing the toilet had a damned seat belt. But it didn't, so I left the safety of the locked door and took the first available seat, which wasn't anywhere near the couch where Zoe sat strapped in, staring at me in complete confusion.

I kept my eyes forward and promised myself that's where they'd stay in regard to Zoe. No more flirting. No more stolen kisses. Definitely no more touching. All that soft skin needed to stay over there, out of my reach, for her own good.

Right. I could do that for her.

If I could give up drinking, then keeping my hands off Zoe Shannon would be a breeze.

Oh, who was I kidding? I was completely fucked.

10

ZOE

Nixon had been in asshole mode for an entire week. He was snippy, cold, and gave one-word answers every time I asked a question. I wasn't stupid—I knew what had happened between us on the plane was the reason. I had my own issues about it, but I wasn't taking them out on him.

He also wasn't sleeping, which I knew because the tea packet I left out next to the honey on the counter every night was always used and disposed of by the time I woke up. He wrote every morning, and by the afternoon, his mood was even worse than the day before, which made our afternoon hikes anything but fun.

His writing notebooks were full of chord progressions, tablature, and even a few scattered piano bars here and there, but there was nothing solid. It was like he'd written sections of thirty different songs, without completing a single one of them.

I'd never really seen his writing process, so I wasn't sure if that was normal for him or not, and I wasn't about to call Jonas or Quinn and ask, so I left him to it. When I wasn't with Nixon, I was online, scouring the internet for a band I could bet my career on.

Today, I'd fallen down a YouTube hole and stumbled onto a new band that—as luck would have it—looked to be based out of Seattle, which would be convenient if Nixon ever saw fit to take us home, or hell, if he'd just send me at this point since he could barely stand to be in the same room as me.

Besides, it couldn't be that hard to find someone else to keep him on the straight and narrow when he was doing a fine job of it all by himself.

Go figure, I'd finally let myself erase the lines between us completely, thrown caution to the wind, and he'd thrown up a wall big enough to be seen from space. It didn't take a mathematician to put one and one together and see that Nixon hadn't liked something about what had happened between us on that plane.

"Are you ready?"

I startled, then fumbled for my water bottle as I knocked it off my desk. Thank God the cap was on. "I didn't realize it was already five," I muttered.

"It is." He leaned against my doorframe, crossing his arms over his chest.

I hated that he looked so damned good. Hated that all he had to do was enter a room and my temperature rose. Hated that he'd flipped the switch back on to my sex drive only to make it perfectly clear I was no longer something he wanted. Hated the fact that I appeared to be the only woman on the planet who turned him off by getting turned on.

Mostly, I hated the way he'd completely frozen me out. I'd given in on that plane, thrown my better judgment out the door without a parachute, and *this* was the result? Even worse, there was nothing I could do about it. He left the room every time I tried to talk to him, and it wasn't like I could just say, "screw this," and leave. I was stuck with Nixon, no matter how badly I wanted him, or how big of a jerkface he was being.

This was my own personal crucible, and my pain tolerance was maxing out.

His eyes narrowed slightly on my computer screen, and I slammed it shut. "Do you want to drive?"

"Sure." He turned and left.

"Good talk," I muttered, taking an extra second to run a brush through my hair and locate my shoes. By the time I grabbed my coat and made it to the garage, he was tapping his fingers on the steering wheel.

It took exactly nine minutes to get to my parents' house, all of which were silent, with the exception of Nixon's playlist streaming through the speakers. Guy had a thing for moody music. Pretty sure his Spotify-recommended playlists were titled *Break My Heart, Another Rainy Monday,* and *Down in the Dumps.*

He pulled into the driveway next to Jeremiah's truck and killed the engine.

"You seriously don't have to come if you don't want," I offered for the hundredth time.

He had the nerve to look taken aback. "I like your family."

"Right." It was just *me* he didn't like, which would make Sunday dinner all the more fun. I steadied my temper with three measured breaths, mentally listed every sweet thing he'd done for me, then followed Nixon up the porch steps. We'd have it out at home, not at Mom and Dad's house.

"We're here!" I didn't bother knocking as we walked into my parents' house.

"Oh good!" Mom called out from the kitchen.

We hung our coats on the rack and headed that way. Mom met us both with hugs, which Nixon handled with so much ease I almost smiled.

"Dad has Levi and Ashley Sandguard in the yard," Mom told us as she fussed over the flowers Nixon had brought her.

It was official—I'd somehow broken him, taking him from a sex-crazed, arrogant rock star with a smirk that could melt the very panties off any girl, to a moody, brooding—fine, he was still a rock star—who wouldn't touch me with a ten-foot pole but brought flowers to my mother.

"Who is Ashley Sandguard?" Nixon asked, sliding onto one of the barstools.

"Next-door neighbor's little girl," Mom answered. "Her mom had to rush Carrie—that's Ashley's little sister—to the emergency room for a pretty nasty cut. Don't worry, everything is fine, she just needs a few stitches."

"So, set an extra place for dinner?" I asked, already crossing the kitchen.

"Already done." Mom waved me off. "And I told your father we're ordering pizza. I hope that's okay with you two?"

"Fine by me," Nixon answered. "Anything you need help with?"

Who the hell was this guy?

"Not at all. But I wouldn't mind hearing how the San Francisco trip went since my daughter's only details included the words *fine* and *okay*." She took the stool next to Nixon's.

Nixon's gaze flashed to mine, and I turned away before I did something uncontrollable, like blush or throw every can in the recycling bin at his stupid, perfect head.

"I thought I heard you pull in," Naomi said as she came in the side door, rubbing her hands. "Jeremiah and Dad—"

"I need you for a second." I grabbed her hand and tugged her into the laundry room, shutting the door behind us.

"You need me to do laundry?" she asked with a furrowed brow.

"What? No. But now that you say it…" I grabbed the basket Mom always kept of household wash, threw it in, and started the machine, then nodded when the sound of rushing water filled the room. Hopefully it would give us another layer of privacy. "I need to ask you something."

"Go for it."

"I…uh…hmmm." Now that I had her here, the question seemed, well, stupid.

"Zoe, I work in the world's smallest health clinic, and we've been friends since we were five. Whatever you need to ask, trust me, I've been asked worse." She leaned back against the washer.

"I somehow doubt that." This was a level beyond embarrassing.

"Does it burn when you pee?"

"What? No!" I shot her a what-the-hell look, and she shrugged.

"See? Already not the worst."

"Can you keep a secret?"

She arched a brow. "Have I ever *not* kept one of our secrets?"

"Even from Jeremiah?"

"As long as you're not asking me to break my wedding vows, I think we're in the clear. What's up?"

I glanced at the closed door, then took a deep breath. "Hypothetically, is it possible to be so bad at sex…well, not even sex, it didn't get that far. Let me rephrase."

Her eyebrows shot up.

"Is it possible to be so bad at foreplay that your…partner," I enunciated that word to keep from saying Nixon's name on accident, "runs away and locks himself in a bathroom until the pilot orders him into a seat because the plane is getting ready to—"

"Nixon did *what*?" Her mouth dropped open a good two inches.

"I didn't say it was Nixon," I whispered in a hiss.

"Yeah, okay." She rolled her eyes. "Because you spend so much time flying around with other people."

I glared at her.

She cringed. "Sorry, you were saying something about the plane?"

"It landed. And…the partner…hasn't spoken more than four consecutive words to me since then, and it's been a week." I hopped up onto the dryer.

"He seriously ran off and hid in the bathroom?" she questioned.

"It would almost be funny if it hadn't happened to me." I nodded.

She bit back a smile. "Oh, it's—"

My eyes narrowed.

"Not funny in the least," she managed to finish with a straight face.

"Seriously, Naomi. I'm probably violating about a dozen NDA's just asking you." I ran my hands over my face.

"Well, since it's *not* Nixon, then that's impossible, right? What might the name of this hypothetical partner be?"

Mom's North Face jacket stared me in the face. "North," I answered.

"Okay, then. Was there any pain involved in this foreplay session with…North?" She turned toward me, her nurse face firmly in place.

"No. I mean, not on my end, and he wasn't exactly complaining either. It's not like I'm a virgin. I'm well aware of what an erection feels like, and trust me—he had one." My face heated at the memory.

"Did anything…weird happen?"

"Unless you'd call having the fastest orgasm of my life weird, then no." My stomach twisted. "Maybe that freaked him out?"

She scoffed. "Trust me, no guy is going to run out because he gets a woman off too fast. Had it been the other way around, that's another story."

My shoulders dipped. "I don't know. He's the one who started it, and then—" I froze.

"Then?" she prompted, but there was concern in her eyes, not a need for entertainment.

"Maybe I pushed him too far," I admitted. "We'd just had this giant discussion on why we shouldn't be doing anything, and then I decided to risk it without letting him in on that choice. Maybe he didn't really want what ended up happening, and he sure as hell didn't want anything else. Or maybe he realized I'm just not what he's used to. Maybe something's wrong with me."

"Look, Zoe. I've seen the way…North looks at you. I would find it really hard to believe that he wasn't interested."

"Well, he sure got uninterested very quickly."

"And locked himself in the bathroom."

"Yep."

"And won't talk to you."

"Nope."

"Which makes living with him exactly how awkward? On a scale of one to ten." She lifted a corner of her mouth.

"About a billion," I admitted. "And we're supposed to leave in two days for the next show. I don't know. Maybe he's used to girls who…you know…take care of him first."

Now I was the one getting a what-the-hell look. "No. Any guy who expects to come first doesn't get to come at all. Those are the rules."

"I think I missed the handbook."

"You were busy taking on the world." She grasped my hands in hers. "I could be wrong, but I'd bet a million bucks that this isn't about you, Zo. It's about *him*."

"He has about a million references that argue otherwise," I muttered. "The only times I've ever heard…North turn a woman down were because he picked someone prettier out of the lineup. I have four years of experience to back that up." I shook my head. "I did something wrong on that plane, and now he doesn't want anything to do with me. It's that simple."

"Honey, that man is sitting in your mom's kitchen right now. If he didn't want anything to do with you, he would have hauled you back to Seattle and gone on his merry way." She lifted her eyebrows at me, like she was waiting for me to see her point.

Which I did.

"How the hell did I even get myself into this situation?" I was always controlled, always colored within the lines, always followed the rules.

"He's fine as hell. If I wasn't married to Jeremiah..." She tilted her head and raised her eyebrows.

"So, what do I do? Just endure the awkward? Every time I try to bring it up, he leaves the room. Clearly, it's not a discussion he wants to have." I rubbed my temples.

"I have no clue," she answered with a grimace. "It honestly would have been an easier answer if you'd just said it burned when you peed. Boys suck."

"Amen. And you can't say anything. Promise." I stared her down.

"Me?" She scoffed. "Hey, did I tell you who showed up at the clinic with chlamydia and no wedding ring?" Her eyes widened.

"What? No! Who?"

"Exactly." Her face deadpanned.

"Point taken," I muttered. "Thanks for listening, especially since you never ask questions like that about my brother." My whole body shuddered in revulsion. Having my best friend marry my brother was pretty cool until I thought about the whole sleeping together part—which was why I tried not to.

We left the laundry room and found Nixon and Mom spreading out the freshly delivered boxes of pizza on the kitchen counter. He looked so...domestic, even with the tattoos spreading from under his collar and wrists.

"You two about done in there?" Mom asked over her shoulder.

"We are!" Naomi answered with a grin as the side door flew open.

"I win!" Ashley scurried in with a mile-wide grin, throwing her hands into the air, as Levi scrambled after her. "Zoe! You're here!"

"Oomph!" I grunted as she hit me with the full force of her hug. "Ashley, you're so tall! What are you now? A senior?" I ruffled her thick blond curls and sighed with a healthy dose of hair envy.

"Ha! I'm in third grade!"

"Well, you've grown at least a foot since I saw you last. Are you hungry?"

"Yes!" She bounced on her toes.

"Zoe. Zoe. Zoe. Zoe," Levi chanted at my feet, his arms raised.

"Levi, Levi, Levi, Levi," I replied with a smile, hefting him up to my hip. This right here was the benefit of Nixon not hauling me back to Seattle and *going on his merry way*, as Naomi had put it. I guided Ashley toward the counter, where Nixon was opening the line of boxes. "Ashley, this is my friend, Nixon. He's a rock star."

Her eyes widened. "Like…a real one?"

"Depends on your definition of real." Nixon's shoulders shook slightly as he pivoted, tossing a smile at the little girl. That smile froze, then disappeared entirely as he stared down at her.

He looked…stricken.

"He's real enough," I promised, ushering her to the first pizza on the counter and turning her over to Mom. "Take Levi?" I asked Naomi.

"Of course." She took her son and smacked a kiss on his cheek.

Nixon stood off to the side, watching Mom help Ashley with her pizza.

"You okay?" I asked him quietly.

"Fine." The answer was gruff as he jerked his gaze to the wall behind my head.

"Are you sure?" Something was off. Way off.

"I said I'm fine," he snapped, just quiet enough that my family didn't hear him.

"Four words," I muttered. "Okay, then. Pizza?" *Keep it professional.* I needed my lines back. My borders. My defenses. The problem was that I didn't want them—not when it came to Nixon. More specifically, I didn't *want* to need them.

He nodded once, and we made our way through the kitchen-counter buffet. I snagged a piece of cheese and one with ham and pineapple.

"Admit it, Zoe, you miss Steve's, don't you?" Jeremiah asked with a hip check. "You might have all the pizza you want up there in Seattle, but it's not Steve's."

"It's not Steve's," I admitted. "You know I only come back for the pizza, right? You're just a bonus."

Jeremiah took two pieces of sausage ahead of me. "Yeah, why do you think I married your best friend. It was the only way I was guaranteed to get to see you."

"Whatever." I hip-checked him back, then headed for the table, Nixon coming up beside me.

He wasn't just tense. He was guarded.

"So, you chose the clarinet?" Mom asked Ashley.

"Yep! I wanted the guitar, but Mrs. Caster said they don't have guitars in band, which doesn't make any sense." Ashley shook her head as we rounded the end of the table.

"Well, I know Nixon plays guitar *very* well," Mom whispered conspiratorially, tossing a wink at Nixon.

Ashley's head whipped in our direction. "Yeah? Can you teach me to play?" Her eyes lit up.

Nixon's plate hit the floor and shattered.

Every head swung his way.

I glanced briefly at the mess, but it was the horrified look on his face that kept my attention. "Hey, it's okay. We'll clean it up."

My family jumped into action, but Nixon didn't move. His body was here, but he wasn't—just like that time in the diner.

"Nixon?" I touched his arm.

He startled, then noticed the mess and dropped down to pick it up. "I'm so sorry." He started to brush the broken shards of pottery into his hand.

"No!" I grasped his wrists. "Your hands."

He slowly brought his gaze to mine, and the utter devastation there would have knocked me to the ground if I wasn't already on it. He looked so lost that my heart physically hurt for him.

"Just give me a second," I said softly, rising to my feet.

He followed my lead, and my father swept in with the broom.

"Dad, I can—"

"I've got it," Dad assured me.

"Don't you worry about a thing." Mom *tsked* and joined in on the cleanup.

"I can't be here," Nixon whispered.

"Okay." I had no idea what the hell was going on inside his head, but this was worse than when he'd demanded we leave the San Francisco show. That had been anxiety. This was blatant desperation.

"I can't. I'm sorry. I can't. I can't." He shook his head and pulled his wrists from my grip, striding for the front door.

"Mom, Dad, I'm sorry." I dropped to help.

"We're fine." Mom stopped me, giving my arm a compassionate squeeze. "Go with him."

I scrambled to my feet and took off after Nixon, grabbing our jackets from the hooks in the entryway and flying out the door.

He stood next to the car, the keys in his hand, but he wasn't getting in.

"Want me to drive?" I asked as I approached.

He nodded, thrusting the keys in my direction. I took them, unlocked the doors, then threw our jackets in the back as I climbed in, shivering against the cold. The engine roared to life, and Nixon slid into the passenger seat, buckling in one smooth motion.

His motor skills are fine.

"Do you want to tell me what happened in there?" I asked, trying to keep my voice level.

"I want you to drive." He stared straight forward.

At least we were up to five words.

"Nixon…"

"We can go straight to the bar, or you can take us home. Either way, please start driving." His hands curled into fists in his lap.

"Home it is," I muttered, putting the car into reverse.

He was quiet the entire ride home, then stalked silently into the house after I parked in the garage.

"Do you want me to call someone?" I asked, following him into the room where he kept his guitars.

"Like who?" he challenged, his head swinging left, then right as he looked over the instruments.

"I don't know. Jonas? Quinn? Something happened back there, and if you won't talk to me about it, then maybe—"

The glare he sent my direction was harsh enough to back me up a step. "I'll what? Talk to either of them?"

"That was the idea, yes."

"I know you mean well, Zoe, but get out." He picked up the first guitar, and my stomach turned over at the possibilities of his next move.

"Nixon, don't—"

"Go." He put it into its case, then stood it against the wall.

I backed out of the room slowly as he packed up the next guitar and stood it next to its sister. I heaved a sigh of relief. He wasn't going on some destructive rant.

The wall was hard against my back as I slid down the surface, parking my ass right outside that door. Each moment that passed without a shatter or a bang, I breathed a little easier.

Until he carried two of them out ten minutes later and marched for the front door.

"Are we leaving?" I asked, hurrying after him.

"Nope. But the guitars are."

I stood at the door and watched Nixon carry the guitars he loved more than anything else down the long, winding driveway and out to the rural highway. Every step he took broke something inside me. I was starting to think Nixon couldn't be won all at once. If I wanted him, I'd have to fight for every piece he'd give me, then go to war for the ones he wouldn't.

I raced to the one I couldn't bear to see him lose and stashed it away, returning to the door in time to see him come back empty-handed, then start all over again until every electric guitar he'd brought to Colorado lay abandoned on the side of the road.

11

NIXON

I TAPPED my phone and the display lit up. 3:23 a.m. and I had yet to sleep, not that I really wanted to anyway. I knew exactly what I'd see if I managed to drift off.

Nix, will you teach me to play guitar?

Maybe the insomnia was actually a gift at this point.

The house was silent as I tossed back the covers and swung my legs over the side of the bed. A few months ago, I would have had options—someone would have been awake and ready to kill a few hours. Hell, three a.m. used to be prime time. Now, Jonas was in Boston with Kira, Quinn was in Bozeman with Graham, and I was in the middle of Nowhere, Colorado, with a woman I shouldn't touch, wouldn't talk to, and couldn't get out of my mind.

Yeah, being sober was *great*.

Maybe some of that tea would help with…something, anything at this point.

I didn't bother with my flashlight as I headed for the door. I'd been up in the middle of the night often enough to know the layout of the room with my eyes closed at this point.

My breath caught as I opened the door.

Zoe was asleep on the hallway floor.

It wasn't like she'd fallen asleep by accident either. She'd brought her pillow and blanket from her room. She'd chosen to sleep here. Chosen to keep watch—or at least use herself as an early detection system for my possible escape.

I raked my hand through my hair. What the hell had I done to this girl? Shutting her out this week had been a last-ditch effort to shield her from the utter wreckage I would no doubt leave in my wake if I got much closer to her, and yet all I'd done was drive her to sleep on the fucking floor.

I dug her out of the cozy nest she'd built herself and lifted her into my arms. She was out cold. The woman didn't do anything half-assed, including sleep. Damn, she felt good in my arms.

A good man would have carried her back to her bed and tucked her in.

I carried her to mine instead.

Her hair fanned out over my pillow as I got her settled, and I smiled. Tomorrow morning, my pillowcase would smell like coconuts and Zoe, which was more than fine by me. I pulled the comforter over her beautiful curves, making sure her soft skin was covered from the nape of her neck to the tips of her toes. It got cold around here at night.

My instincts told me to climb in and warm her with my own body. To pull her close and hold tight. To stop pushing her away and instead, savor each second I had before I inevitably fucked up a relationship I wasn't even in. She was only here, putting up with my shit, because she was being paid to be. And still, I couldn't slow the rate of descent as I spiraled toward her, caught up in some unrelenting force that kept us on what felt like a collision course.

Zoe was strong, but she was also tender, where I was a mess of thorns and barbed wire. Getting tangled up with me could only end one way for her. I wouldn't just ruin her reputation, I'd ruin *her*.

I sank into the winged armchair as she roused slightly and adjusted the blanket. She didn't wake completely, just burrowed a little deeper into my pillow and sighed with what sounded like contentment.

I envied her ability to sleep so restfully almost as much as I was determined to protect it. I hadn't slept a full night in over a decade without some form of self-medication. As penance went, I'd gotten off easy.

Nix, will you teach me to play guitar?

God, that little girl had shredded me tonight. It wasn't that their faces looked the same, because they didn't. But that hair had stopped me dead in my tracks, and when she asked me to teach her... My stomach curdled for the hundredth time since dinner—or lack thereof.

Why the hell had I gotten a chance to play when she didn't? It wasn't fair. It would never be fair. I'd taken one look at those guitars tonight and all I'd seen were the moments she'd been deprived of. Moments she deserved way more than I ever did.

The sun had turned the wall a dusky shade of pink by the time I checked my phone again. Six fifteen. Thursday, October second. We had to leave for Vegas tonight, followed by the Tacoma show. Not sure who the hell had booked that one, but I must have been drunk to agree to it.

Shit. We had a show tomorrow, and I'd just thrown out my eight best guitars.

Thursday. Trash pickup day.

"Fuck," I muttered, rising to my feet and grabbing a hoodie from the top of my dresser. Did I want to play? No. But I wasn't about to blow a show and make Quinn and Jonas look like assholes either. All of this would be for nothing if I didn't get my shit together and play, which meant I needed to get out to the curb before trash pickup.

Icy air blasted me in the face as I opened the front door, and I shut it as quietly as I could, so Zoe might be able to get a little more sleep. She'd lose her shit if she caught me leaving without her. Not like the bars or the liquor stores were open this early anyway.

The driveway was long, but that was part of what I loved about this property. Even if someone was dedicated enough to track me down, it was impossible for fans to gather at the front door.

My heart stumbled when I reached the road.

My guitars were gone.

"Fuck!" Thank God wildlife didn't handle cell phones, because the deer munching their breakfast a dozen yards away had a stellar view of my tantrum.

I started back to the house, huffing a warm breath into my hands to warm them, all the while exhausting my mental list of curse words. Not only was that almost a hundred grand in equipment, but I'd have to send someone to my apartment to check the inventory there. There was no chance of me playing a guitar I'd never held before during a concert. None.

The smell of coffee filled the entry and grew stronger as I made my way into the kitchen.

Zoe sat at the kitchen island, her cell phone and planner both on the counter before her, going over today's agenda as she took in her morning ration of caffeine.

That woman was as constant as the tide, but instead of it annoying the shit out of me, like it had a couple of months ago, it was almost…comforting now.

She didn't so much as glance up as I made myself a cup of coffee.

"I didn't mean to wake you," I said, by way of apology.

She lifted her eyebrows but kept those green eyes locked on

her planner. "Seven words. My, how verbose you are this morning."

"Got it. I'm an asshole." I took the stool next to hers but didn't crowd her.

"You're something," she said with a sigh. "And you didn't wake me. The alarm did." She tapped her phone a few times, bringing up the motion-activated camera footage of me leaving.

"You saw me leave?"

"Apparently." She flipped to the back of her planner, where she kept her notes, found whatever she was looking for, and returned to the day's agenda.

"And you didn't come running after me." It was a question and statement all in one.

"Nope. I figured you were either going for a run or wanted to test the patience of the local bear population. And let's be honest, I'm not keeping you from a bar. You could have sneaked off whenever you wanted over the last two months."

I tried to process her statement but kept getting hung up on the middle of it. "Wait, there are *bears* around here?"

She tilted her head, then sighed so hard the pages moved. "I'm not even going to dignify that with a response."

Okay, fans I could handle, but *bears*? I was liking this property a little less now. "I may have caused a problem," I said slowly, the words tasting like vinegar on my tongue.

"Oh?" She sipped her coffee and flipped the page to tomorrow, where she already had sound check and a radio station interview blocked out before the show.

"Well, it's trash day."

"No, it's not."

My brow puckered. "Yeah. It is. Thursday is trash day."

"Nope." She tapped the little sticker on the top of tomorrow's page with the icon of a trash can. "It's tomorrow. Which probably explains why there were no cans out on the street when you went to see if you could salvage your guitars."

I blinked. Of course she knew. If I'd been capable of embarrassment, I probably would have turned red, but that ship had sailed years ago—the first time a fan had posted naked pictures of me passed out in a hotel.

"Let me guess, your guitars are missing?" she asked, scanning between her phone and the planner, then narrowing her eyes at her phone. "Who the hell added that?"

"I wouldn't say they're missing as much as I would acknowledge that they're not where I left them." I leaned over slightly to see what had her confused.

"There's a meeting added before tomorrow's show, but I didn't put it there. *This* is why I keep my own planner." She shook her head. "So, someone took the guitars you tossed out like trash? *Shocking.*"

"Right." Despite my current lack of guitars, I almost laughed. She'd managed to throw sass at me without so much as looking in my direction. Even her profile was beautiful. Her hair was piled on top of her head in a knot, exposing the long lines of her neck and the stubborn set of her chin. "Unless you think the bears—"

Now she shot some side-eye my way.

"No? Okay. Then yes, someone took the guitars I tossed out like trash." I repeated her words verbatim, minus her sarcastic tone.

"Now I have to call the office as soon as it opens," she grumbled.

"I know. And...I'm sorry. Someone will have to go to my place and get at least four guitars from my studio. I'll have to juggle and retune a few while Jonas does the whole introduce the band thing he loves to do after the second set, but I can do it with four." I scratched the three-day scruff I had growing on my face.

"I have to call the office for the appointment, not the guitars," Zoe corrected me, then sipped her coffee.

"I know you're pissed at me, but please don't tell me you

expect me to play some off-the-rack instrument tomorrow." Because that wasn't happening.

"Your guitars are in my room." She opened her email on her phone and flipped through.

"What?" I put my mug on the counter.

"You heard me. Your guitars are in my room, but you're not getting the acoustic back until I'm sure you won't set it on fire. Oh, good. The plane will be ready for us any time after three. I know you want to spend as little time in Vegas as possible, but any later than that and you won't be able to make it to dinner with Jonas and Quinn."

She'd gone out there last night and brought the guitars back. Apparently, she'd rescued the acoustic before I even had the chance to haul it out with the others, which showed exactly how messed up my thinking had been last night. My chest tightened as my emotions bounced between relief, gratitude, and more than a little shame. This was yet another one of my messes she'd had to clean up. She'd known I'd regret my tantrum this morning and sheltered me from the consequences.

I turned her head as I cupped the back of her neck, then kissed her. It was chaste—I kept my tongue behind my teeth— but I put every ounce of my gratitude into it before pulling away slowly. Need flared, shooting down my spine and spiking my heart rate, all from a simple brush of her lips. "Thank you," I whispered.

Yeah, we were sure as hell on a collision course for something, and her eyes showed it, too, as she glanced down at my lips, skimming her bottom one with her tongue before looking away.

"You're welcome. So that means you'll need to be packed by noon," she stated, like nothing had happened. "The new leathers I ordered for you are already waiting in Vegas, and your therapist will be waiting after the show, as requested."

My eyes narrowed slightly. How the hell could she ignore the kind of reaction her body was having? Color flushed her cheeks, there was a slight hitch in her breath, and she shifted her weight on the stool, yet she'd already moved on to the day's travel plans. "Are you really going to pretend I didn't just kiss you?"

She scoffed. "Just taking a page out of your book. Now, we have a meet-and-greet scheduled—"

I took her face in both hands and filled her mouth with my tongue, kissing her with every ounce of skill I'd picked up from years of nameless women. *Zoe.* She wasn't faceless, nameless, or forgettable. There was a hint of peppermint on her lips as she melted into the kiss, her hand gripping the front of my hoodie.

So. Damn. Good. Kissing her only got better and hotter every time. I could have spent the next year of my life doing nothing but kissing Zoe and it still wouldn't be enough. I wanted more than a kiss. I wanted to taste every inch of her body, then come back for seconds, thirds, fourths. I wanted to feel her orgasm while I was buried deep inside her, to hear my name tumble from those lips, to wear little half-moons in my skin from her nails.

I wanted her, which was precisely why I stopped kissing her, yanking my mouth away before I could change my mind. Thank God I was wearing sweatpants, or I would have had to readjust. Then again, they didn't exactly help me out in the camouflage department.

She blinked rapidly as her eyes came back into focus.

Let her ignore that one.

"You were saying?" I asked, struggling—and failing—to keep my breathing steady.

"I woke up in your bed this morning," she said, a clear challenge in her eyes.

My jaw ticked, and I fought the urge to walk away. "You did." My voice dropped.

"Any idea how I ended up there?" Her eyes softened, the plea obvious.

"Maybe it was the bears." Kissing the hell out of Zoe was

one thing. Discussing whatever this was between us was…something else. I'd already told her she wasn't a game. How much more could she want? I turned my head and took a long drink of my coffee, uncaring that it was probably scalding the shit out of the vocal cords I'd need later.

"Right. Be packed by noon." Zoe slammed her planner closed and stood.

No matter what I did with this woman, it was wrong. Shutting her out was wrong. Kissing her was wrong. Doing more would be even worse. But that little flash of pain in her eyes trumped them all.

"I put you there," I admitted, catching her wrist. She didn't tug it away. "I found you sleeping on the floor, and I…" My eyes squeezed shut as I sucked in a deep breath. "I hated seeing you like that. Hated that I put you in that position. So, I put you to bed." I slowly brought my gaze up the length of her body to meet hers.

"In *your* bed," she whispered.

"It was closer."

She scoffed and tugged her wrist free.

"I wanted you in my bed." I stood, taking the vertical high ground if I couldn't hold the moral one. "I didn't get in with you or anything. I just…wanted you in my bed."

Her eyes flared in surprise. "I would have rather woken up next to you than alone in your bed."

A dull ache spread through my chest, sharpening into something simultaneously painful and sweet. "That's a really bad idea." But it sounded really good.

"Why did you run away from me on the plane and then freeze me out for a week?"

"Can we talk about something else?" I cringed slightly.

"Sure. What happened at my parents' house last night?" She stared me down even though I was a head taller.

"For fuck's sake." I rubbed my hands down my face.

"Pick one, and I'll let the other slide for now," she offered.

"And if I don't?"

She swallowed, then lifted her chin a good inch. "Then you can find someone else to stay with you, because I can't help you if you don't talk to me."

I swore under my breath as I realized how badly I didn't want her to go. There were only two people in my life I couldn't walk away from—Jonas and Quinn. I cared too much about them. But Zoe had shot right up there without permission. Which was probably for the best, since I never would have given it.

"Fine." The stool squeaked against the floor as I moved it back under the counter and stepped away from her. Maybe it made me a coward, but I went for the easier of the two. "I thought it was best to put some professional distance between us, given the direction things had gone."

"Because you didn't like kissing me?" Her brow puckered. "Because I'm not sure if you noticed, but you just kissed me again. Twice."

"Didn't like kissing you?" I sent up a quick prayer for patience. "If you'd like to come over here, I'll let you feel exactly how much I like kissing you."

She came closer.

I jumped back. "Fuck! Would you please let me be honorable for once in my damned life?"

"Explain." She sank onto the stool.

"I want you." My chest eased a little with the admission, and I raked my hand over my hair. "Let me be perfectly clear. I want you naked, under me, in my bed, on this counter, against that wall, in the shower, on the porch swing in full view of the wildlife—"

"I get the picture," she blurted, her blush deepening. "So why run to the bathroom like you need to wash the taste of me out of your mouth? Was it all just to prove how far I'd let you go? I thought you said I wasn't a game."

"You're not!" My mouth hung open for a second before I managed to snap it shut. "That's not what happened. I went to the closest room with a lock because I knew if I stayed on that couch, I would have been inside you in the next thirty seconds."

Her lips parted.

"Understand now?" I put the island between us. "I didn't want to use you like that. Can you honestly tell me you wanted to fuck me with the crew on the other side of the door?"

She drew back slightly as her brow furrowed in thought. "Well, I wouldn't have used that word, but in the moment, I'm not sure I would have cared if the press was on the other side of the door."

I groaned and gripped the edges of the counter. "That's the problem. You weren't thinking. I was *barely* thinking, so I did the responsible thing and gave us both time to clear our heads."

"Which took a week?" She folded her arms across her chest. She wasn't wearing a bra.

Great, now I was going to start drooling. "I might have a slight communication problem."

"You think?" she snapped. "And it's not *using* me if I'm clearly on board with it."

That brought me up short. "You're…on board with it? So many inappropriate plane comments are rolling through my mind right now."

"Nixon!" She pushed away from the counter, then sighed. "Okay, you're right. Looking back, I probably would have been a little mortified. About the audience. And the location. After the fact. Not during. You have a way of switching off my common sense."

"Exactly. I have f—" I grimaced. "Been with a lot of women. I've never really cared if they regretted it afterward because they were all clearly in the consent column before and during."

"I get it. You're a rock star. Everyone wants it." She put up her hands and rolled her eyes.

"That's not what I mean, and you know it. I care if you regret this, Zoe. I care about what you think. I care about being in the right state of mind when it comes to touching you, because I care more about your feelings than I do about getting my hands on you, which, trust me, is a *first*." I pointed at her. "And don't you dare pull that shit about not wanting you, when you know it's not true. I want you so badly that I'm hard the second I smell a damned coconut!"

"Well, I bet you're fun in the produce aisle." A ghost of a smile curved her lips.

"I've been banned by your local grocery store."

She laughed.

"I'm a mess. You're on the management staff. I heard what you said up there, loud and clear. I know how important your job is to you. It's...complicated, and I was trying to put some distance between us for your own good."

She studied me carefully. "Are you done now?"

"I don't know," I answered as truthfully as possible.

"Well, I do." She swallowed. "I want whatever this is."

My eyes widened and my heart stumbled. "You want... What about your job? I mean, I'd never let Ben fire you, but I know you're worried about perceptions."

She took a deep breath. "I've decided if you're willing to be real with me...then I'm willing risk whatever the consequences might be."

I stared at her in openmouthed shock. She thought I was worth the risk. Me. The guy who'd proven himself as anything but reliable. Perfect, gorgeous, rule-abiding Zoe wasn't just coloring outside her lines, she was obliterating them. For me.

"Say something," she begged, her voice slipping to a whisper.

You'd better earn it.

"All right," I said with a nod.

"All right?"

"We have two shows in the next six days. Let me get through them without…" *Alcohol. Drugs. Sex.* "And then we'll see. I need to know I'm not using you."

Every inch between us went tight in the quiet.

"Okay," she finally agreed, breaking the silence but not the tension. "But…" She winced, looking away before steadying herself and meeting my gaze. "But if you end up using someone and it's not me, I don't know—"

"Won't happen." There was zero chance in hell.

"I'm sure you mean that, but I'm not exactly new to backstage, Nix."

I came around the island and took her face in my hands. "You're new to *this*, just like me. And I'm telling you that I don't want anyone else."

For now. The flash of sadness in her eyes said it for her.

"I promise. No one else." I'd never offered that to another woman in my life. Then again, I'd never met one I wanted to keep for myself either.

"Okay." She stood, brushed her lips over mine, and walked away, scooping up her planner and phone. "Now get packed."

"Just like that?" I asked.

"Just like that," she agreed. "You made me a promise. I trust you to keep it. It's that simple. One week."

"Six days!" I countered as she walked out, tossing me a grin over her shoulder.

These were about to be the longest six days of my life.

12

ZOE

THIS HAD BEEN the longest six days of my *life*.

I had to give it to Nixon. If he'd been trying to heighten the tension between us, then mission accomplished. I couldn't stop thinking about kissing him. Couldn't stop fantasizing about what would happen once tonight's show was over, and we were on our way home to Colorado.

Then again, he'd probably want us to wait until tomorrow, just to be sure he could handle the aftermath of the second show on his own the way he had the first. He'd kept his word. No alcohol. No drugs. No other women. And while he'd occasionally brush his lips over mine when we were alone, he hadn't taken it further, even after the first show. Plus, I was pretty sure he enjoyed torturing me.

Like right this very minute.

I didn't need to turn around in the dark, hidden little spot I'd found offstage to know those were his hands on my hips, his lips at the shell of my ear, his chest pressing against my back. The second he touched me, my entire body started to hum.

And it was humming.

"What are you thinking about?" he asked.

"The bass guitar is bringing them down," I lied, motioning to the stage, where a local band was opening. Not that it wasn't true. Seven to One was pretty damn good. The vocals were hot, lead guitar impressive, and the drummer was on point. They had the sound, the talent, and the looks...except for the bass. I'd watched about a hundred videos of their live shows, and they all told the same story—the problem was the six-foot-three model with shit timing.

"Really?" He leaned forward, molding my curves to his frame. There was another act before Hush Note went on, which meant we had a little over an hour.

"Don't you think?" I reached up and tangled my fingers in his hair, turning slightly so my mouth brushed his jawline. Six days of mental foreplay had me ready to back him against the wall, regardless of who might see us. Six days of hidden looks, barely there touches, and secret smiles. He hadn't so much as given me a proper kiss, and I was starving for it—for him.

"He's dragging the tempo," he agreed. "But what I really think is that you're trying to kill me in this dress." He swept his hand from my waist to my thigh, ruffling the light, flirty material.

"I thought you hated the dresses," I teased.

"I hate my inability to concentrate when you're in a dress." He nipped my earlobe.

The curtains moved to our left, and Nixon stepped to my side, putting a friendly but professional distance between us.

Quinn and Jonas appeared.

"Here you are!" Jonas grinned and clapped Nixon on the back. "Checking out the competition?"

"They're not competition," Quinn noted, her attention

focused on the drummer, then slipping to the bass guitarist. "The bass is lagging."

"Told you!" I swatted Nixon's chest. Not that it mattered, since they were already managed, though still unsigned by any label.

"I didn't disagree!" Nixon smiled down at me, and my heart stuttered.

This was going to be bad. Maybe not now, but eventually. There was no way something that felt this wild ended with anything but heartbreak. I knew it. I just didn't care.

"I want your opinion on something. You got a second?" Jonas asked Nixon.

"Yeah." Nixon turned toward me, blocking me from sight. "I'll see you in my dressing room? I have to change my shirt."

"I'll be the one in the dress."

His smile hit an all-time high for sex appeal.

Yeah, you're screwed.

He winked, then turned and walked back through a set of curtains with Jonas. I shook my head to clear it from the sight of those new leather pants and focused on the band.

"You have a good ear," Quinn said, coming up next to me, her sticks protruding from her back pocket.

"Thanks." It was a huge compliment coming from Quinn, who was pretty much as brutally honest as they came. "They're already managed, but poorly. It's a shame."

"You're smart too." She watched me carefully, and I had the feeling she saw way more than I wanted her to.

"Thank you?" My gaze drifted sideways.

"Too smart to get yourself tangled up in Nixon." Her tone softened.

My gaze jerked to hers, and I felt the blood drain from my face.

"Shit," she muttered. "I really wanted to be wrong."

"I'm not...tangled." I knew exactly what I was getting into.

She sighed. "Look, I love Nixon like a brother. You know that. But you should cut your losses and run. He's not stable." Her words were at odds with the kindness of her tone.

"I'm the stable one." I fidgeted with the pass that hung around my neck. "I'm not blind. My eyes are wide open to everything he is. And besides, we're not..." I stumbled. "We haven't..." If my tongue would have cooperated, that would have helped.

"You haven't slept with him?" Her eyes narrowed.

"No. Not that it's any of your business." I turned to face the band but felt the weight of her stare.

"Good." She rubbed the bridge of her nose. "If it were anyone else, Zoe, I wouldn't care. But I've watched Nixon go through women like a river for the better part of a decade. He doesn't alter course. Doesn't give concessions. And when he hits the self-destruct button, he takes out everyone in his path. Jonas and I just know when to head for the high ground."

"He doesn't scare me." I shrugged, my stomach flipping at the fib.

"He should." She tilted her head. "You really haven't slept together?"

"No."

"Huh." Her expression shifted into confusion for a second. "That's not like him."

"I know."

My cell phone buzzed, and I looked down to see a message from Ben. "I have to go."

Quinn nodded, then touched my elbow as I turned to leave. "Zoe, I need you to know that I think you'd be incredibly good for him. I'm not trying to protect him by warning you off, I'm worried for *you*."

"I know." I forced a smile and headed for Nixon's dressing room. Quinn was protective of Jonas and Nixon, everyone knew it, but in this instance, she really was looking out for me.

I waved to the roadies I recognized as I walked down the hallway. Thank God this was just a two-show stint, and I only had Nixon to worry about. I'd never been a tour manager. I couldn't even imagine handling a whole tour the way Ethan did, but that was exactly what I'd be doing for whichever band I took on first. I'd come into Hush Note when they were already big enough to have Ethan on the road and Ben in the office. It would take me a few years to bring one act, let alone several, up to a level even close to that.

Ben broke away from Ethan when he saw me coming. "Did you get a chance to listen to Seven to One?"

"Bass player needs to be replaced."

He grinned and nodded like a proud father. "He does. Which is why I'm guessing they'll be looking for new management soon."

"How soon?" A little bubble of excitement fought through my practical pessimism.

Ben lifted a shoulder. "I would guess it's going to take the other members another few months to figure it out. Timing might be right."

"You think?" My head swam with the possibilities. In a few more months, I'd be looking to sign my first band.

"I do, especially since the Berkshire brothers formally gave me the approval to promote you once this is over."

"Really?"

"As of this morning. They're really impressed at how well Winters is doing."

"Well, that's all him." My heart jumped. It was really happening.

"And you. Seven to One would be lucky to have you, kid."

It didn't matter that I was twenty-six years old, I'd always be a kid to Ben.

"Are you talking about me again?" Nixon asked, coming up behind me.

"The world doesn't always revolve around you, Winters," Ben lectured but smiled. "You look good, though. Feeling good?"

"Absolutely," Nixon answered, flashing that million-dollar smile. "Straight and narrow too. Shannon here is quite the disciplinarian. Keeps me solid."

I rolled my eyes.

"Glad to hear it. She's going to make a lucky band even luckier when she branches out on her own here in a few months, although I hate to lose her." His smile dipped. "You sure I can't talk you into another year? At least until the new interns are potty trained?"

I laughed. "I think you'll do just fine."

Nixon tensed beside me, and my stomach sank.

"Fine then. Think about what I said, though. They might be worth keeping your eye on," he said to me, then clapped Nixon's shoulder. "You really do look good."

"Thanks," Nixon answered as Ben left, heading the opposite direction.

"Nixon—"

"Not here," he ground out, then plastered a smile to his face as a group of venue staff passed by. His hand splayed over the small of my back, ushering me down the hall. The touch was possessive but nothing out of the ordinary to onlookers.

The gaggle of women outside Nixon's dressing room perked up as we turned the corner, but he ignored them all, passing by the security guard with a nod as he led me into his dressing room and shut the door.

"You're leaving?" he asked, pinning me in place with his gaze.

"No. Not exactly." I tucked my hair behind my ears and leaned back against the counter. Why was it that dressing rooms all felt the same? "I'm staying at Berkshire, but I won't work for Ben anymore."

"You're not leaving Berkshire. Just me." He cringed. "Just *us*. As in, the band."

"You're not my band, Nixon. You're Ben's. I'm getting promoted, not leaving you."

"Why didn't you tell me? Why am I hearing about it in the goddamned hallways?" He laced his fingers and linked them above his head.

"Because I just heard about it in the hallway, and until it was set, I wasn't allowed to say anything! Nothing was official, at least not until right now." I took a deep breath, trying to remember there were staff members and fans outside that door. "I take my job very seriously."

"I'm well aware." His eyes widened as his mouth fell slack. "Holy shit. That's the deal you made with Ben, isn't it? When this"—he motioned between us—"started, you said you made a deal with Ben. I just didn't press the issue. You made a deal about *me*."

Heat rose in my cheeks. "Yes. The deal was that if I got you through the shows already on the books, I'd get my own band to manage, as long as the partners agreed." My voice fell to a whisper.

"February," he said softly, his arms falling to his sides.

"February." I nodded.

The space between us crackled with tension. I just couldn't tell if that crackle was electricity or the warning that sounded just before you fell through the ice.

Three heavy knocks sounded at the door.

"Come in," Nixon called back.

Chris, the security guard, popped his head in. "Sorry to bother you, but there's a woman out here who's pretty insistent that she see you."

My stomach pitched and rolled. So far, he'd kept his word, but how long would it be before I was too complicated, too physically unavailable for him to stick around for?

"Not interested," he answered Chris, but stared straight at me.

"Okay. She's not typical, if that makes a difference. She's older than your usual…you know," Chris added.

"Still not interested," Nixon responded.

The nausea in my stomach subsided as Chris shut the door.

"I'm not leaving you," I said softly, pushing off the counter.

"For another few months," he retorted, pulling his shirt over his head and tossing it onto the couch.

"You knew you only had to keep me around through the February shows." My mouth went dry at the sight of those familiar, cut lines, all brilliantly inked in various shapes and patterns. "Remember? You didn't even want me here."

"I didn't like you then!" He marched toward me, but I held my ground. "When were you going to tell me?"

"As opposed to liking me now?" I fired back. "I was going to tell you when Ben—my *boss*—told me I could!" I raised my finger to point but ended up tapping him lightly on the chest.

"I like you just fine, Zoe. One day, you might start to believe that."

I lifted my chin. "You want me. There's a difference."

He cocked his head to the side and dragged his heated gaze up my body in blatant appraisal. I ignored the way my breasts tightened and my blood grew hot. "Spoiler alert, Zoe. I've *always* wanted you. I've dreamed about stripping these dresses off you for years."

My lips parted. He noticed.

"You're not going to say the same?" He lowered his lips until they grazed mine.

"I've never seen you in a dress."

He grinned. "Smartass."

"Every woman I know wants you," I whispered. "You make every eligible bachelor list. Every sexiest man. Every hottest musician. You're well aware of your own appeal."

"I don't give a shit what every other woman wants. I'm asking *you*." He sucked my lower lip between his, then scraped it along his teeth before releasing it.

"Yes, I've wanted you since the day I met you." The admission came in a rushed whisper, but it was there.

He smiled, long and slow. "Good. It's nice to know we're on equal footing on that issue." He turned abruptly and tugged a new shirt from the hanger. That one would end the night with whatever fan in the crowd caught it. He'd stopped wearing his own shirt out years ago.

"You walking me to the stage, Shannon?" he asked.

Shannon.

"Absolutely."

He slung his favorite Les Paul over his back, then opened the dressing room door. "They're all yours."

The stagehands marched in to begin the evening routine of ferrying Nixon's guitars to the stage. Once they'd all been taken, Nixon held the door for me.

"Thank you," I said, walking through it.

He followed, putting his hand on my lower back. *Right where it belongs.*

"I'm still pissed at you," he whispered in my ear as he waved to a wide-eyed fan with a backstage pass.

I turned my face, bringing us dangerously close for being in public. "But you still want me."

His jaw ticked.

"Nixon!" a woman shouted behind us, her voice shrill and high.

It was nothing out of the ordinary, but Nixon's hand tensed on my back.

"Nixon! Please!" the woman shrieked.

We both turned at the same time to see a middle-aged blonde trying to barrel her way past security.

"Look, a show before the show," Quinn quipped as she

stepped from her dressing room and joined us.

Nixon's eyes hardened in a way I'd never seen before as he stared at the screaming fan.

"Nixon!" she wailed as Chris looped his arm around her stomach, keeping her from charging our direction. Something about her triggered my memories, but I wasn't sure what. Security kept a list of rabid ones, the fans who crossed the line, so surely, she wasn't one of them.

"Nix?" Chris questioned, avoiding her flailing fists.

"Not interested," Nixon responded, his voice as cold as his eyes.

He turned us back around and walked, his muscles so tight I thought he might snap before we made it to the stage.

Jonas walked out of his dressing room, much to the delight of a group of fans corralled off the hallway. Nixon loosened up as the trio stopped to sign a few autographs and snap pictures. I bit my tongue when one woman offered up a part of her body to be signed. My own body rebelled at the thought, flaring uncharacteristically with a jealousy so hot I lifted my fingers to my face to feel if my skin registered the temperature change. It did. I didn't want his hands on her, or any other woman, for that matter. I wanted him to be mine.

I exhaled a sigh of relief as Nixon chose her arm.

Quinn glanced between Nixon and me, lifting an eyebrow and mouthing *tangled* before turning to sign another autograph.

She was right, I was tangled. I wanted him for more than a few months. Somewhere between his penthouse in Seattle and the ranch in Colorado, between the private jets, the dressing rooms, and my mom's kitchen, I'd fallen in love with him. No wonder I was willing to break all the rules.

"So, you won't be running," Quinn said softly as she came to my side.

"It's too late for that," I whispered.

Her eyes flared, and her shoulders tensed as she glanced

again between Nixon and me, as if that charged, crackling space between us was a tangible thing. "God help us all."

"It will be fine," I argued, forcing a smile to my face as Nixon and Jonas finished up.

"You have to keep a clear path to the high ground. It's the only way to survive him," she warned quickly and quietly as the guys headed our way.

"This is where I leave you," I said to Nixon, who appeared calm and collected to the average viewer, but I knew better. That little spark of panic in his eyes, the set of his jaw, the flicks of the pick across his knuckles…he was most definitely not fine.

And it was my fault. I should have told him I was leaving, should have broken that rule too. Had I ruined everything before we'd had a chance to try?

He nodded. "See you after the show."

I caught his hand after Quinn and Jonas had already turned, then looked up into those dark eyes with as much conviction as I could possibly will into mine. "I have wanted you since the first day I met you. I listened to you play long before that. We've never been on equal footing. You blew me away through the radio of a pickup truck in the middle of Colorado when I was eighteen years old, Nixon. I wanted you long before you ever laid eyes on me."

His eyes widened slightly, but I saw that spark in his eyes settle. His jaw loosened. Then he nodded and pressed a hard kiss to my forehead, despite our very public setting.

"Zoe," he whispered against my skin, like it was the answer to a question I hadn't asked.

Then he walked off with his bandmates to do whatever it was they did before the show.

They were knee-deep in the middle of the third set when I realized why that shrieking fan had bothered me so much—she had curly blond hair.

Just like Ashley's.

13

ZOE

I SCROLLED through the latest contract offer with a little more force than necessary, skimming my fingers over the trackpad of my laptop as I sat at the dining room table.

I'd waited six days for Nixon.

Then seven.

Now eight.

He'd been quiet since we'd come back to Colorado, or maybe *focused* was a better word. He'd been kind, ridiculously courteous, and even conceded to my movie pick without complaint last night. He'd been…professional.

Not once had he brought up the deal I'd made with Ben, or the rather embarrassing confession I'd given him before he'd taken the stage in Tacoma. He didn't mention the woman with the curly blond hair, or that we'd earned a curious stare by more than one roadie when he kissed my forehead.

Nixon was cool.

Nixon was calm.

Nixon was collected.

I was the one going out of my fucking mind. I was in love with him, and there was nothing I could do about it. My heart had abandoned all logic, all reason, and embraced the complete madness I'd brought myself into.

The grandfather clock in the family room chimed ten, and I scrolled on, mentally formulating the precise rejection for this particular offer. Ben might be proud of me and ready to set me free, but he wasn't done handing me the grunt work, which was just fine with me, since it wasn't like I had anything else to do.

Nixon appeared in the doorway and stretched, revealing the strip of his stomach that carried the tattoo, *Apathy is Death.* If that were the case, I wouldn't be dying any time soon, because the heat that licked through my belly at the sight of his abs was anything but apathy.

"How much longer are you working for?" he asked, bracing his palms on the doorframe.

"Just about done," I replied, forcing my eyes back to the screen.

"Is it important?"

"No. Just reading an offer so I can reject it tomorrow." *Something you're familiar with.*

"Okay. Well, I'm going to head up to bed," he said.

"Good to know." I could have sworn I saw him crack a smile from the corner of my eye, but it was gone before I looked up.

"Want to come with?" His voice went all gravelly.

"I'm sorry?" I looked up at him and raised my eyebrows.

"Do you want to come to bed with me?" There was nothing but pure intent in his eyes.

"Is that a trick question?"

He stalked forward, his gaze lazily traveling over my baseball tee and pajama pants. "It's been forty-eight hours."

I turned in my chair to stare up at him. "Okay, I'll play your little game. Forty-eight hours since…" What? The concert? Ben's little reveal? My single-sided confession?

"Since I walked off the stage." He braced one hand on the back of my chair and the other on the table. "Forty-eight hours and"—he glanced at the clock on my laptop—"three minutes."

"Aww, look at you, telling time," I teased, giving his cheek a little pat.

He turned his face and pressed a kiss to my palm, then raked his teeth over the pad of my thumb and swirled his thumb over the sting.

My breath caught. "You have my attention."

The smirk that played across his face sent my heartbeat through the roof.

"Nixon," I warned. If this was his new form of getting under my skin, I was going to lose my shit.

"I'm level. I'm steady. And the only craving I have is for you. There's zero chance this has anything to do with the show, or the high, or even jet lag. I've been counting down every single minute since I walked off that stage—hell, from the moment you said you wanted me first. In a few months, you won't even be on staff, which knocks another barrier out of the way. Therapist said to give it a day, so I gave it two."

I swept my tongue across my suddenly dry lips. "It's been forty-eight hours."

He nodded. "So, I'm asking you again, Zoe Shannon, if you'd like to go to bed with me."

This was actually happening.

"It doesn't actually have to be bed." He leaned in and brushed his lips over mine. "I can adapt pretty easily. This table will do just fine. That wall over there? Even better. We've got a few couches, the kitchen counter too. Or I can take you straight down to the floor."

"Yes, please." I was going to combust right here in this chair.

"Which one?"

"All," I managed to say. "All of it. Yes."

"Thank God," he muttered, then kissed me hard and deep.

I looped my arms around his neck and held tight as he stood, helping me to my feet. He took my mouth with sure, rhythmic thrusts of his tongue, mimicking exactly what we were headed for, and my body liquified.

"I want you in my bed the first time," he said against my mouth.

"The first time?"

"And maybe the second, even the third." He kissed me between words as we stumbled out of the dining room and up the wide staircase. The moving part was all him, I was too busy kissing him back, unleashing the need I'd kept such tight reins on, to notice where my feet went.

We made it to the landing of the staircase before he gripped my ass and lifted me into his arms. I locked my ankles around his waist and kept kissing him, groaning at the taste of orange soda and Nixon as he carried us up the remaining stairs and into his bedroom.

I felt the bed at my back and unhooked my ankles, kicking off my slippers in the process. I should have worn better underwear. Should have broken out some explicit lingerie—not that I owned any. Nixon didn't seem to mind as he yanked his shirt off and slid over me, bringing his hips to rest in the cradle of my thighs.

I raised my arms, and he did the rest, sending my shirt to join his on the floor.

"Lace." He palmed my breasts, then lowered his head and sucked my nipple into his mouth, flicking it with his tongue as he held it gently between his teeth. I gasped, spearing my fingers into his hair as he moved to my other breast and did the same.

His hand slid beneath my back, and my bra came undone. It landed somewhere to the left.

"God, you're gorgeous." From the look in his eyes, he meant it. There was only appreciation and hunger in his gaze.

"You are," I said, my voice thin as I trailed my fingers across his shoulders.

He flashed me a wicked grin, then kissed a path across my breasts, taking his time with each peak as I arched beneath him. Then he moved down my body, stroking the curve of my waist with his hands, moving to my hips and thighs.

His eyes met mine in unspoken question, and I lifted my hips with a nod.

He hooked his fingers in the waistband of my pants, then drew them down my legs, leaving me in nothing but my underwear.

"I'm going to devour you," he promised with a hand on each of my thighs.

"Only if you do it without your pants on." I eyed his gray sweatpants and arched a brow. "Equal footing, remember?"

He doubled down, taking off *everything*. Sweet Lord, he was a masterpiece. The weight he'd picked up in the last few months showed in every line of his muscles, to include the curve of a really nice ass. His abs weren't just lean anymore, they were stacked, roped, tapering into a V that made my mouth water, and strong thighs—and *whoa*. Yeah, he was perfect *everywhere*.

My gaze flew to his.

"Now you have the advantage." He parted my thighs.

"I'd say you're working with a pretty nice advantage yourself." I lifted my knee, running it along the outside of his thigh.

He laughed softly, dipping to kiss the inside of that knee, then slowly, methodically worked his way up the inside of my thigh. My breaths grew choppier with each inch he gained. At this rate, I'd be hyperventilating before he even got me naked.

"So soft," he said against the sensitive skin of my inner thigh.

My hips rolled, urging him higher.

Again, his eyes met mine, and I nodded, arching so he could remove the last scrap of fabric between us. My thong hit the floor, and a heartbeat later, his mouth was between my thighs, his fingers parting me wide for his tongue.

"Nixon!" My fingers clutched at the covers, gathering fistfuls of fabric as my anchor. His mouth drove me higher, the pleasure so intense I gasped for every breath.

"I could stay here all night." He hooked my knees over his shoulders like he was going to do exactly that, then proceeded to push me to the edge of madness, licking and sucking at me until I was on the verge of orgasm, then backing down until I caught my breath.

"Nixon," I begged, rocking my hips as I rode that edge of knife-sharp pleasure, the tension inside me coiled almost painfully tight.

"Zoe," he replied, swirling his tongue around my clit, then stabbing deep.

"Please!" I arched.

"Did you want something?" He swirled again, and I whimpered.

"You know what I want!"

"What was that?" He gave me another long lick, and my hips bucked. "You taste so damned good."

"Nixon!" He really was going to keep me here, on the verge but not over it. If there was control to be had between us, he held it all, and the way he locked eyes with me, holding my stare as he flicked his tongue across my clit, told me he knew it. "Let me come!"

Hunger so deep it bordered on ravenous filled his gaze as he sucked my clit between his lips and used that tongue to catapult me into the hardest orgasm of my life. I screamed—it might have been his name—as the first wave crashed over me, unleashing the tension he'd so carefully built. Again and again, it crested, lessening in intensity each time as he worked me down, until I was finally limp.

Then he started again.

It came quickly this time, the pleasure spiraling to a breaking point. I needed him inside me, needed him to feel the same way I did right now. "Nixon, I want you."

"You have me."

"I. Want. You." I tangled my fingers in his hair, tugging lightly.

He groaned, then prowled up my body. "Are you sure?" Every line of his body was taut, the muscles of his shoulders rock hard as he waited for my answer.

"More than sure." My hands slid down the powerful ridges of his back.

He nodded, then reached into his nightstand and brought back a foil packet. "I'm clean," he promised. "I get tested every—"

I kissed him quiet. I didn't want to think about the reasons behind that testing—of how many women had come before me...would come after me. "I trust you." I did. I'd spent every day of the last few months with him. He'd never intentionally hurt me.

Unintentionally...well, that was an inevitability.

He nodded and ripped the packet open, then slid the condom on with practiced ease.

"And I'm clean too," I blurted, my nerves getting the best of me as he positioned himself at my entrance.

"I figured." A smile ghosted his lips.

"And on birth control." God, he was right there.

"I know."

"You know?" My hips rolled.

He hissed, moving his hand to hold the curve of that hip. "I've seen the pills when we travel."

"I just made this awkward, didn't I?" I cupped the side of his beautiful face and skimmed his lower lip with my thumb.

He nipped the flesh lightly. "You couldn't make it awkward if you tried. I want you too badly, just the way you are."

"Good." I melted from the inside out, my muscles relaxing beneath his rigid frame.

"Tell me you're sure," he demanded.

"I'm sure. I want you. I want this." I arched up and kissed him, rocking gently.

"Zoe," he groaned, flexing his hips and sinking into me inch by inch.

I gasped as he filled me, stretching me tight until his hips met mine.

"Holy fucking shit." He panted against my lips, holding himself completely still within me, giving my body time to adjust to his size. "Zoe. I don't even have words for the way you feel."

"I know." He summed it up perfectly. There were no words for this, no way to describe the incredible feel of him inside me.

I moved, and he took the hint, withdrawing, only to drive inside me again.

We both moaned.

His hips started a slow, deep rhythm I answered with my own as we came together again and again. Each thrust was better, sweeter, harder than the last.

I was never going to get enough of this.

He drove us toward that peak with steady intent, and even when I urged him to take me faster, he just grinned and drove deeper, adjusting the angle so I felt him in every nerve, every cell in my body.

Only when my thighs began to tighten again did he pick up the pace, watching me with an intensity that pushed me higher, faster.

"Nixon." I clutched at his shoulders as I felt that familiar spiral of pleasure coming undone.

"I love how you say my name." He swung his hips faster, harder.

I love you. I barely managed to keep the words behind my teeth as he reached between us and pushed me over the edge with his fingers.

I flew, chanting his name as the orgasm pulsed through me in waves of color, but nothing compared to the look in his eyes as he watched me.

"Zoe," he whispered as he let go, chasing his own release with wild abandon, following me over before I'd completely come down.

He collapsed, and I held him, savoring his weight, his gasping breaths against my neck, the shudders that wracked us both as we struggled to recover.

Within a few breaths, he rolled us to the side, locking his thigh over mine and cradling the back of my head as our breathing slowed and heart rates lowered.

"I think I might be dead," he said a few moments later, pressing a kiss to my forehead.

"Really?" I leaned back enough to lift my eyebrows at him. "Shame. I remember you saying something about a shower."

His grin was completely and utterly wicked. He carried me to the shower, and we started all over again. Who needed sleep?

14

NIXON

I SLEPT. *Holy shit*, I slept.

The sun streamed through my bedroom window as my eyes opened, and a quick glance at my phone confirmed it. I'd slept through the whole night.

No nightmares.

No insomnia.

Just Zoe.

Zoe, who was still asleep in my arms, her back tucked up against me, and the sweet little curve of her ass pressed up against my dick, who agreed this was the best way to wake up.

Not now, I told the unruly bastard. I'd been inside her three times last night, and she needed a hot minute to recover. I'd never been with a woman I wanted more the morning after than the night before, but here I was, fighting off the craving to take her again.

The sun shimmered through her hair, dancing over every shade of red like a living flame as I slid my hand from beneath the silken strands. So soft. Everything about her was so damned soft.

She was my opposite in every way. It went far past comparing the contrast of my inked hands on her flawless skin, or even the supple curves of her body to the hard planes of mine. Her heart and her mind were wide open, where mine were locked away for the safety of the general public. Her past was all picket fences, where mine was barbed wire. Her family was a step away from a sitcom, where mine wasn't even suitable for HBO. She was diligent and goal-oriented, where my work ethic ebbed and flowed with the tide of my moods. She was as constant as the North Star, and I was fickle on my best days. She was my better in every single way.

The only place we matched was in the bedroom—or the shower, to be fair. Hopefully, I'd get to test that theory later in the kitchen, the dining room…the list of places I wanted her was endless. Here, we were more than just compatible. I'd never lost myself in someone the way I had with Zoe last night. Never cared more about someone else's pleasure than my own. Never spent the night sober, that was for sure.

And yet, while that same fire of need was churning through me, demanding I wake her up with another orgasm or two, my heart was at peace just holding her.

At peace.

There was nothing more I wanted in this moment than the soothing fire of this woman.

The sweet feeling of contentment swelled in my chest and melody came alive in my head, a yearning that transformed into gratitude. I pressed a light kiss to her bare shoulder, then slid out of bed as quietly as possible, grabbing my pants off the floor so I wouldn't wake her with the sound of the dresser drawers shutting.

Then I took my acoustic to the sunroom and settled into the song.

Apparently, I'd found my muse.

———

"WHAT DID YOU THINK?" I asked Jonas two weeks later, once I'd worked up the guts to email him the rough cut of "Merciful Fire."

"It's good. *Really* good. Your hat is right there, honey—" I heard shuffling in the background as he helped his daughter.

"Go sled. This can wait." I was good with any reason that delayed this conversation, which was a first. Usually, I shared my music with zero reservations, but this one was different.

"No, I'm here. We're still waiting for Kira. Plus, I'm slightly afraid that if I hang up, it will be weeks until I hear from you again," he added with no small note of censure.

"Sorry. I'll be better about picking up the phone," I promised. It wasn't that I didn't want to talk to my friends as much as I felt like I was different here—Nixon 2.0—and I was just as apprehensive of the change as I was protective of it.

"Yeah, right. So, what does Zoe think?"

I took him off speakerphone and lifted the phone to my ear, then leaned around the wall of the living room to make sure she was still engrossed in whatever contract she was currently negotiating.

"Nix?"

I sighed. "She hasn't heard it."

"Really?"

"Really." I dropped onto the couch and stared out at the snow-covered Rockies. We'd gotten about a foot last night.

"But...it's about her, right?" he guessed, his tone dropping slightly.

"Maybe," I admitted gruffly.

"Nixon, we've been friends for a long time, and unless

you're hiding a whole collection of sh—crap somewhere that I don't know about, you've never written a song for a woman."

Silence filled the line.

"Can I take that as a confirmation?" he asked.

"Not if you're going to get pissed." I let my head fall back on the cushions.

"I'm not. I just thought you didn't…play with women on our staff," he said slowly.

"Play." I scoffed at the way he flipped the language around just because he was a dad now. "Yeah, well, I'm not playing. Not with her. It's…" *Serious. Addictive. Perfect. Infuriating. More necessary than air.* "It's complicated."

"You're telling me you wrote that song and you're not *playing?*"

"If you're asking if I'm sleeping with her, then that's none of your business." What was between Zoe and me was private. It had been two weeks of easy, open communication, no fighting, and the most mind-blowing sex of my life.

"Fuck," he muttered.

"Daddy!" I heard Vivi exclaim.

"Don't repeat that to Mommy," Jonas begged.

"Mommy already heard!" Kira's voice came through loud and clear. "Hi, Nixon."

"Tell Kira I said hi."

"He says hi," Jonas muttered. "Look, I'm trying not to be *that* guy, when you're obviously happy—"

"Then don't," I countered. "She's only on staff for the next two months. Once we're through the Houston show, she's leaving the Hush Note account and taking on her own bands."

"Oh." His tone changed completely. "Good for her."

"Yeah. She works really hard. She deserves it."

"She does. And when you need advice, call." There was some more shuffling and the sound of a door opening.

"What makes you think I'll need advice?"

"Given what I saw at the Tacoma show, I think it's safe to say that this is the longest relationship you've ever had—"

"It's not a re—" *Shit, it so was a relationship.*

"And there's bound to be a few struggles when she's no longer assigned to be at your beck and call. She's not like one of the girls milling around the dressing rooms, Nix."

"I know that!" I snapped.

"Good. I gotta go, but you should play her the song. It's pretty fu—phenomenal."

"Thanks." I hung up with him just as Zoe walked in. She was in jeans and one of my hoodies—which hit her low on the thigh. Relaxation looked good on both of us. "All finished?"

I sat up, tossing my phone on the coffee table to free up my hands. I'd learned fast that she was hands-off during the workday, but once she got through her daily to-do list, which was longer than my yearly one, it was *play* time.

"Yep," she said, flipping through the letters in her hands as she came closer. "Just going through today's mail. Nothing big. Looks like just a few bills." Her brow puckered. "This is weird." That was saying something considering she'd been responsible for quite a few unsavory pieces of my mail in the last few months.

"What?" I asked, gripping her hips and pulling her toward me. Everything could wait. I needed to hear her scream my name again in this room. The acoustics were incredible.

"It's from a law firm, but it's addressed to you." She flipped the envelope over, showing the forwarding sticker that brought it here. "Did you get sued again?"

"That was *one* time, and it was bullshit."

She lifted her eyebrows at me. "You spray painted that woman's house."

"True, but in my defense, I thought it was mine. And I was twenty-three. And drunk." I leaned back and tilted my head to see the return address.

"I'm not sure that makes it any better," she teased.

Howell and Johnson, Attorneys at Law. My stomach fell out. *It's not him, just a letter. Not him. Not him.*

"Have you ever been sued for paternity?"

But it was in her hands, a thin layer of paper away from touching her—affecting and infecting her.

"Nix?" Her hand cupped my face, and I jerked my gaze to hers. "I was just joking. But...have you? You know? Ever been sued for paternity?" Her brow furrowed, and concern darkened her eyes.

"Hell no. Never been that wasted." I shook my head. I had to get that letter out of her hands. He wasn't allowed here. Wasn't allowed near her.

"Well, I guess that's good." She cringed. "Not that you wouldn't make a great dad. I think you would. Just not..." She bit her lower lip.

"When I was wasted every night and all day in the summer?" I forced a smile to my lips.

"Exactly." She tilted her head and watched me carefully. "Do you even want kids?"

"I'm not sure a kid would ever want *me*," I responded, my hands flexing on her hips.

"Every kid would want you," she whispered, trailing her fingers down the beard I'd quit shaving after the last show. "And I bet you'd make some beautiful babies when the time is right."

My heart cranked over, but I was too focused on the letter to reply.

"Anyway." She withdrew her hand and ripped open the envelope.

"Practice." I yanked the letters out of her hand and threw all but one onto the floor, then filled my hands with her incredible ass and lifted her to straddle me.

"I'm sorry?" she mumbled through the fabric of my hoodie as I stripped it off her.

"You say babies, and it makes me want to practice making them." The hoodie hit the floor as I slipped the letter between the couch cushions.

She grinned. "You always want to practice."

"Makes perfect." I held the nape of her neck and brought her mouth to mine in a kiss that took us from playful to burning in less than a second. The bone-jarring panic that had accompanied that letter fell away, replaced by a primal demand that bordered on desperation.

I needed her *now*.

It took minutes for our clothes to come off and a condom on, and then I was inside her, where the world made sense. Fuck me, she was hot, and tight, and always so incredibly wet, so perfect. This was where I wanted to live—right here with her, where nothing else mattered. Where nothing else could touch us.

I kissed her hard as she rode me, arching my hips to meet her. She slowed the pace when I would have pushed it. Gentled her strokes when I would have driven her faster and harder. Ran her fingers through my hair and pulled back enough to look in my eyes, smiling.

The woman was going to drive me to the brink of madness, but I was here for it.

I sat back and let her take the reins, pulling her with me so I could use my hands, teeth, and tongue to work her into a frenzy. Watching her come was even more gratifying than my own orgasm, and I made sure she got there twice before I plummeted over that edge, groaning her name.

Our breathing slowly returned to normal as I cradled her against my chest. She traced the scar along the top edge of the wings that stretched across my chest.

"Jealous lover?" she asked softly.

"Bar fight."

She lifted her eyebrows at me.

"Other guy started it." I shrugged, then kissed her. "What

about you?" I trailed my finger down the silvery line at her side. "Old jousting wound?"

"Bear fight." She grinned.

"You're a dork." But I laughed.

"Appendectomy when I was ten." She sat up, depriving me of her skin but giving me a fantastic view of her breasts. "Which tattoo was your first?"

I hesitated, and nearly gave her the lie I'd quoted to every magazine for the last decade. Instead of pointing to the side piece of Icarus mid-fall, like I usually did, I drew her fingers to the small clock that rested under a wing above my heart.

"Really?" Her gaze flew to mine. "I thought it was…"

"If you thought it was Icarus, then why did you ask?" I held her hand against my chest, giving her the only piece of truth I was capable of, which was more than I'd offered anyone else.

"I don't like getting my information secondhand." Her index finger circled the clock, pausing on the Roman numerals at the second and hour hands. "Seven twelve."

"Yep." My heart clenched. "You going to ask me why?"

Those green eyes pinned me in place. "Do you want to tell me?" The little lift at the end of her question shredded my soul. She was always so hopeful.

I shook my head, crushing that hope.

"Then I'm not going to ask," she whispered, cupping my face. Her kiss was soft but a little sad. "The irony of you being inside my body when you won't let me in here"—she tapped my temples lightly—"is a bit too much for me right now."

With that, she slid off me, picking up her discarded clothing and the mess I'd made of the mail, then leaving me to my own shitty thoughts and a letter I needed to burn.

WE STAYED in Colorado as November rolled into December. I liked it here, where we were far from the cameras and the tabloids. The only parties included ugly Christmas sweaters, from which I abstained, choosing to wear a sweatshirt I'd had made of Jeremiah's face.

Zoe's mother laughed her head off, drawing every eye in the crowded community center.

Naomi drew a mustache on her husband's printed face.

Zoe rolled her eyes and told me she wouldn't kiss me while her brother's face was rubbing up against her, so I ditched it twenty minutes into the party. Nothing was worth missing out on Zoe's kisses.

I stealthily avoided Peter, who never let an opportunity pass without suggesting he join Hush Note on backup guitar. Apparently, he wasn't aware that Jonas currently occupied that position.

"So, when are you two headed back to Seattle?" Naomi asked, sipping on whatever green liquid filled the punch bowl.

Zoe turned a questioning gaze up at me. "Oh, I don't know. Nix, when *are* we going back to Seattle?" It was a discussion we had every few days.

"When we feel like it." Was I hindering her from scouting out new bands? Probably. Was I blatantly using any excuse I had to stay here with her in our little snow globe? Absolutely. I was twenty-three weeks sober and in no rush to jump back into the lifestyle that jeopardized that. Plus, living in Colorado had the added bonus of living with Zoe—an issue that would eventually rear its head when we went back.

"Such a defined answer," Naomi teased.

"Is this sarcasm from the same woman who walked into the kitchen counter when she first met me?" I wrapped my arm around Zoe's shoulders.

"That was before I knew you. Sigh. The good old days."

"Your family is mean," I complained to Zoe.

"At least you know my family. We've been together for—" Her eyes popped wide, and she pressed her lips between her teeth.

Ah, yes, the *together* label she'd studiously avoided using when dancing around the topic of our relationship. That little ache in my chest flared up at how worried she looked, so I went through a quick comparison in my head to Quinn and Jonas, who were the only examples I had.

Zoe and I lived together. Slept together. Fought both for and against each other, depending on the subject and day. Grocery shopped together. Watched movies together. Showered together. I didn't want anyone else and didn't see that changing anytime soon...or at all. We were here together, and we'd go back to Seattle together. Yeah, we were together. At least we'd better be after my lawyers threw a shit fit while arranging her Christmas present.

"Months," I said softly. "We've been together for months. And trust me, you're not missing anything when it comes to my mother. Now, how about you let me take you home so we can go be...together again."

"You're lucky my dad is across the room." Zoe smiled.

"I'm lucky for far more reasons than that." I pulled her closer.

"I'm lucky you're leaving, because you two are nauseating," Jeremiah interrupted, coming into our little circle with a sleepy Levi on his shoulder. "And don't talk about my little sister like that." He shivered. "I mean, I get it. You're a tatted-up rocker, but come on. There are families around and you're using words like 'together.'"

"Shut up." Zoe rolled her eyes. "You guys headed home?"

"Levi needs to go to bed," Naomi said with a nod.

"And Daddy needs to be *together* with Mommy," Jeremiah said, wiggling his eyebrows at his wife.

"Eww." Zoe cringed.

"And on that note." I hefted her over my shoulder, applauded myself for not smacking her ass, then carried her to the coatroom, successfully avoiding both Peter and his wife.

Naomi and Jeremiah followed us out.

"Crap, I forgot my purse," Naomi said over the stack of Tupperware containers she carried.

"Coatroom?" Jeremiah asked.

Naomi nodded. "Left-hand side."

"Here, I'll take him," I said, stepping forward to take Levi out of his arms.

"You sure?" Jeremiah asked.

"I won't drop him," I promised.

"Thanks." Jeremiah transferred the sleeping boy to my arms, and I carried him the rest of the way to their car, then buckled him into his car seat with a few quick motions.

When I looked up, Zoe was watching me with a mix of surprise and confusion. I kissed her quickly and tucked her into our car.

"You made it," Zoe told me a few minutes later while I handled the snowy roads. "Your first Legacy Christmas party. I'm impressed."

I shook my head and smiled but kept my eyes on the road. "I bought you a Christmas present."

"Oh yeah? I bought you one too."

"I bet mine is better than yours." I smirked.

"If it's just you in a big red ribbon, I'm not interested."

I laughed. "You're a liar."

"Maybe." She tensed as we rounded the corner into our driveway. "When we go back to Seattle, will we still be... together? Or is this a Colorado thing?"

I slowed the Rover down, stopping completely when the house came into view. "What do you want it to be?"

"You first." Her chin lifted despite the fear in her eyes.

That ache was back, throbbing behind my ribs. Damn, she

was gorgeous…and mine. "We're together wherever we go." I put the car in park and reached for her hand. "I'm going to fuck this up. I don't want to, but I know I will. I know I already do on some days. But I want this. I want you in my bed, and I don't just mean in Colorado. I want you with me in the hotels, in my apartment in Seattle—or yours," I rushed to add.

She shook her head. "You don't want to see my apartment."

"I do. I want to be wherever you are." It was the most honest thing I'd ever said to her.

Her lips parted, and she smiled. "Good. Because I feel the same."

"Thank fuck." Every taut muscle in my body relaxed.

"Oh, come on, like anyone has ever told you no." She picked up my hand and kissed the back of it.

"I've never cared enough to put myself in a position for someone to say it." Did she know everything about me? No. But she knew more than anyone else. That was enough for now.

"We can't stay here forever, you know. I can't always tour with you. I won't be outside your dressing room, fending off the women lined up to take my place." Her grip tightened.

I leaned across the console and kissed her until we were both panting. "No one else," I repeated the promise I'd made months ago.

"No one else," she said against my lips. "Just like that?"

"Just like that." I pulled back so I could see her in the dashboard lights. "And we can come here whenever you want. We never have to leave, as far as I'm concerned. Fly to Seattle for meetings, go out on tour, whatever."

She looked at me like I was nuts. "No, we can't."

"Yes." I looked her in the eye. "We can."

Two little lines appeared between her eyebrows.

"You know I'm shit at following the rules, and I'll just buy you a second present to open next week. Merry Christmas." I looked pointedly toward the house.

She glanced back and forth in confusion.

"I bought it. The house. The land. All of it. Except the bears. Turns out, those aren't for sale." I held my breath as she sucked hers in.

"You bought the house...as in, *that* house? The McClaren house?" Her voice broke.

"We can call it whatever you want, since you're on the title too. I was going to give you the whole thing, but just in case I fuck this up, I have the legal right to park a camper on the front lawn and loudly beg your forgiveness."

"This had to have cost millions."

"A couple." *Three.*

"We weren't even officially *together* until twenty minutes ago!"

"I didn't say my attorneys approved of the decision." I shrugged. "I like it here. I want to know we can come back whenever we want, so I bought it. Merry Christmas. Accept your gift." Was it always this hard to give a woman a present?

"I didn't get you anything near this big!" she sputtered.

"You're welcome." I grinned, then drove us into the garage and parked. She was still slack-jawed when we made our way inside.

"Seriously, Nixon..." She shook her head, looking around like it was the first time she'd seen it. "This is too much. I bought you a new strap for your Les Paul because the other one leaves a welt on your shoulder." She sighed.

My chest tightened. "Really?"

She nodded, pursing her lips.

"You noticed the welt." I pulled her against me.

She nodded again.

"You're incredible, and I can honestly say that's the most thoughtful gift I've ever been given." I dipped to kiss her.

She put a finger on my lips. "Don't say that until you see it. I had it personalized."

I grinned. "Oh yeah? What does it say? Nixon? Sex God? Yes, oh yes, please, yes?"

"Not exactly." She arched an eyebrow, and I waited. "It says, 'Zoe's.'"

My mouth dropped for a second, and she laughed.

"Just kidding," she rushed. "I got you two. That one was the joke."

"Until I wear it in Houston and you're the one answering the questions," I teased, meaning every single word. I lifted her by her ass, and she locked her ankles around my waist, Grinch sweater and all. "What does the other one say?"

She set her lips to my neck, and my grip tightened. "'Still Zoe's.'"

We didn't make it to the bedroom.

15

ZOE

I WAS BLISSFULLY, madly, totally in love with Nixon. Every day, it got just a little harder to keep it in, but I wasn't about to scare him off when he'd come so far. He challenged me every day, worshipped my body every night, then wrote music in the mornings while I worked.

It was the kind of perfect we knew couldn't last—hiding away in our little slice of heaven—but we held onto it with our fingernails. Nixon had paid millions to keep it—to give me equal footing in this one space we both owned. But even this house couldn't prevent the calendar from turning, and February came, no matter how hard we both tried to hold it at bay.

He wore the "Zoe's" guitar strap I'd bought him as a joke instead of the real "Nixon" one that had been his actual present for the Houston concert a few hours ago, and according to the thirty-seven emails in my inbox, the world had noticed. But hey, he was asleep at my side without a welt. Deliciously naked and weltless.

We probably should have let the post-show buzz run through him, but he'd given me that look the second we walked through the door, and I'd jumped him.

Five shows. Six months. He was still sober.

My job was at its contractual end, and we were headed into uncharted territory.

At least, we would be next week when we headed back to Seattle. I couldn't do my job from here—not to begin with. Plus, the band had a few studio days set aside now that Nixon had handed in three songs for the upcoming album. "Worry and Ruin" was my favorite of the three, followed by "Palm of my Hand." "Blue Castles" was right up there, though. I loved everything he wrote.

I pulled the sheets up over my breasts and flipped to the next email, then replied with the line we'd agreed to use. *Our relationship is private and therefore will not be commented upon.* I hadn't even wanted to go that far, but Nixon had turned that smirk on me and asked if I was embarrassed to publicly admit we were in a relationship. So there, another statement fired off to another person who had zero business asking.

On to the next email. It was an event request for July. I wouldn't be on the Hush Note team when we got back to Seattle, but that didn't stop me from glancing ahead at the band's calendar. They'd be in the middle of the tour but might be able to swing it.

Where would I be in July? I flipped back to my personal calendar and scrolled to summer. I'd no doubt be fighting to split my time between the office in Seattle and wherever I could meet up with Nixon. There was zero chance I'd be able to go three months without seeing him.

I grinned at the little tabbed reminder that popped up on July 12. Nixon: One year sober. I'd definitely have to fly to wherever he was on that day.

Nixon roared, jolting upright, his chest heaving as he fought to catch his breath.

I gasped and my phone hit the bed, throwing us back into darkness. By the time I hit the bedside lamp, Nixon was out of bed and shoving his legs into a pair of shorts.

My heart thundered. This wasn't the first time, but it had been a few weeks.

Something told me the further we got into spring, the more often they'd come. The closer he'd get to reaching for a sleep-aid that wasn't my body.

"Nix?"

"I'm okay. Go back to sleep, babe." He walked out of the bedroom without another glance my way.

I sighed, then slipped a robe on and headed downstairs for what had become a little too routine. He already had the teakettle on.

I took out the box as he grabbed the mugs.

Neither of us spoke until the tea was steeping.

"You're not okay," I whispered across the island, breaking the silence.

"I'm fine," he argued, running a hand over the scruff of his beard.

"You just woke up screaming."

"Won't be the last time," he muttered, stirring honey into his tea.

"That's not *fine*."

His jaw ticked as he slid the honey over the granite so I could use it.

I caught it, then added some to my own cup, shaking my head. "I hate this—"

"You don't have to sleep next to me."

I drew back, despite the soft tone he'd used. "Let me finish. I hate this *for you*. What happens in the nightmares?"

Terror flashed across his face before he managed to mask it. "Let it go."

"If you don't talk about it, you'll be a wreck by the summer." I rounded the island and put the honey back into the cabinet.

"I'll handle it."

I leaned against the counter, facing him. "No, *we'll* handle it, because that's what people do when they're in a relationship. But I won't be on tour to make you tea, and I can't help you if you don't let me in."

He turned, folding his arms across his chest. "I let you in."

"No, you don't. You let me skim the surface, but you never let me in." I was starting to wonder if he ever would, or if this was as close as he'd let me get.

"I bought you a house!" He backed up a step.

"Nixon." I groaned, putting my hand on his chest. "Baby, that's not what I mean."

"How much more *in* do you want?" he challenged, pain mixing with leftover fear in his eyes. "I bought you a house. With me. You want my bank account? I'll get you a card. You want a key to the penthouse? Wait. You already have that. You want your name plastered on my chest in front of a hundred thousand fans—"

"I want you to tell me why you have nightmares!"

"I want you to tell me why you can't ignore your email for twenty-four goddamned hours! Neither of us sleep, but mine is an issue and yours is what?"

"Work!" My head snapped back, but I kept my hand on his chest, right over his pounding heartbeat.

"You promised to take the week off," he reminded me.

My mouth opened and shut a few times before I sighed. "You're right. I did. I'm sorry. But that still doesn't touch the reasoning behind your nightmares."

Deflect. Deflect. Deflect. I'd gotten pretty used to Nixon's go-to move in a fight.

"Let it go," he begged, his voice dropping.

I glanced at the powerful chest under my hand, the physical proof he was healthy. Then I blinked at the clock inked beneath my fingertips. *7:12.* "I thought you said this was your first tattoo?"

His brow puckered. "It was. Why?"

"Huh." I lifted my eyes to his, but I couldn't see much in those dark depths in this lighting. *Go figure, even his eyes are hidden from me.* "That's the day you went to rehab. Talk about a coincidence."

The way his muscles tightened told me it wasn't. "Zoe. Baby." He took my face between his hands. "Let it go. Please."

"I don't understand." I was missing something. A piece of a puzzle that was all one color and mixed in with a thousand just like it.

"You don't have to." He shook his head gently.

"Yes, I do!" I snapped, the frustration bubbling over and pricking my eyes. "That's part of being together. Helping each other. I'm supposed to understand. I'm supposed to help you."

"Why?" He retreated again. "Why can't you just accept that there are things about me you don't get to know? Things I don't share with anyone?"

"Because I love you!" I shouted, my voice breaking.

His face slackened.

"Because I love you," I repeated, this time softer as my vision blurred. "Because I fell for you, and now I'm yours. My family is yours. My hometown is yours. My entire career has been wrapped around yours. And it hurts, Nixon. It *hurts* to know I don't even merit a visitor's parking placard in your head when you own me, body and soul." I batted away the tears that streaked my cheeks.

"God, Zoe." He moved toward me, tense with an emotion I couldn't name.

I stepped back, but he followed, holding my face between his hands and brushing the tears away with his thumbs.

"Don't cry. Fuck, I didn't mean to make you cry."

"I can't help it." I blinked rapidly, hoping to make the tears stop. "I love you. You have to let me in. This won't work if you don't let me in."

He pressed his lips to my forehead. "I know. I know. I know." The words came between kisses as he moved down to my temple. My cheekbone. The corner of my mouth.

Then he took my mouth like it was…his. And the little alarm of logic flared in my brain. *Deflecting.*

But I didn't care. I'd told him I loved him, and he hadn't run. Hadn't laughed. Hadn't made a quick joke and rolled his eyes. Hadn't declared this all some sick joke he'd been playing since August. He was kissing me like I was the most precious thing in the world to him. Like I was more necessary than air.

He kissed me like he might love me, too, and I let him.

He lifted me to the counter and stepped between my thighs, kissing me over and over, tangling his hands in my hair, then sweeping them down my body. My breasts, my waist, my thighs —I felt him everywhere, as though he couldn't touch me enough.

He untied the satin belt at my waist and parted the fabric but didn't slide it from my shoulders. My head rolled back as he pressed openmouthed kisses to my neck, lingering on every spot he knew would make me gasp as his hand slid up my thigh.

My body melted under his.

His fingers swept between my thighs, and we both groaned.

"You want me." His voice was a step above a growl in my ear.

"I always want you." There was no use denying it. Whether it had been an hour or a day, it didn't matter. My body responded to his the second he touched me.

"I don't deserve you," he said against my mouth.

"Yes you—" He stopped my words with another kiss, this

one deeper and hotter as his fingers set me on fire, ceaselessly building that tight coil of need within me until I was ready to snap, ready to scream, clawing at him for more because it was right *there.*

He slid a finger inside me, then two, and I whimpered. It wasn't enough.

"I need you." I shoved at his waistband.

"I'm here." He dropped his shorts, and a second later, I felt the head of him against me.

I grasped greedily at his back as he drove home, sliding to the hilt and filling me with one smooth thrust and ripping a cry from my lips.

He stilled, tensing unnaturally.

"What's wrong?" My hips rolled, and he moaned but held tight, pinning me to the counter.

"I'm bare." He rested his forehead against mine, clearly fighting for control. The condoms were upstairs.

"I'm on the pill," I reminded him. "It's okay." It was a hard line for him, but in that moment, I didn't care. I'd just given him my soul. He could break his rule for me.

"Zoe." His eyes squeezed shut. "Fuck, you feel too good."

"Either you trust me, or you don't." I would never trap him with a baby or set my career back by starting a family before I was ready with a man who clearly didn't want one.

His eyes snapped open. "I trust you."

"I love you." Then I was the one kissing him to keep from answering, because the statements weren't equal and I knew it. There was no equal footing here.

He tangled his fingers in my hair and moved, taking me hard and slow, both of us straining for the other as we came together over and over, each thrust better than the last. The kiss broke, both of us breathing heavily, sweat beading on our skin as the pleasure wound tighter and tighter.

I fought it, holding his gaze as I held his body, knowing that, in this moment, our need for the other was equal. Then his hand glided across my thigh, then between them, and he used his thumb to tease me to the edge.

My body trembled, my muscles locking tight around him.

"Yes. God, yes. You're right there. So beautiful." It was the look in his eyes as he said it that shoved me into bliss.

I unraveled, coming so hard I lost my grip on him, but he held me tight, finding his own release just a few thrusts later.

After we were cleaned up, he carried me to bed, then stripped my robe off and curled his body around mine, fading quickly to the deep even breaths of sleep.

The clock changed number after number before I realized we hadn't even drunk the tea that had taken us downstairs in the first place…yet he was passed out and at peace.

The nightmares. The buzz. The constant refusal to go back to Seattle—to real life. The insatiable need with which he reached for me in the middle of the night, often pulling me from sleep with his mouth and hands…

You naïve little fool.

He'd replaced one addiction for another.

I'd become his fix.

My sleep was restless, and when I woke for what felt like the hundredth time and the sun was already up, I slipped from the bed, careful not to wake Nixon. He looked younger when he slept, peaceful in a way he never was while awake, which only seemed to make his nightmares even less fair.

I dressed in my own room, though it really wasn't mine anymore. It was just where I kept my clothes. Nixon and I hadn't spent a night apart since October.

How could I have been so complicit I didn't think to press pause—to pump the brakes? I'd challenged the house, sure, but I hadn't refused it. I'd accepted everything he'd given and thrown my heart into these last few months with the knowledge they'd come to an end.

I'd tortured myself with the question of whether Nixon wanted me. If he needed me the way I did him. I'd never asked myself if he *should.*

The full cups of tea were the only evidence of what had happened last night, and within a few minutes, I had them in the dishwasher, my body on autopilot while my mind raced.

"I didn't hear you get up," Nixon said as he came up behind me and enveloped me in his arms, and like the lovesick girl I was, I pressed a kiss to his bicep, just beneath where his sleeve began.

The doorbell rang.

"What the fuck? It's seven o'clock in the morning. I'll get it." He kissed the top of my head, then headed for the door.

I put my coffee mug under the Keurig and pressed brew.

"What the fuck are you doing here?" Nixon shouted from the entry hall.

I abandoned my coffee and raced for the door.

"I've got it," he called over his shoulder at me, his back filling the majority of the doorway.

"Is that her? Maybe she can talk some sense into you!" a woman shouted.

My stomach pitched.

"You don't get to speak to her. Not now. Not ever," he snapped. "Get the hell off my property."

"I'm not going to hurt her, for Christ's sake," the woman argued.

"Mr. Winters—" a deep voice interrupted.

"I'm not giving you a chance to hurt her. Get. Out."

I eased to Nixon's side, getting my first clear view of the porch. A tall, well-dressed man grimaced behind a middle-aged woman with curly blond hair.

"Tacoma," I whispered, then looked up at Nixon.

Blatant horror stared back at me.

16

ZOE

"Zoe," Nixon begged.

I wasn't sure what for. Did he want me to walk away? To ignore that the very fan who'd tried her best to claw her way past Chris was now standing on our front porch in the middle of Colorado?

"Zoe," the woman said with a shaky smile, a plea in her eyes.

Guess everyone wanted something today.

"Ms. Shannon." The man stepped forward with an outstretched hand. "I'm Richard Howell."

Attorneys at Law. A mental picture of the envelope flashed before my eyes—the envelope I'd never finished opening.

Nixon's jaw flexed. "Get. Out. You're trespassing."

"What can I do for you?" I asked the man, avoiding the woman's beseeching stare as my brain gave me rapid-fire answers I didn't want.

Nixon had lost his shit when he'd first seen Ashley. He'd

denied knowing this woman even though he'd clearly met her. Same hair.

"Do you have a kid?" I asked Nixon, my eyes narrowing.

His flew wide. "No!"

Wide but honest.

"I'm his mother," the woman blurted, earning my surprise.

"Stepmother," Nixon corrected through gritted teeth.

What the hell?

"If we could just come in for a moment," Richard addressed me, not Nixon.

"Over my dead body." He moved to shut the door.

I stepped forward, blocking him.

"I represent his father," Richard told me.

"His father is dead," I retorted, only to be met with two very confused faces…and one very guilty one. My stomach did a dive roll and my cheeks heated. "His father isn't dead, is he?" I asked Nixon's stepmother.

"No." She shook her head, her gaze darting between Nixon and me. "Please, Nixon. It's been ten years—"

"I don't know how you found me, but you're not welcome, and the answer is no." Wrath shone from his eyes as he moved, positioning himself slightly ahead of me.

Putting himself between us.

I stepped back into the house. If Nixon truly hated this woman that much, there was a good reason.

"It was the guitar strap," she said softly.

"I'm sorry?" Now she had my attention.

"It said *Zoe's*," she replied. "All you have to do is google Nixon's name with Zoe and Berkshire Management comes up. You're his manager?"

This just reached a whole other level of creepy.

"Not exactly."

"We ran a property search, and you came up in title with an

LLC," she explained. "So, we flew out immediately, just hoping you might listen."

"I think you'd better go now." I took Nixon's wrist and tugged. I wanted answers, and I wanted them *now*. But I wanted those answers from him.

I tugged at Nixon's wrist again, and this time, he came.

"I know you hate him, Nixon, but it was an accident!" she begged, moving forward.

"An accident? Like the time I *accidentally* hit myself in the face with the edge of the table?" Nixon sidestepped, putting himself between us again.

Holy shit. My heart stopped.

"Nix—"

"Or how about that time I *accidentally* broke my wrist falling off my bike? Or wait, shit, that was the nonexistent tree house, right? Isn't that what you told the doctor?"

"He was drunk," she said softly. "He's been sober for—"

"He was sober when he blackened my eye at eleven, and again at twelve, and—"

"Enough!" she shrieked.

The nightmares. I sidestepped enough to see them both, bracing my hand on the rigid muscles of the small of his back.

"What happened to Kaylee—"

"You don't get to say her name!" Nixon roared, and I flinched.

"It was an accident," she repeated. "He's waited ten years—"

"What do you want me to do, Cheryl? Want me to go visit him? Absolve him of his sins? Because that's not going to happen. And it's not like Washington State has a parole board, so at least I know he'll do the time."

"We actually managed to get a hearing with the Clemency and Pardons Board," Richard said slowly. "It's very rare, and it's why we're here."

Nixon's head snapped back like he'd been slapped, and silence filled the entryway for a handful of heartbeats.

"Nixon, please," Cheryl begged. "He's so sorry. You should talk to him. He's changed. And if you would just speak at the hearing—"

"You have to be fucking kidding me. It will be a cold day in hell before you get me to speak for that son of a bitch. I hope he dies in there. And if you ever come near Zoe again, I'll dedicate my life to ruining yours. Do you understand me? The only reason I haven't is because I thought you were weak, not cruel, and we both paid the price for it. His price isn't paid yet." Nixon swept me behind his back, retreating into our house and slamming the door.

My heart galloped.

"If they're still there in five minutes, call the sheriff." Nixon threw the deadbolt and strode off, headed toward the living room.

"Nixon!" his stepmother screamed.

I glanced between the door and Nixon's retreating back. Only one path guaranteed answers. Problem was, I didn't want them from strangers—I wanted Nixon to tell me. Wanted him to let me in.

Steadying my heart with a deep breath, I followed Nixon into the living room where I found him pacing in front of the windows, tapping a message out on his phone.

"Let me guess, you want know what that was about." He didn't even look my direction as he finished and tucked the phone into his pocket.

"Of course, I do." I wrapped my arms around my middle. "Why did you lie to me?"

He stilled, turning to look at me with the flattest eyes I'd ever seen. "I never lied to you. Not once."

"You told me your father was dead."

"No, I told your parents my father died. You read it in a

magazine or in the troves of whatever file you keep on me with my damned SAT scores. For all intents and purposes, he's dead to me. I never lied to *you*." He dropped his hands, then walked past me, headed for the stairs.

"Where are you going?" I followed him.

"We're leaving," he announced, flinging the bedroom door open.

"Why is your father in jail?" I asked from the doorway.

Nixon paused, then shook his head as he yanked a bag from the top of the closet and threw it onto the bed. "This discussion is over. Get packed."

I felt his words like a direct blow to my heart. "You can't just ignore what happened down there."

He scoffed. "No, *you* can't just ignore it." The sound of drawers opening and shutting filled the space as he threw his clothes into the bag. "Please, Zoe. Let this go."

Like hell.

"Why is your father in jail?" I repeated. "Is it for hurting you? Is that what those scars are really from?" I gripped the wood of the doorframe to keep from crossing the distance between us and tracing those scars.

"Those are bar fights. Just like I told you. He was never stupid enough to leave marks on me," Nixon answered with another shake of his head.

Bile rose in my throat. "But he did beat you."

"Every summer, when I was there for visitation," he replied casually, grabbing the shoes from the bottom of the closet.

"Why did you go back?" I flinched at the sound of my own words. "I don't mean that it was your fault. It wasn't your fault. Did your mom know?"

"I told her after the first summer." He glanced at me, but there was still nothing recognizable about him in those eyes. "It didn't really start until I was seven or so. And my mother liked her summers free. When she questioned him, my father told her I needed discipline. Said I was out of control. My father...he's very convincing."

"Nixon," I whispered, imagining him as a boy, small and vulnerable.

"Don't do that," he snapped. "Don't pity me. I'm the last person who deserves it."

"It's not pity." It was compassion.

"Like hell it isn't." He ripped his phone charger from the wall, stuffing it into his bag. "And I'm the one who chose to go back as I got older. I'm the one who stopped telling my mother when it escalated. This is just as much on me. If I'd pressed the issue, she would have done something. She's...flighty and *naïve*, not inhuman."

"It's never on you!" There were missing pieces here, that's why I couldn't put it all together, but I didn't know what to ask. Didn't know what he'd even answer. But I had to try. I couldn't let him put on the *I'm fine* mask only to wake up screaming beside me tonight. A name—Cheryl had said a name. "Who is Kaylee?"

The blood drained from Nixon's face, and he froze like a statue, his hands on the edges of the duffel. It was the same face he'd worn when Ashley had come over. But he liked kids. Loved Levi. He buckled a car seat like a pro...like he'd done it before. Cheryl's hair—

"You don't have a kid, you have a sister." My hand fell from the doorframe. "Don't you?"

"Had." The admission was low, the sound grating over my heart like a thousand tiny cuts.

"Had?"

He pulled another piece of luggage from the closet, then started on the clothes hanging there. His motions were quick and jerky but efficient, as though his body was on autopilot. As though we weren't in the middle of a storm he'd held at bay for far too long.

"Nixon!" I moved inside the room—our room. How long before he shut the door in my face too?

"What?" he shouted, turning to face me, his hands out. "What else could you possibly want to know, Zoe?"

"Everything," I answered softly. Suddenly, the room didn't feel like ours anymore. Maybe it hadn't ever really been ours. Just like his heart, I'd only borrowed the space that was ultimately his. Now I was trespassing. "I want to know everything."

"Everything," he mocked with a sneer.

"Yes." This was the Nixon I'd seen backstage and across the conference table for the past four years—the egotistical, callous, pompous asshole. He had the mask in place so seamlessly I couldn't help but wonder if I was the only one who saw it for what it was—a scab over a sluggishly bleeding, festering wound. Somewhere between the two—that's where *my* Nixon lived, and he'd shut me out.

"You want to know about my little sister?" He folded his arms across his chest and glared at me with the same face he'd shown Cheryl. The face that sent everyone running.

"Yes." I leaned back against the wall next to the door.

"Really." There was that dismissive scoff again. "Why? What good will it do? She's dead. She's not coming back. She had eight summers in this shitty world before he snuffed her out like a weed he found growing in the sidewalk. Is that what you want to hear, Zoe?"

"I want the truth. No matter how ugly or sad it is." I swallowed and stuffed my hands in the pockets of my jeans to keep them from shaking.

"He killed her! It wasn't an accident. I don't give a shit that he was drunk, or that the charges were dropped to manslaughter and abuse. I don't care that he swears it was only the one time, or that Cheryl is so desperate for that asshole's love and approval that she still claims it was an accident. I've seen the report. The force with which she hit the bottom of the stairs could only have come from being thrown down them."

I gasped and pressed my lips between my teeth.

"Still want the truth, Shannon?" He lifted his brows.

"Yes," I whispered. I'd take whatever he'd give me because I knew this moment wouldn't come again. "I want to know what makes you who you are, Nixon."

"Jesus, you really are just like everyone else!" He shook his head. "My head isn't public property! The only person who owns the rights to my past is *me*." He thumped his chest.

"I only want to help you!" I pushed off the wall.

"Bullshit! You want to crawl inside my head and try to fix me!"

I floundered. "That's…that's not true. Do I want you to *be* fixed? Yes. I love you. I want you healthy, and I want your nightmares to stop, and I want you to be okay. But I don't care if I'm the one who fixes you, Nixon."

He tilted his head as a corner of his mouth lifted. "Right. So, you don't want to be the one who unlocks my secrets? The one who gets in here"—he tapped his chest—"and turns me into a changed man?"

"That's not fair." I wanted all those things romantically. To be the woman he trusted with his secrets because he wanted to.

"What if I made you choose?"

"Between?"

"Between fixing me and loving me?" He motioned down his body. "Just like I am. Right now. Addictions. Nightmares. General asshole. The whole package."

"I already love you." I moved forward, and he retreated.

"You love who you think I can be. Who I've been here in this house. But it's not enough for you, because I'm not perfect. I'm not…*healthy*. So, you chip, and you dig, and you ask, and you prod at me, like I'm the next square to check on the Zoe's gotta-fix-it list. I'm the phone you can't put down at night. The mess you can't quite clean up."

"That's not true." I lifted my hand to my chest, right above the tearing sensation behind my ribs.

"It is. We both know it. You're literally only here to keep me from fucking up. Maybe your heart got tangled up in the process, but the mission has never changed. So, I'm asking you to choose, Zoe Shannon. Would you rather fix me? Or love me?"

My feet were still on the floor, but I felt gravity shift as he stared at me, waiting for my answer. I loved him, and not only the version of him who existed in this house. I loved all of him. But I was also smart enough to know my love might not be enough to hold him. I might not be enough—not in the long run. And he'd still have the nightmares long after I was gone. Still carry the weight of his past.

"Choose." He shrugged, like it meant nothing.

"It's a ridiculous hypothetical."

"Choose."

"Fine." I ran my hands over my face. "If it came down to me loving you, or me standing aside so *you* could be healthy enough to love someone, I'd choose that. I'd fix you."

"Right." He turned away from me and zipped the first bag. "Right," he repeated to himself. "Well, so much for love, huh?"

"That's not what I mean. You can't just make me stop loving you." I couldn't even stop it if I tried. Loving him was a force so strong there was nothing I could do to protect myself.

"Sure I can." He zipped the second bag.

Gravity shifted again, turning my stomach inside out. *And when he hits the self-destruct button, he takes out everyone in his path.* Quinn's warning sounded in my ears like the wail of an emergency alert for a flood that hit two minutes ago.

I'd failed to climb to higher ground, and now he'd drown me.

"Nixon," I whispered as he calmly sat on the bed, putting on his socks and shoes.

"You see, I'm somewhat an expert on how to kill love." He didn't bother to look at me as he tied his shoes. "You just remove yourself from the equation. If that's not enough, you dole out a little neglect and maybe just a hint of what could be considered abuse. Give it some time, and *voila*, no love." He stood.

"I love you."

"For now." He shrugged. "But you asked for the truth, and let's be honest—damn, did you work your ass off to deserve it. So here it is: I'm the reason she's dead."

"Why would you think that?" I ignored the blatant dig at my character and concentrated on his confession.

"Because it's true."

"I don't believe that."

"I don't give a shit what you believe." He lifted one of the bags to his shoulder. "He never touched her—at least when I was there. He saved all that shit for me. I figured it was because she was a baby. Or because he loved her. I loved her too. It was impossible not to. And I went. Year after year, summer after summer, I went just so I could be with her, so I could protect her, like big brothers are supposed to." He sighed. "And then I turned eighteen."

"And visitation ends." I drew the obvious conclusion.

His gaze flashed toward mine. "It was the first time in my life that I didn't have to explain myself. I was an adult. Besides, he always took my phone when I got there, and I had too much college shit to organize to let that happen. He couldn't touch me anymore, and I convinced myself—like the selfish bastard I am —that he'd never hurt Kay—" He flinched. "He loved her in a way he'd never loved me, and hey, you don't hurt someone you love, right?"

My chest tightened, making it almost painful to breathe.

"She cried at graduation when I told her I wasn't coming for the summer, but I promised I'd teach her the guitar. I bought one for her with the money I'd been given for graduation—Mom was never in short supply in that department." He adjusted the bag on his shoulder and reached for the handle of the luggage. "Then I turned down every offer but Washington, because it meant I'd be close enough to see her. You got that one right back in Seattle—first person to see it."

I didn't feel like I'd scored a point, not with the loss I saw coming from a mile away.

"I gave it to her on her eighth birthday, but he was there, and I didn't stick around long enough to even show her how to tune it. It was too big for her anyway. I should have gotten her a kid-sized one." His face crumpled for a breath before he locked his jaw and lifted the suitcase to the ground. "She was dead a week later."

"I'm so sorry." I swallowed back the lump in my throat for what they'd both been through as I walked to the end of the footboard and lifted my hand to his chest. His heart was racing, his muscles tight.

For a second, our gazes collided, and he was there. He was still mine.

Then he froze me out with a single blink. "Why? It wasn't your fault. It was mine. I've always done whatever was best for me, Shannon." He focused on the wall. "Anyway, there was no record of my abuse, no pattern to go on, so it was ruled as manslaughter. He got thirty years. I got back the guitar I'd given her. I don't even have a picture of her." That last part faded into a whisper.

The acoustic. He didn't say it, but I knew it from the bottom of my soul—the acoustic was hers. It was Kaylee's. I didn't know what to say, what to do, or how to even begin helping him. "It wasn't your fault."

"I chose not to go. She died. That's a pretty easy line to draw."

A car honked outside.

"That's my ride. Amazing that even a town as small as

Legacy has Uber." He walked right past me, as though my hand hadn't been touching him. As if I wasn't even there.

"Where are you going?" I followed him into the hallway.

"Back to Seattle," he answered over his shoulder. "I figured we should leave the Rover here in the garage, but now that we're traveling separately, you can do whatever you want with it."

"Traveling separately?" This wasn't happening. I couldn't fathom a world where Nixon would actually walk out and leave me. Somehow my legs got the message and raced after him.

"Well, yeah. I asked you to drop it. I asked you to pack. I asked you to choose." He was already in the entry hall when I caught up to him. "You chose."

"This isn't how this works!" I shouted, reaching for his arm.

He shrugged me off. "It takes two to decide how a relationship works, and I decided we're not in one anymore. You don't want me, Zoe. You want whatever little picture it is you painted of me inside your head."

"That's not true! I love you!" And he was maliciously, purposely breaking my heart.

"And whose fault is that? I never asked you to!" he snapped. "And this is exactly why. Consider it a mercy that it ends here, Shannon. Before the tours and the media and my inevitable decline decide to do it for us. Besides, it will make it way less awkward on the occasions I have to come into the office if it all just stays...here." His gaze skimmed the exposed timbers and rock walls.

"Don't leave me," I whispered. "Don't do this." Already, I felt the cracks in my soul widening, splitting apart under his reckless hands. *You don't hurt someone you love, right?* That's what he'd said. But he'd never loved me.

He'd used me, and I'd let him.

"The plane will be back tomorrow. Or whenever you're ready to leave. Don't hurry on my account." He swept his gaze over me like it was the last time, like he'd need to remember.

"Oh, and don't worry about the guitars. I'll have Ben send his new Shannon for them." He let go of the suitcase only long enough to twist the handle on the door and open it.

New Shannon. Because I was replaceable.

"Just like that?" I challenged, throwing the words that had defined just about every stage of our relationship back at him.

"Just like that."

"Funny how you accuse me of trying to fix you when that's all I was *to* you—a fix." Something ugly erupted from the fissures in my soul, pricking at my eyes.

He stiffened in the doorframe but didn't turn. "Good. You're finally learning. You might survive the industry after all. See you around, Shannon."

He didn't even slam the door as he left. The sound of my ruin was the soft *click* of the door shutting behind him and the silence that followed. He didn't care enough to scream. To fight. To hold on.

Apathy is Death. That's what he had inked across his stomach, and that's what this was—his emotional apathy, my death. The months of waiting, the celibacy, the monogamy, the effort... it wasn't affection. Wasn't love or even attachment or devotion. It was the price he'd paid to attain his fix.

And now he'd find a new one.

17

ZOE

I DROPPED my bags just inside my apartment door, then stood on the little patch of linoleum that served as my entryway, staring at the space that no longer felt like home.

Or maybe I didn't feel like me anymore.

This apartment belonged to BN Zoe. Before Nixon. I was someone else entirely after him. *That's exactly what this is*, I thought as I slowly walked to my couch, falling into the soft cushions. This was a new era—after Nixon.

I'd stayed in Colorado for two days. First, because I couldn't believe he wasn't going to walk back in that door. Couldn't believe he'd thrown away our entire relationship on a hypothetical question. Would he have stayed if I'd answered selfishly? Chosen to keep him for myself, wounded and hurting? That entire day, I'd done nothing but cry and stare out the window, waiting for him come back.

It hadn't been until the next morning, when I'd woken with tear-swollen eyes, that I remembered Nixon never came back.

Nixon never made the first move. Our entire relationship, first professional then personal, had been based on me chasing him. I was the one who'd tracked him down. I was the one who'd told him I wanted more. I was the one who'd risked my reputation in an industry that wasn't known for second chances. I was the one who'd pried his secrets loose. And I was the one he'd left behind to clean up the mess, as usual.

Nixon didn't come back. Not for me. Not for anyone. That would take a vulnerability he wasn't willing to expose.

That second day, I'd spent doing my job. Packing the things he'd left behind and shutting up the house. Trying like hell to close the gaping wounds he'd left in my heart, only to accept it was useless. There was no suture in this world strong enough to hold me together.

I fell to my side, curling up on the couch and clutching one of the throw pillows to my chest. I wasn't brokenhearted. I was emotionally eviscerated, bleeding out.

Tears turned my vision blurry and I let them fall, not bothering to wipe them away as the trickle became a steady stream. No risk. No reward.

I'd risked.

I'd lost.

I'd been too blind to see I'd let myself become the fix for the very addiction I'd been assigned to guard him against.

He'd failed me, yes. But I'd also failed him. In that, we were perfectly matched. My phone rang, and I ripped it from my back pocket.

Naomi. I hit decline and put it on the coffee table. I wasn't ready to talk about what had happened. I wasn't sure I ever would be. There simply weren't words for this kind of pain. No way to explain the complete and total devastation that came with giving every part of yourself to someone who took that gift and twisted it.

Twenty minutes. That was all it would take for me to get to

Nixon's penthouse. I even had a key. Twenty minutes, and I could fight. I could make him listen. I could use the explosive chemistry between us to solder us together, broken pieces and all. I could break down those walls of his, just like I had so many times before.

But I was just so damned tired—too tired to keep chasing a man who didn't want to be caught. Didn't want to be open. Didn't want to love me.

I fell asleep there on the couch.

I woke the next morning and declined every call that came in. None of them were from him anyway. Jeremiah. Naomi. Mom. Even Ben. I declined them all, wishing I could find a way to do the same to a world that waited outside my door. The world where Nixon wasn't mine anymore…if he ever had been.

Two days later, someone pounded on my door.

I tried to ignore it, but after ten straight minutes, I hauled myself from the couch and walked to the front door, passing the bags I had yet to unpack.

"I'm not leaving until I see you, Shannon." Ben's voice came through the wood.

Shannon.

My heart clenched, but I yanked open the door to see my boss standing there in jeans and a sweater.

"Damn," he muttered, giving me a quick once-over. "Okay. Get in the shower." He walked into my apartment and shut the door himself.

"I'm sorry?" I folded my arms across my chest.

"We have an appointment in a little over an hour, so get in the shower." He lifted his brows.

"No, we don't." I shook my head.

"Look." He hauled out his cell phone and opened it to the office calendar. Sure enough, we had an appointment.

"I'm not even supposed to be here," I groaned. "I'm still on vacation time."

"Get. In. The. Shower." He crossed his arms and stared me down.

"Fine," I answered, just because it was easier than fighting with Ben. I didn't have the energy for it.

"And put on something that doesn't smell like you've been wearing it for a week!" he called after me.

"Picky, picky," I mumbled.

Forty-five minutes later, I emerged from my bedroom, showered, with dried hair, minimal makeup, and dressed in jeans and a silk blouse.

"Feel better?" Ben asked from the kitchen, where he'd loaded the dishwasher.

"Sure. Like putting a Band-Aid on a bullet wound." I flashed the fakest smile in the history of fake smiles.

"Uh-huh." He shook his head. "Let's go."

Thirty minutes later, we sat in a private booth in the balcony of a downtown club, both nursing sodas as a crowd milled beneath us, waiting for a show to begin.

"I can't believe you hauled me out to listen to a band." I trailed my finger through the condensation on the outside of my glass.

"I can't believe I had to." He sipped his drink and looked out over the crowd.

"You know what happened?" Here it came—my downfall.

"Given that stunt Nixon pulled in Houston with that guitar strap, the fact that he's locked himself inside his penthouse, and your general state of devastation, it's not too hard to put together."

"Are you firing me?"

His gaze swung back to mine. "Why would I fire you?"

"For sleeping with a client. Not exactly professional of me, was it?"

"No, it wasn't, and no, I'm not going to fire you. Remember, as of last week, I'm no longer your boss. You're a manager in your own right." His mouth tightened. "Do I think your choice was reckless, foolish, and stupid? Yes."

"I know," I said softly.

"I know you do, which is why I didn't bring it up." He shrugged.

"Everyone knows." I rolled the glass between my palms.

"Yep. Nixon Winters wore your name across his chest. You weren't exactly discreet there, Zoe."

Zoe. Not Shannon. My gaze rose to meet his.

"You made a choice, and like it or not, you have to deal with the consequences, which, in this case, appear to be a broken heart and some office gossip." He nodded once. "But I'll be damned if I watch the young woman I just spent four years training waste her potential because she fell for a guy too damaged to hold on to her."

I swallowed, trying to dislodge the lump growing in my throat.

"Kelly Rowland, Mary J. Blige, Celine Dion, and Usher," he said, as the lights flashed and a cheer went up from the crowd.

"I don't follow." I shook my head.

"All artists who married their managers." He shrugged. "You're not the first to fall for a star. You won't be the last. Now hold your head up and get back to work."

"I still love him," I admitted.

"I figured. Do you see that changing any time soon?" He tilted his head.

I shook mine. Getting over Nixon wasn't something I saw on the horizon. I wasn't saying never, but definitely not now.

"Then, again, hold your head up and get back to work. You've earned it. Take it." He nodded toward the stage as a band walked on.

I dragged in a heavy breath. Ben was right. Nixon was gone. I could cry for a week, a month, or the rest of my life. It wouldn't change anything. All I could do was put one foot in front of the other and wait for the pain to lessen. "I'm not sure where to start."

Ben grinned as the first notes of a familiar song rang out, and my gaze jerked to the stage.

"You can start by telling them their bass player sucks."

18

NIXON

I SAT at my dining room table, staring down the barrel of a bottle of Crystal Skull, imagining the taste of the vodka on my lips, the slight burn as it would slide down my throat, the blissful stupor that would come next.

Buying it had been easy without Zoe at my side.

That was a lie. It would have been easy to buy it at any point in the last six months. I'd chosen not to. Chosen not to sneak away. Chosen to please her, to make her proud of me...to make me proud of myself.

But the pain of recovery was nothing compared to the utter agony shredding my chest, screaming with the constant reminder that Zoe wasn't here. I wasn't enough for her. Wasn't healed. Didn't fit into the lines she drew for her life.

My phone rang. Jonas.

Decline.

Quinn.

Decline.

I sat there for the next hour, my focus bouncing back and forth between my phone and the bottle. I could call her. I could fix this. I could beg her to fix me, to love me. But I couldn't guarantee I'd actually, eventually, *be* fixed. This was simply who I was.

Facing a life without Zoe felt as impossible as that first day at rehab had been, starting down a path I couldn't imagine reaching the end of. But the reasoning behind the two were so different I couldn't compare them.

The alcohol had to go. It was killing my body, my mind, and my friends. It was slowly wiping away every ounce of my talent and led to the shittiest decisions of my life.

But Zoe... She was none of that. She was as clean as freshly fallen snow at our house in Colorado. As honest as a compass. As good for me as a full night's sleep, even though the last thing I ever thought about was rest when I got into bed with her. Everything I'd written about in that damned song. The only reason I couldn't have her was my own inability to let go of my past.

And even as pissed as I was that she couldn't just love me as I was, that she felt like she needed to *fix* me, I wanted to be whole for her...even if I couldn't have her.

Standing, I grabbed the bottle, pocketed my phone, then twisted the top of the Crystal Skull as I started to walk. I lifted the bottle to my nose and inhaled sharply, swinging the door open.

Then I poured the entire thing into the toilet, my chest clenching at the steady *glug* as it emptied. My phone rang as the last of the liquor left the bottle.

Unknown.

Maybe it's her.

"Hello?" I answered it, tossing the bottle in the trash.

"Mr. Winters?"

"Yes?" My jaw ticked. Of course it wasn't her.

"This is Richard Howell. I was hoping I might get you to change your mind about talking at your dad's hearing."

"My father murdered my little sister. If you want me to talk at his hearing, that's all I'll say." I hit end and let go, the phone falling into the toilet with the vodka before I flushed.

———

A month. Thirty fucking days. Seven hundred and twenty hours.

That's how long it had been since I'd left Zoe standing in the entry hall of the only place that had ever really felt like home.

Don't leave me. Don't do this. Those were the words that haunted my nightmares now. Instead of seeing Kaylee's curls, it was Zoe's auburn tresses wrapped in my father's fists. Zoe's fingers reaching for the banister. Her broken body at the bottom of the kitchen stairs.

On the worst nights—and there'd been a few—I'd woken from the dream gasping for air, my hands outstretched like I could catch them both. One of them I'd failed, and the other one I'd abandoned.

"Mr. Winters?" the wannabe Shannon asked, snapping me out of my thoughts. She was straight out of college, with that first-year oxymoronic mix of ball-busting confidence and naivete that all interns seemed to be issued when they started at Berkshire.

"What?" I snapped, looking over the Seattle skyline and wishing it was the Rockies.

"Quinn's here to see you."

"I'm sorry?" Last time I checked, Quinn was in Bozeman. We weren't due in the studio until next week.

"She said Quinn is here to see you," Quinn called out from

inside the penthouse, walking right past wannabe Shannon onto my deck.

"So I see." I lifted my open bottle of orange soda and drank, wishing it were something a little clearer and a little more like vodka.

Quinn plopped down on the chair next to me and gave me a blatant once-over, clearly assessing my sobriety, just like everyone did now that Shannon was gone. But she wasn't gone, was she? She was working in this very city. Living within a twenty-minute drive. Going on with her life because I'd forced her out of mine.

"Will you need anything?" Wannabe Shannon asked, flashing a smile that implied anything meant *anything.*

"Go play with your dollhouse, Malibu Barbie." Quinn waved her off without even looking. "How long are you stuck with the intern?"

I shrugged. "She's only here during the day. I'm being weaned off supervision. You want something to drink?"

"Not if it's that orange shit."

I leaned to the right, opening the mini fridge that was built into the outdoor cook station, and handed Quinn a bottle of water. "WBS keeps it stocked."

"WBS?" she questioned, twisting the top.

"Wannabe Shannon."

"You're unreal." She rolled her eyes and took a drink. "I saw her, by the way."

"Oh yeah?" My heart—whatever was left of it—clenched.

"Yep. She signed that band she loved. What are they called... Nine to Five?"

"Seven to One," I answered. Good. At least her career was moving forward. She'd gotten what she needed out of her deal with Ben. "Did you seriously fly here to tell me that?"

Quinn watched me carefully, taking in the way my knee

bounced and my fingers drummed on the soda bottle. "I was already here, which you'd know if you ever checked your damn phone. It's spring break, and Graham and Colin wanted to spend it in the city. Meanwhile, I stopped into Berkshire to sign something."

I scoffed. "Bullshit. You stopped into Berkshire to see Zoe."

"Guilty." She shrugged. "She looks like shit, and you're even worse."

"I'm fine." I willed my body to stop fidgeting.

"Try saying that to someone who doesn't know you." She snorted. "What the hell happened in Colorado? You two were wrapped around each other in Houston. You wore a guitar strap with the woman's name on it, for crying out loud. Three days later, I find out you're locked in your penthouse like a hermit and won't even let the housekeeper in."

"I let Jonas in," I argued.

"Because he has a key," she retorted. "One he had to fly out here from the East Coast to use."

"Yeah, well. I've always been an asshole, but in my defense, I would have opened the door if she'd told me she was running to Jonas to tattle." I still felt like shit for pulling Jonas away from his family once again.

"Jonas was scared you'd fallen into a bottle." She leveled me with her stare. "Imagine his surprise when he burst through the door to find the only thing that had fallen was your phone into your toilet."

"I'm sober. Fucked up, maybe. But sober." Barely. The first twenty-four hours had been touch and go, but I'd locked myself away up here. "And I apologized to Jonas."

"It's not about that. You know you have an open invitation at both our houses. Pretty sure Kira has already stocked three cases of orange soda on the off chance you finally admit that you might need a little support."

"I'm fine." I was going to tattoo that shit on my forehead pretty soon.

"What happened to you and Zoe?"

"What did she tell you happened?" I rolled the bottle between my hands and told my chest to simmer down with the whole heartache shit.

"Is this high school?" Quinn shook her head. "I'm not carrying a note to fourth period."

"Pretty sure everyone just texts now." Except Zoe. No calls. No texts. No carrier pigeons or emails. My guitars had arrived at the penthouse two days after I left Colorado, along with a bag of things I'd left behind. Leave it to Shannon to keep picking up my shit after I was gone.

"She said what happened between you two was private." Quinn lifted the bottle of water like she was looking through it.

"Did she?" My hands paused.

"She did." Quinn put the water bottle down. "She also said I was right, and she should have gone for higher ground."

My head whipped toward hers. "What the hell is that supposed to mean?"

"My best guess is it means that she got too close, you couldn't handle your feelings, and then you hit the self-destruct button." She lifted a brow. "How close am I?"

I looked away.

"That's what I thought."

"She thinks she needs to fix me." I started rolling the bottle again. "I told her to choose between loving me just like I was and fixing me. She chose to fix me, because that's what she does. Something isn't perfect? Zoe to the rescue. Someone doesn't work? Zoe's on it. She'd rather know she accomplished her mission than stick it out with a mess she can't manage."

"No way. If someone walked away, it was you. That woman loves you."

"She only thinks she does," I argued.

"Right, because you're an expert on the way women think? What *she* thinks?"

"I know enough about women—"

"In bed!" Quinn snapped.

"I've never taken you to bed, and I know you pretty damn well."

"Thank God for that," she muttered, then sighed. "What did she say exactly?"

"Do we have to do this?" I shoved away from the table and walked to the railing, turning to lean against it the same way I had every morning when Zoe had taken her coffee out here.

"Yes, we do! You broke that woman, Nix, and from what I see, you're just as shattered. So yeah, we have to do this. What did she say?" She folded her arms across her chest.

"Fine. She said if the choice was between her loving me, or her *stepping aside* so I could be healthy enough to love someone, she'd choose that. She'd choose to fix me, rather than love me."

Quinn's face slackened. "She really said that."

"Yeah. She tells me she loves me and then less than twenty-four hours later, she's dropping that shit."

"Restating that she loves you?" Quinn's eyes narrowed. "Is that what you mean by *dropping that shit*?"

I bristled. "She'd rather fix me than take me as I am."

"Well, let's ignore for a second that you're pretty messed up, shall we?" She stood. "Listen to what she said. She loves you so much that she's willing to break her own heart, if that means you'll be able to experience love, even if that means she's not the one you love. That's some pretty heavy self-sacrifice."

"That's not…" I ran my hands over my hair and tried to find the words. "Who the hell does that? I wouldn't trade her love so she could go love someone else." Screw that.

"Isn't that what you're doing?"

I sagged against the railing. "I don't know what I'm doing."

"At least we can agree on that."

"What if there's no fixing me? What if this is just the way I am?"

"You still going to therapy?"

"Every Thursday like clockwork," I replied, cringing at the sight of Wannabe Shannon's silhouette crossing the far window. Fuck, I missed Zoe. I missed her smile, and her laugh. I missed her sense of humor and wit. I missed her kisses, and her body, and the smell of her shampoo.

"How is that possible without your phone to keep you on that clockwork?" Quinn challenged.

"I bought a paper planner." I shrugged. "They're really quite practical."

"Wow. I'm not touching that statement with a ten-foot pole." She slid her phone out of her pocket, checking a message. "Sorry, that's Graham."

"She accused me of using her like a fix." The admission slipped out as a whisper.

"Are you?" Quinn's eyebrows shot up, and she put her phone back.

"I..." Touching her was the ultimate rush. Being inside her was the sweetest oblivion possible, where nothing else mattered but how good I could make her feel. "I don't know. I mean, it's more than that. I don't have words to describe the way I feel about her, but when it comes to sex? I don't know."

"I'm impressed that you recognize it." Quinn nodded. "I think there's a certain level of addiction we all have for the people we love. I live off the sound of Graham's voice, his touch, his smile." She sighed. "I don't know where that line is for you, but I bet your therapist does. And there's a word for what you feel—it's love."

Love.

The perpetual ache in my chest grew, sweetened even through the pain. *Shit.* Yeah, I was in love with her. "I'm no good for her."

"You should probably let her decide that, don't you think?"

"Maybe I should let her find someone capable of loving her the way she deserves. Someone who doesn't have to be fixed."

"Yeah, well, if you can live with knowing she's out there with someone else, kissing them, loving them, marrying them, making babies with—"

"Holy hell, stop!" I rubbed at my chest.

"Right. There's your answer. Now Colin wants pizza, so why don't you grab the new phone I left you on the kitchen counter and join us?" She nodded toward the door.

"Leave the penthouse."

"I'll hold your hand the whole time, big boy." She wiggled her fingers. "Come on. There's life out there, and while I'll ignore your possession of a paper planner, I do insist that you power up that phone. It's already set to your old number. Unless you've decided to go back to mailing letters instead of texting?" She raised her eyebrows.

"You're lucky I'm hungry."

———

"Not interested," I told Chris as I walked by the gathering outside my dressing room a few weeks later.

We weren't supposed to be at this festival, but the whole thing had come together as an impromptu fundraiser, which meant I was backstage in the middle of Chicago, with about an hour to showtime.

"Noted."

"Jonas never has this crowding issue," I said, my hand on the door handle. Pretty sure Zoe broke me, because none of the women even looked appealing. I just wanted them all gone.

"With all due respect, Nix, Jonas never set that precedent." He lifted his heavy black brows, clearly insinuating that I had.

"Right. Well, let's change—" The words died on my tongue as I looked down the hall.

Zoe.

She was maybe twenty feet away, talking to the band she'd signed. Her heels were high, but she'd foregone her typical dress for a tightly tailored black pantsuit that cupped every curve the way I wanted to. She smiled at the lead singer, and my heart stopped, then thundered.

That's not her romantic smile, it's her professional one, I reminded myself, but it didn't help. That clawing, insidious little knife in my stomach was jealousy. That kid was barely old enough for the beer in his hand, and he hadn't earned a smile from the woman I loved. He didn't know she liked honey in her tea, or that salted caramel ice cream was her favorite. He didn't know her over-organization was the result of the first man she'd ever loved telling her she'd never be good enough. He didn't know her favorite pajamas were the panda ones that made her look like a fucking sorority girl at a sleepover, or that her underwear always matched and was ninety percent lace. He didn't know how she tasted, how she sounded right before she came, and if he did, I was going to kick his ass and break the fingers on his left hand so he couldn't even strum that little guitar of his.

He sure as hell didn't know how it felt to slide inside her bare, skin on skin, with nothing between us but my own goddamned walls. That torture was mine, and mine alone.

"You see something you might be interested in down there?" Chris asked.

"More than interested."

"Thought so."

I turned my head to find him smirking at me. "You knew. You knew she was here."

He nodded. "Why do you think Jonas pushed so hard to play this show?"

I looked past Zoe and her band and found both Jonas and

Quinn leaning out of their respective dressing rooms, watching. I tilted my head at them and narrowed my eyes.

Jonas lifted his brows and slipped slowly back inside his dressing room. Quinn just grinned and nodded toward Zoe, then stood to watch what I was going to do about her.

Well, I'd always done my best work in front of an audience. I blew out my breath on a long sigh and nodded to myself. Then I strode down the hall like I owned it and came up behind her. The scent of coconuts hit me straight in the dick, and I almost smiled. I wasn't broken. I was in love.

"Zoe."

Her shoulders straightened, then rose and fell once before she turned toward me, arching her neck slightly to look up at me. I was indecently, intimately close, and I wanted the baby rock stars behind her to note it. "Nixon."

Words. I needed words. Quickly. But, fuck, her eyes were the knockout punch, stripping the common sense straight out of me.

"What's up?" She arched her eyebrows in annoyance. As if I meant nothing. As if I hadn't made her scream my name so many times she'd gone hoarse that first week. As if she didn't love me.

"I'm in love with you." It was easier to say than I'd imagined. Way easier. Effortless.

Her eyes flew wide.

"Holy shit," one of the baby rockers exclaimed. "That's Nixon Winters."

"I am in love with you, Zoe Shannon," I repeated, just in case she hadn't understood me across the scant inches that separated us.

"Heard that part." She did that little head tilt of hers that signaled her inner debate.

"And?" I would have given anything to be inside her head.

"And she obviously doesn't feel the same," the drummer replied. "Awkward."

"No one asked the daycare crowd." I didn't look away from

the confusion swirling in those green depths for fear I'd lose my chance if I lost eye contact.

"Hey, we're like, seven years younger than you. That's it," another one chimed in.

"The fact that you know that when I don't even know your names is why you're the daycare crowd. Now quiet down and let the adults speak." A smile tugged at the corner of my lips.

"He's sorry, boys," Zoe sang. "Don't talk to them like that."

"He's not," I replied. "They're protective of you. Is that because you got them into the show, or because they're immeasurably grateful for you making them fire their shitty bass player?"

"Both." There it was, the tiniest smile. "What do you want, Nixon?"

"You."

"We tried that once already, remember? Now, go get ready. I know you're supposed to be on stage soon." She lifted her chin.

Because she knew my schedule. Hope flared in my chest.

"We can do this in my dressing room, or right out here in the hallway. I don't care." That was a lie. I clearly preferred my dressing room, but I'd make do.

"And if I choose not at all?" Her voice softened.

"I'll stand here as long as it takes. I just need you to hear me out." I was going to smack Jonas upside the back of the head when I got ahold of him. If he'd warned me, I would have been prepared with something better than that.

"You're really going to hold up the show? Make an entire stadium full of fans wait?" She shook her head. "What will Jonas say?"

"I'm good with it," Jonas said from behind me.

"Me too," Quinn added.

"You're not helping," Zoe replied, her gaze still locked on me.

"I'd argue otherwise," Jonas countered.

"God, I've missed you," I whispered. My hands formed fists to keep from reaching for her. "I've missed every single thing about you."

Zoe sighed in complete exasperation. "Fine. Ten minutes."

"Fifteen," I argued.

"Nine." She arched a brow.

I muttered a curse but nodded. Something was better than nothing.

"Don't worry, I'll watch the kids," Jonas offered as Zoe and I headed for my dressing room.

She gave Chris a hug, which he quickly ended when he saw the look on my face, then she flung open my dressing room door and marched inside with me close on her heels. She looked around briefly, then hummed and sat on the edge of the counter.

"What were you expecting to find?"

"New Shannon." She braced her palms on the counter as I approached. "Stop right there. That's close enough. What the hell was that out there?"

"There's no new Shannon." I halted.

"Oh, come on, I know Monica was assigned to be your…Shannon."

"Her name is Monica?"

"What did you think it was?" She drummed her fingers on the edge of the counter.

"Wannabe Shannon." I shrugged. "But she's not you. There's no new you." My voice dropped.

"At work or in your personal life?" Every line of her body radiated tension. Anger.

That little flare of hope sparked brighter. She was jealous. "There's been no one since you. There won't be anyone after you. It's just you."

She blinked, quickly schooling her features, which I deserved.

"I'm in love with you, Zoe." I started all over again.

"Stop saying that!"

"No. It's true. I'm in love with you. We have to figure this out."

"Why? Because we have a ridiculous house together?" She lifted her brows. "Or because Monica doesn't know how to make tea? Or do a good enough job at sucking your—"

"Because you still love me!" There was no way a woman like Zoe gave her heart away and then yanked it back so quickly.

"Don't be so sure about that." She folded her arms across her chest.

Damn, the woman was a walking piece of frustration, and she knew exactly how to get under my skin.

"I told you I would fuck this up. That I didn't know how to do this." I motioned between us. "And I'm not against parking a camper on the front lawn of the Colorado house like I threatened, but you haven't been back there since I left."

"Keeping tabs on me?"

"Yes!"

"Why?" she fired back.

"Because you're mine!"

"The hell I am!" Every line of her body went taut.

"Fine, then I'm yours! Better now?" I ripped my hand over my hair.

Her eyes fluttered shut. "Nixon, we can't do this to each other. We just can't. Even if you can take it, I can't. It physically hurts to be this close and not touch you."

"Then touch me." Four strides—that's all it took to haul her into my arms. I poured everything I had into that kiss as our mouths met and opened, my longing, my need, and my love. It was all there for her to do whatever she wanted with it. She laced her hands behind my neck and kissed me back like it might be the last time.

At the bittersweet taste of that desperation, I pulled back, gentling the strokes of my tongue to lazy swirls around hers.

"I missed you every minute of every day," I said between kisses.

She shook her head and pushed at my chest. "Nothing's changed." Her eyes met mine, and there was so much sadness mixed into the anger that an ache developed in my throat.

My body screamed in protest, and my heart lurched as I put precious inches between us, but my head was in control this time. "Everything has changed," I assured her. "Everything but the way I feel about you. I'm in therapy. I'm sober. I'm *not* sleeping with Monica or anyone else. I don't need you to keep me sober, Zoe, I just need you, period."

"You hurt me." She bit out every word as the accusation it was.

My gut knotted. "I know. I'm really sorry. I'm going to do everything in my power to make sure it doesn't happen again."

"I don't believe you."

Ouch.

"I'll earn it." I ran my thumb over the soft skin of her cheek.

"You'll earn it?" Sarcasm saturated every word.

"I'll *earn* your trust," I promised. "And honestly, I have to earn my own first. When you said that you were my fix, it struck a chord."

"Was I? Am I?" She tensed. "I mean, look at what just happened."

"Maybe," I admitted, stroking her lip with my thumb. "There's nothing that compares to what it feels like to touch you."

Her eyes flared in surprise.

"What? I've told you that before."

She studied me carefully. "You said maybe. You didn't deny it."

"Working on that whole emotional availability thing," I said slowly. "And until I can be sure that you're not my current drug of choice, I'm not putting either of us in the position to feel that way."

She glanced pointedly to where our bodies were aligned.

"Right. This is why I'm going to need another few months."

"To do what?"

"I need to get through the spring...start the summer without the yearly downward spiral. Need to hit my year mark without leaning on you. That way, I know I can do it on my own, and you'll know you can go slay the management world without stressing out that I'm going to lose it on tour without you. Plus, I kind of ignored the whole wait-a-year-before-starting-a-new-relationship advice, but I wasn't expecting you—expecting this."

"So, you're what? Asking me to wait?"

"Yeah. I guess I am." It hadn't been planned, but seeing her again clarified the path. Waiting was the only logical course to take. For both of us.

Her gaze shifted as she made her choice. "What do the numbers on your clock mean? The one on your chest?" She tapped her index finger right above the ink.

The urge to shut down hit hard and fast, but I pushed it aside and focused on her eyes. "Seven twelve. July twelfth. Kaylee's birthday."

Her brow furrowed. "You went to rehab on her birthday."

I nodded. "I tried a few times before, but I never made it through. The day she would have turned eighteen, I signed myself in and I stayed." She would have been old enough to leave on her own. She wouldn't have needed me.

Zoe weighed my answer for a few very long, very quiet moments. "So, you need about three months."

"Yes."

"I'll think about it."

"You'll think about it?" I didn't know whether to be frustrated or relieved.

"I said I'll think about it." She shrugged, then pushed at my chest. "Your ten minutes are up."

"Come on, let's get you back to the Mickey Mouse Clubhouse brigade." I stuck out my hand, but she didn't take it.

"They're not that young," she muttered, headed for the door.

"Yeah, they are. But you chose well. They might be almost as good as us one day." I followed after her.

"Cocky bastard." She shook her head as we walked into the hallway.

"At least you know what you're getting into."

"Yeah. That's part of the problem when it comes to you." Her voice dropped.

"Three months," I repeated, devouring the sight of her and memorizing every single detail. "It'll be over before you know it, and then it's you and me."

"What makes you think I'll wait it out?" She arched an eyebrow as she backed away, but there was a spark in those eyes.

"Because you love me." I folded my arms over my chest and watched her retreat, battling every instinct in my body to throw her over my shoulder and race back to Colorado.

"Hmm. Is that so?"

"It is, and I love you." I didn't give a shit who heard us in the hallway. "Three months, Shannon."

"Yeah, I heard you the first few times. Bye, Nixon." She pivoted and walked off toward her band, pausing as Quinn said something in her ear. Zoe nodded, then disappeared around the corner.

"How did it go?" Jonas asked as we walked with Quinn toward the stage twenty minutes later.

"Guess we'll see what happens in the next three months," I answered, adjusting my guitar strap. I'd passed over the *Nixon* one she had made for me and chosen the one that read *Zoe's*.

"Okay then." He clapped the back of my shoulder.

"Hey, I have something I need to do in a few days, but I was thinking I might take you up on that invite afterward. Maybe come to Boston for a while? If the offer still stands."

"It always stands. It will be really good to have you." He smiled. "Plus, it will give me time to bully you into putting 'Merciful Fire' on the album."

"I'm all for it," Quinn chimed in. "It's good."

"Not a chance in hell." Zoe hadn't even heard it yet.

"We'll see."

19

ZOE

"So, you're together? Not together?" Naomi asked.

"Yes? No? I'm honestly not sure." I hit the speakerphone button and put the phone on my counter as I dug around in my refrigerator to find something for dinner. "I think we're in limbo."

"Limbo?"

"Yeah, limbo. You know, the place between heaven and hell—"

"I know what limbo is. I just don't understand how you're in it."

"He asked me to wait three months." I pulled out the takeout I'd ordered two nights ago and gave it a whiff. Smelled good to me. Plus, it was already eight thirty and I was starving. Getting Seven to One off the ground had me working around the clock, but we'd had some summer festival proposals sent our way today, so it was looking up.

"And you said you'd think about it."

"What else was I supposed to say?" I popped the leftovers into the microwave.

"Oh, I don't know. Anything that would have given one of *People*'s Sexiest Men Alive a clear answer on whether or not he's allowed to go sleep with other people?" Her voice rose.

"He won't." I watched the plate spin round and round inside the microwave, debating what I'd thought was a cute little comment three days ago. "And if he does, then I guess we have our answer, don't we?" Just the thought of it made my stomach curdle, but I was done feeling responsible for Nixon's choices.

"Are you sleeping with other people?"

"No!" I turned and yelled at my cell phone, like Naomi was actually in the room with me.

"So, you're not officially together, but you're not sleeping with other people."

"Exactly. At least that's what I think is going on." The heart-break I'd come back to Seattle sporting eight weeks ago wasn't as sharp since I'd seen Nixon in Chicago. It wasn't completely healed, either. I missed him more than I wanted to admit.

Way more.

The every heartbeat kind of more.

But that was to be expected, right? It wasn't natural to spend every waking moment with someone for six months and then be okay when they cut you off cold turkey. In that way, I guess I was addicted to him too. And as much as I wanted to believe it, I wasn't sure he'd stick to the three-month plan. There was every chance he'd leave for the tour and not look back.

Ironic, but I was supposed to be happy. I finally felt like I was making something of myself when it came to my career, but I'd lost something I hadn't realized I'd even wanted, something that was scarily close to a need.

"He'll come back," she said, way more confident about it than I was.

"How do you know?" Nixon was anything but predictable.

"I've seen the way he looks at you. He'll come back. Did you know he deleted Instagram?"

"So Monica was telling me." The microwave beeped, and I took out my leftover pasta, stirring it.

"That's New Zoe?"

"Nixon calls her Wannabe Shannon. She's Ben's new intern, whose favorite hobbies include texting me every five minutes to ask questions about Nixon and frequenting TMZ to 'make sure the band doesn't have negative exposure.'" I snorted.

"She's young. Give her a break."

"Her father is Donald Berkshire. Trust me, she doesn't need one." I opened the refrigerator again and stared at my drink options, then bypassed the lone bottle of orange soda on the door for some lemonade. God, I missed him. "Tell me how Levi's doing."

Naomi filled me in on the happenings around Legacy as I ate and threw in a load of laundry.

Then the doorbell rang.

"Hold on a second, someone's here." I walked the ten feet to my front door and looked through the peephole. "It's Monica."

"Be nice."

"I'll call you right back." I hung up with Naomi and opened the door. "Monica, it's almost nine o'clock. What's up?"

"Sorry." She blew her hair out of her eyes and sighed. "I spent all day getting his royal assholeness packed to leave for Jonas's in two days, where, spoiler alert, I don't get to go." I had to give it to the girl—she looked exhausted.

"Jonas isn't a big fan of interns creeping around his kid," I said as gently as possible. It was good Nixon was headed to Jonas's, not only for the support but for the distance. Now I wouldn't be tempted to drive over and climb into bed with him at two a.m.

She nodded. "I know. I just thought I'd be doing higher-level stuff, not packing Nixon's guitar straps. Did you know that he has one that says *Zoe's* on it?" She lifted her eyebrows.

"Yeah, I did." I grinned. "It was supposed to be a joke. Long story."

"Well, he made me pack it." Her shoulders fell. "Is this what it's really like? Babysitting the creatives?"

"No. Nixon's on special handling orders for a few months, that's all. Then he'll go on tour, and Ethan will be responsible for his royal assholeness." I opened my door wider. "Do you want to come in? You look like you need to sit down."

"No, but thank you for the offer. I just came by because Nixon wanted me to hand deliver this to you." She leaned over and hefted a new guitar hardcase from next to the door.

"He sent me a guitar?" I took it from her.

"Maybe it's just a case. Who knows with him." She shrugged. "Is he always so grumpy in the morning? I show up at nine a.m. as instructed, and he bites my head off for the first few hours."

I put the guitar case on the other side of my door. "Is he sleeping?" My brow furrowed.

"How would I know? I don't spend the night there."

Thank God for that. Guess she really wasn't New Shannon.

"Here. Come in for a second." I motioned her forward, then shut the door and walked around the Formica peninsula and into my kitchen, where I dug out an unopened box of tea. "Put this on the counter when you see him tomorrow."

"He drinks tea?" She looked skeptically at the box.

"He does." I nodded.

She glanced from the box to me and back again. "You don't have to pack his clothes."

"Not anymore." I never packed his clothes, but I wasn't about to say that to her.

"How did you get to manage your own band?"

"Went to law school while being Ben's assistant for four

years…only three of those were while I was in school, though. Keep showing up, Monica. You'll be fine."

"Thanks." She slipped the tea into her massive shoulder bag.

"No problem, and if Ben doesn't run you ragged while Nixon's gone, pop over to my office and I'll…show you some contracts or something."

"Really?" Her eyes lit up.

"Really."

"Thank you!" She adjusted her bag and headed for the door, then paused with her hand on the handle. "Oh, I'm supposed to tell you something."

"Okay?"

"Nixon said that's not a gift, just a loaner. He called it collateral." She pointed to the guitar case. "And you're supposed to keep an eye on TMZ tomorrow, because he bets a whole year of your property taxes that something is going to pop up." She gave me a smile, then waved and let herself out.

TMZ. He had to be kidding me.

I laid the guitar case flat, then undid the latches and opened the lid. The case may have been new, but the guitar wasn't. The honey-gold tones were all too familiar. My heart somersaulted, and I called Naomi back.

"He'll come back," I said, a smile lifting my lips.

"Did you talk to him?"

"No, but he sent me a message." I smiled and ran my finger over the polished wood of the body he'd called collateral.

It was Kaylee's guitar.

―――――

"WHO KNEW ABOUT THIS?" Ben shouted down the halls of Berkshire Management the next afternoon.

I abandoned the contract I'd been reading and rolled my chair to the edge of the broom closet that served as my office.

Leaning my head out of the doorway, I blinked at the sight of Ben stomping toward the collective group of cubicles that housed the interns.

"Berkshire! Did you know?" Monica's head popped above the cubicle.

"About?"

"Seriously, the one day you don't live on TMZ?" he snapped. *Nixon.*

I pushed off the doorframe and rolled back to my desk, clicking for a new tab on my internet browser and pulling up TMZ.

There was a photo of Nixon—*in a suit*—walking down a set of concrete steps with Jonas and Quinn behind him, dressed similarly. All three had on sunglasses, but it was absolutely them. I clicked on the picture, and the headline blew up on the next screen.

Confirmed: Hush Note guitarist Nixon Winters leaving a hearing at the Washington State Clemency and Pardons Board with his bandmates, Jonas Smith and Quinn Montgomery, earlier today.

My stomach pitched.

I scrolled furiously, but the article was short, because there was nothing to report. Though the hearings were open to the public, Nixon hadn't been spotted until leaving the building, and only the results of that hearing—not the transcripts—would be released.

"The answer is 'no comment'!" Ben bellowed. "Can someone please get Amy Manson on the phone?" The band's publicist.

Nixon had gone to the hearing.

I scrambled for my phone, not giving a shit if it hadn't even been a week into this wait-three-months thing.

Zoe: Are you okay?

I tapped my fingers on my desk, waiting for a reply.

"I told Zoe Shannon!" Monica's voice rose above the noise.

Awesome.

Nixon: I miss you

Zoe: Not what I mean.

Nixon: I know

I wanted to reach through the phone and throttle him for not giving me an answer, but if I actually had my hands on him, I knew that wouldn't be the outcome. My chest tightened, thinking of him taking that step, knowing that while he'd had the support of his friends, I hadn't been there with the same.

"Shannon!" Ben was headed this way.

Zoe: I'm serious.

The three little repeating dots were going to be the death of me.

"Did you know?" Ben asked from my doorway.

"Know what?" I folded my hands over my cell phone screen, and Ben narrowed his eyes.

"You know what! Did Nixon tell you he was going to a legal hearing today? That picture is everywhere."

My phone buzzed with an alert.

"Nope, he didn't."

"Berkshire said—"

"That Nixon wanted me to keep an eye on TMZ today?" I shrugged. "If we represented sports stars, they'd want us to watch ESPN."

His face tightened.

"I didn't know," I reiterated.

"Do you know what it was about?"

"I can't be a hundred percent sure." My smile was fake, and we both knew it.

"Was he involved in something—"

"No." Was that really the first conclusion everyone jumped to? "Nixon didn't do anything wrong. Nothing that happened in there can have any legal ramifications, and it's not like we have any morality clauses anyway."

My phone buzzed again.

Ben glanced from my hands to my face, then pushed off my doorframe and headed back into the hallway. "Someone get me Amy Manson!"

I uncovered my phone as soon as he was out of sight.

Nixon: I read a statement to the board about the abuse

Nixon: He wasn't even in the room before I left

The tension in my chest eased a bit. He hadn't been forced to see his father.

He was really doing it—the work to get better. He wasn't avoiding his past or shutting himself away in his apartment...or our Colorado house...and he was doing it sober, with his friends to back him up.

The ache from missing him threatened to consume me as I typed out a reply.

Zoe: I'm proud of you.

Nixon: I love you

My fingers hovered over the keys, but I just couldn't go there. Couldn't give him that power again. The first time I'd given him those words, he'd destroyed me in less than a day. It didn't matter that my heart lodged in my throat every time I thought about him, not when it came to the very real need for a little self-preservation.

My phone vibrated.

Nixon: 3 months

I swallowed. That, I could handle.

Zoe: Three months.

20

NIXON

DAMN, my girl was beautiful. I leaned over my guitar and scrolled through her last couple of Instagram posts, and sighed like the lovesick fool I was. Three weeks down...too many to go.

The only reason I'd opened my account back up—after deleting all the bullshit I hadn't posted over the last few years—was hearing that Zoe had finally gotten one. It was the closest I got to her.

Her emerald-green eyes stared back at me through the screen, mid-laugh, with her arm around Naomi at Puget Sound. Guess she'd finally taken some much-needed time off. Missing her wasn't even an emotion anymore as much as it was a state of being. Add to it the fear that she wouldn't wait, wouldn't take me back, wouldn't want to handle the shit that being with me would inevitably heap on her, and I was hanging on to my sanity by a thread.

But it was a thread, which was more than I'd had this time last year. I was usually mid-spiral by the first week in May.

"Zoe post another picture?" Jonas asked, walking onto his porch and handing me an orange soda before taking the chair next to me.

"What makes you think it's Zoe?" I asked, giving her one last look before shutting my phone off.

"You follow three people, and if you're looking at Quinn or me like that, we've got problems." He picked up his guitar and retuned the E.

"True." I glanced at the notebook that sat on the small, wrought iron table between us. "Where were we?"

"Chorus." He took a swig of his iced tea and set it back down. He strummed the same progression we'd followed with the first. "How about we split that first line here—" He tapped the paper.

"You're the only thing—the only thing that matters," I sang.

"Yeah. That's good."

I wrote the new variation down as he strummed it out, then penciled in my next thoughts as I spoke them aloud. "In this parade of mad alibis—a thousand little lies—intentions fall like confetti."

Jonas stopped strumming and looked over at me. "Damn."

"Or we could flip it—"

"No, that's perfect. We should have sobered you up years ago." He grinned. "Mad alibis. Nice."

"Whatever." I scribbled down the chord progression before strumming it out. Had to admit, my brain was on fire now that it wasn't constantly weighed down. Did every song I write have a hefty dose of Zoe in it? Yeah, but most of my thoughts did too.

Jonas read off the paper and nodded as he moved through the melody. "Let's repeat the hook here."

I nodded as he sang it back. "You're the only thing—the only thing that matters." His eyebrows raised as he followed up with the next lines. "Holding me steady with little more than a memory—the only thing—the only thing that matters."

I had a full-out smile by the time he put his spin on the end. "It's good."

"Yeah. Like...single good. Like 'call Quinn and get on a plane so we can record it' good."

"The album's already finished, and besides, we don't even have a second verse yet."

"Screw that. We'll finish the song and unfinish the album. It's not due to drop for another six weeks. I'll call Ben and have him deal with the production side." Jonas stared down at the spiral notebook. "What are we going to call it?"

I never went for the obvious titles. It just wasn't my style. "How about 'Mad Alibis'?"

Jonas's smile spread slowly across his face "Yeah. Yeah, that's the one." He lifted his brows at me. "Now, how about sneaking a little 'Merciful Fire' onto the album too?"

"No." My fingers picked at the lead-in from memory. "Too personal."

"Man, I hate to break it to you, but you're in a long-distance 'maybe' relationship with a woman you don't even talk to. *Too personal* might ease those waters right now."

"I'm not putting a song about Zoe on an album when she hasn't even heard it." I shook my head.

"Yeah, and 'Mad Alibis' isn't about her?"

My mouth opened and shut a few times.

"Exactly." He laughed.

The back door opened and Vivi raced out, a bundle of pure energy as she zipped up her jacket. "I finished my homework!"

"What exactly are they giving kindergarteners these days?" I questioned.

"Don't get me started on the math." Jonas groaned, but he was all smiles for his little girl. "Good job, honey."

She ran her fingers over his strings. "Did you finish?"

"Almost!"

"Can I hear it?" She bounced on her toes.

"Sure," I answered for Jonas, then took it from the top, working through the harmonies once he hit the chorus.

Vivi clapped when we ran out of material. "I love it! You play really well, Daddy."

"Thanks, honey, but you know, Uncle Nixon plays even better."

"Really?"

"Really," Jonas nodded emphatically.

"You're better than Dad?" Vivi eyed me skeptically.

"Singing? No. Playing, yes." I was shamelessly proud of my hands.

"Dad bought me a guitar." Her bright eyes met mine. "Can you teach me too?"

My entire chest seized. I took a deep breath and let it out, keeping myself in the here—the now. She wasn't Kaylee. I'd never get that chance back. I'd made my choices, and she'd paid a price neither of us had foreseen. Maybe it wasn't my fault—I was still working through that—but I'd been a factor all the same.

"Honey, Uncle Nixon is—" Jonas started, obviously seeing my distress.

"Sure, I'll teach you," I interjected.

"Thanks!" She rewarded me with a grin, then threw her little arms around my neck.

"Any time." I squeezed her back, and she raced off to play.

Jonas gave me a speculative once-over.

"What?"

"Just picturing you as a dad." He gave me that hopeful look he'd been fond of since I'd come to Boston.

"Don't." I shook my head. Not that a green-eyed baby would be the worst thing in the world, just…not any time soon. I could barely picture the next six months as it was, and that was even knowing we were due to start a moderated tour schedule the first of July. But maybe one day. As long as Zoe was on board.

"Scared of diapers?" he teased. "Or the whole commitment thing?"

I scoffed. "I'm just scared I'll be better at parenting than you are, and I'm trying to give you the upper hand for a while."

He rolled his eyes. "Yeah, okay. Let's get back to that second verse."

I fell into the music a little deeper than usual, and before I knew it, we were dropping the single.

———

Two months into the...whatever kind of break this was...I sat at a conference table at Berkshire Management with Quinn and Jonas, going over all the details for the tour that started in two weeks.

"That will give you time to hit up the radio station," Ethan said, flipping the page on the stapled packet we'd been given.

I turned mine absentmindedly, keeping one eye on the glass wall as another person who wasn't Zoe walked by. We'd been in this room for an hour, and still no sign of her.

"...at which point Nixon will put on a pair of rubber duck feet and peacock feathers...*Nixon*!" Ethan snapped.

"What?" I whipped my head toward him.

"You'd better start paying attention before you agree to a music video dressed like a really bad rendition of Elton John." Jonas laughed.

"She's not here. Stop looking," Ethan lectured. "So that does it for the LA trip. Turn the page—"

"What do you mean, she's not here?" I challenged.

"She's on the road with Seven to One. Because they listen during meetings and let their manager do her job." Ethan stared me, silent, for all of ten seconds. "And...we're in Vegas for one night."

Well...shit. Disappointment wasn't nearly a good enough

word to describe the way my stomach sank. I drummed my fingers on the conference table and tried to pay attention.

A few minutes later, Quinn placed her hand over mine to stop the incessant movement. "Do you need a fidget cube?"

"He needs a redhead," Jonas muttered, turning his page in time with Ethan.

I glared at him.

"...things are still in motion by the time we're in Phoenix because Rising Tide just canceled on us as an opener. His wife went into labor early. Anyone have suggestions?"

"Seven to One," I said, after raising my hand.

Quinn laughed. "You have it so bad!"

"No can do. They're booked for the entire month of July and into August," Ethan stated.

"They fucking *what*?" I dropped my packet onto the table.

"They. Are. Booked," Ben chimed in from the doorway. "We'll see if we have anyone in-house, and go from there."

"And their manager is on the road with them?" My blood pressure spiked.

"Seeing as they're nowhere near the size that demands a separate tour manager, yes." Ben sank into the chair across from mine.

She'd booked out her band until August, knowing our three months was up in July. What the fuck did that mean? My fingers went double-time on the table as my mind whirled. Had she made her choice?

Had she not understood what I meant by sending Kaylee's guitar to her? That thing was collateral on my heart. Shit, had she decided I came with too much bullshit? Fallen out of love with me?

Quinn's hand covered my own again, but she didn't tease me this time.

I stopped my fingers, but my concentration was shot as we

finished the meeting with a note from Ethan to check the final drafts of our riders at the back of the packet.

Who the hell cared about our nitpicky dressing room demands when the woman I loved had just extended our separation by a *month*?

"What the fuck does that mean?" I asked the universe as the three of us left the conference room.

"It means she's working," Jonas answered.

"Bullshit. Go figure, the first time I let myself fall for someone, they can't be bothered to—"

"To what?" Quinn interrupted with a bone-crushing glare. "To put her entire career on hold while you sort your shit out?"

I blinked.

Jonas punched the button for the elevator, then flipped to the back of the packet and read down.

"I thought you were on my side, here," I said to Quinn.

"I am, as long as you're not being an idiot. If you'd wanted some simpering groupie who had nothing better to do than follow you around, you would have chosen one, but you didn't. You chose an ambitious, intelligent woman who is currently in some pretty pivotal months of her career, so if you have to adjust your little deadline, then do it. You remember what it was like when we were first starting out. Why are you making that face?"

"Because there's a perpetual toddler living inside him who hasn't been told no for the last ten years," Jonas noted, flipping another page.

"Accurate," I admitted, following the other two into the elevator as it arrived. "I'm allowed to be disappointed."

"Yeah, you are." Quinn rolled her packet and swatted me on the chest with it. "Just. Don't. Be. A. Jerk."

"I miss her!"

"Well, the entire office will be sure to tell her that when she checks in." Jonas nodded toward the raised eyebrows of the receptionist, and then hit the button for the parking garage.

"She's not going anywhere, Nix." Quinn cringed. "I mean, emotionally. Not physically, obviously, since she's not here right now."

"You don't know that. Contrary to popular belief, I'm not easy to love." My voice dropped.

"Yeah, you are," Quinn replied softly. "Remember when we were in Chicago, and you two had that whole hallway encounter?"

"Obviously." Jonas turned another page.

I shot him a glare.

"When she came out of your dressing room, I asked her if she was all right, or if she'd learned to climb for higher ground yet," Quinn said as we reached the garage and the doors opened.

My eyes narrowed slightly, not quite following.

"She said, 'you don't need to climb for higher ground when you're the dam.'" Quinn raised her eyebrows at me, and we filed out of the elevator. "Get it? You're the river. She's the dam. She knows she's the one who can hold on to you. No other girl has ever come close."

My chest tightened. "That doesn't mean she wants me."

Quinn rolled her eyes. "Fine, then let's pretend she's a hydro-electric dam. You need her to contain you. She needs you to turn the lights on." She grinned and swatted my chest again. "However you want to say it, what's between you guys isn't one-sided. You need each other."

"Or we could cut the metaphors and check out Nixon's rider," Jonas suggested, waving his packet. "Every addition in the last two weeks has initials, and unless your initials are ZS and you added chamomile and valerian root tea to your list, I'm pretty sure it's safe to say that your woman still loves you."

"See?" Quinn's smile widened. "You got tea!"

It wasn't a tour date or even a phone call, but I'd take it, because at some point in the last two weeks while those riders were being finalized, Zoe had not only thought about me, she'd taken time out of her day to make sure I had everything I needed. It wasn't her heart with a ribbon, but it was something.

"I got tea," I said with a smile.

21

ZOE

"YOU MADE IT!" Monica waved forward as I raced toward the back entrance of the stadium. "Quick, they're almost three-quarters through the set list!"

I flashed my backstage pass at the venue staff, and the security guard stepped aside, letting me through.

"Barely!" Philly was *hot* in the middle of July, and I'd been racing since I landed a little over an hour ago.

"You look great," she said over her shoulder, walking me through the hallway.

"Thanks." I'd pulled my hair up to avoid the summer humidity of the East Coast and forsaken my usually professional concert attire for a simple sundress because, for the first time in two months, I wasn't working tonight.

Tonight, I was a fan.

"Which one is his?" I asked as the dressing room lineup started. "Never mind. Hey, Chris!"

"Zoe!" Chris swept me into a bear hug before setting me back on my feet.

I noted the lack of women outside the door. "Did the crowd clear out for the show?" I asked, motioning to the empty wall.

"He doesn't let anyone linger. Hasn't the whole tour. He'll sign autographs, but the only other person ever in that dressing room is Brad."

"Brad?" My head snapped toward Monica.

"New intern gets Nixon duty," she said with a smile. "I'm assisting Ethan."

"Nice! Moving up, I see!" I walked into Nixon's dressing room and took a deep breath. There were two empty cans of orange soda on the vanity, and his favorite T-shirt lay forgotten on the arm of the couch. I ran my fingers over the soft cotton.

Three months were up.

Time to see if he'd followed through on his promise, or if he'd grown weary of falling asleep alone at night. My heart plummeted at the possibility. I should have told him I was coming. Should have given him the chance to tell me not to.

"You ready?" Monica asked from the hallway.

"Right. Yeah." I dropped my shoulder bag at the end of the love seat and hurried out. My heart pounded faster with every step we took toward the stage. They were on the second verse of "Sweetness" when we reached the wing.

Monica handed me a set of earplugs, and I put them in as the stage came into view.

My breath caught at the sight of Nixon. His shirt was still on, which was odd for this late in the concert, his head bent, watching his fingers work over the frets. He was totally and completely in tune with the music. I'd never seen him look so good. The muscles of his forearm rippled with his fingerwork, and the look of intensity on his face was enough to make me shift my weight.

I knew that expression. I'd been on the receiving end of it

every time he'd been inside me. He made love to me just like he played that guitar, with sure hands, expert fingers, and single-minded focus.

A mix of longing and need unfurled in my belly. These last three months had been incredibly busy, but there wasn't a moment where Nixon hadn't been on my mind. With the new album out, it was nearly impossible not to see his face or hear the music.

The song ended, and Monica said something into her walkie-talkie.

Jonas touched his earpiece, then nodded once but didn't look our way.

"What was that about?" I asked.

"Nothing," she answered with a sly grin.

Nixon nodded to whatever Jonas said to him, then headed to the opposite wing, where a stagehand waited with a new guitar.

I backed away from the light as he headed toward center stage, facing me fully for the first time. There was no way I was taking the chance he'd see me until after the show—not with things so up in the air between us. I was too professional for that.

The lines of his face were tight with concentration as he adjusted the shoulder strap. It read *Zoe's*. I couldn't help but smile as hope blossomed in my chest. He still had it. Still used it at least once a show.

"He had one made for every guitar," Monica said over the noise of the crowd.

My eyes popped wide, but she just nodded.

Nixon adjusted the microphone as the lights fell, leaving him in the lone spotlight. What was he doing? He never played without Quinn and Jonas. And was that…it was. The guitar was an electric acoustic.

"I lost a bet with Jonas earlier today," Nixon said, his voice echoing into the stadium. "Turns out, there are indeed seventy-two steps up to the Rocky statue, not seventy."

The audience roared, and I smiled. He always knew how to work a crowd.

"So, here I am, paying up, because I didn't check Google... and he did. Cheater." His thumb strummed over the strings. "So, I owe him a song, and this is the one he's been trying to get me to play for the last eight months." Another strum, changing the chord.

My breath hitched. We were in Colorado eight months ago.

"I'm one year sober today—" The cheer from the crowd was deafening and took a hot minute to die down. My eyes pricked, and I had to blink the blurriness out of them. God, I was proud of him, especially today. "Thanks, guys. Someone I love told me once that there was nothing more romantic than pouring your heart out in public. So, this one is called 'Merciful Fire,' and it's about the person who made this last year possible."

My jaw dropped as the song started—fully acoustic.

His hands moved across the strings, bringing the melody to life, and I felt it resonate in my chest—my very soul—as he began to sing.

"Wandering through the mountain air," he began, his voice strong and clear. "Snow blanketing the ground, falling in your hair."

My breath caught. *Legacy?*

"Your name is my only prayer to a God who stopped listening under summer's glare."

Every muscle in my body went tight, my fingers flexing with the need to touch him.

"Your warmth singes my soul. Brands me, marks me, welds me whole. Red strands of silk between my fingers, lace and desire—"

Red hair. Lace. Oh my God.

"You banish the pain, cleanse my sins with your merciful fire."

The man who'd never written a song about a woman had written one for *me*.

My hands flew to my mouth as the emotions of the last year swept over me, filling every cell in my body with the simple truth that I loved this man. I would always love this man. There was no getting over Nixon Winters, even if I wanted to.

And I didn't.

Not now. Not ever.

———

I PACED BACK and forth in front of Nixon's vanity about forty minutes later. I'd left the wings during the last song in the encore, which also happened to be the biggest hit off the new album—"Mad Alibis."

I loved it just like everyone else in the country. I'd had the song on repeat enough times to know it word for word, had heard enough of the uproar at Berkshire when the group added it to the album last minute, but hearing it live, watching Nixon's fingers fly over his guitar, took my love to a whole new level.

But this reunion wasn't something that should take place in front of an audience, so I'd left during the second chorus, and here I was, waiting for Nixon to show up.

Hot mess. I was a flaming hot mess. Nervous. Excited. Terrified. All of it. I wasn't stupid; I knew creatives wrote songs about ex loves and old flames. That could very well be the case with "Merciful Fire," especially since he'd written it eight months ago. But he'd stood up there with my name across his chest, which had to mean something, right?

The door flew open, bouncing on the hinges.

"Call the car around back," Nixon demanded, his voice rushed as he stripped the guitar off his very shirtless back. "I want to be at the airport in the next—" He froze, his eyes widening when he saw me.

Shit. I was interfering with his travel plans.

"Hey." I swallowed, my eyes eating him alive. Sweat shined on his skin, dipping into the lines of roped muscle. He'd clearly kept up the workout routine.

"Hi." He set the guitar in the nearest stand without bothering to look, but luckily it didn't topple over.

"Congratulations on the one-year."

"Thanks."

A line of stagehands filed in, marching between us as they put the rest of his guitars on their stands, but Nixon kept his eyes on me. "Thanks, guys," he muttered as they made their way out.

"So, you're leaving?" I tucked my hair behind my ears, only to remember I'd pulled it up. My cheeks caught fire.

"I have a plane waiting at the airport." His gaze raked over me, and heat prickled at my skin in its wake.

"Water, and a towel," Brad said as he walked into the room. He glanced between the two of us, put the offerings on the table, and backed away. "I'll just…uh…lock this." He closed the door behind him on the way out.

The feet that separated Nixon and me felt like miles.

"Where are you headed to?" I tried to keep my voice as level as possible.

"Miami."

I startled. "That's where I'm supposed to be."

"I know." A corner of his mouth lifted.

"Oh." That meant—

"I took a look at your tour schedule and knew you didn't have time to come see me, so I carved out a few days to come spend with you. I was going to surprise you."

"I surprised you first," I whispered. He'd been coming to me. My heart rate kicked up to a full gallop.

"I noticed." He took a step, then paused. "Does that mean you made a decision? Or are we still at *I'll let you know*?" Fear flashed through his eyes.

"I'm here, aren't I?"

"Zoe," he practically growled.

"You wrote a song for me." I fidgeted with the backstage pass that hung around my neck.

"I've written about ten songs for you, only two of which you've heard. I'm kind of in love with you, if you hadn't noticed." His jaw flexed. "Now, would you please put me out of my misery?"

He was still in love with me. Suddenly, breathing was a million times easier.

"Of course I want you, Nixon. I love you." Like there had ever been another option. Wanting him was a given, like the sun rising in the east or the Colorado River flowing to the Pacific. It just was.

"Thank God," he muttered, already closing the distance between us.

He didn't stop once he reached me. He only paused long enough to pick me up before pressing my back against the wall and kissing me senseless.

I clutched his neck, holding him to me as he kissed me over and over, our tongues picking up where we'd left off months ago without skipping a beat.

Yes. I locked my ankles around the small of his back and kissed him like my life depended on it because it did. This man was my life. I loved my career, loved the industry and the rush of the music, but the last three months had taught me that none of it mattered without this—without him.

"I'm all sweaty," he said against my lips.

"I like it." I grinned.

His smile matched mine for one elated heartbeat before his mouth was busy at my neck. I whimpered as my body liquified, turning molten as he palmed my breast.

There was a knock at the door.

"Nix, Jonas wants to add 'Merciful Fire' to the Atlanta set list," Ethan called through the door.

"Go away," Nixon snapped, then brought his mouth back to mine in an even deeper kiss.

I rocked against him, using the wall as leverage. *Now. Now. Now.* The demand built to a fever pitch, the result of too many months without him.

Another knock sounded.

"Nixon, the car is here," Monica called out.

"Okay," he answered, sliding a hand under my dress to cup my ass. "Damn, I've missed everything about you, but this makes the top ten." His voice dipped to that sandpaper-rough tone that sent my temperature skyrocketing.

"So, do you want me to tell the driver you're on the way?" Monica asked.

Nixon sagged, resting his forehead against mine.

"How private is that plane?" I asked.

"Very," he answered, a wicked gleam dancing through his eyes. "Want to get out of here?"

"Yes."

He didn't even pause to pack his guitars.

EPILOGUE

FIVE YEARS LATER

NIXON

THERE WAS something to be said for being snowed in over spring break, but it took on a whole other level when there were seven energetic kids under your roof and only six adults.

One of those kids skid by, sliding in his socks across the hardwood of our Colorado home.

"Whoa!" I reached out from the kitchen and caught Jonas's oldest son about a second before he met the wall. "You can't go sledding with a broken head, my man."

"Okay, Uncle Nixon!" Like a wind-up toy, he scurried off toward the mudroom as soon as I released him.

"Vivi, get your mittens!" Kira shouted over her shoulder as she followed after her son. "Thanks, Nix. He's a little reckless."

"He's a menace," Jonas corrected her, already in his snow pants.

"Takes after his dad," I said with a grin, grabbing my hat off the counter.

We had so many people in this house that the crowd spilled out of the mudroom and into the hallway beyond. The noise was easily as loud as our last concert, which had been in August.

Cutting down the tours to summers had worked out just the way we'd hoped—giving us all time to spend with our families, time to enjoy what we'd worked so hard to build.

"Uncle Nixon, I can't find my gloves!" Colin yelled over his little sister's head as Quinn bundled the four-year-old up like she was about to face off with a Yeti.

"There's a bin full of extras on that second shelf." I pointed to the one on his left.

"Thank you," Graham said as he passed by, clapping me on the back with his empty hand, their youngest slung under his arm like a football.

"Learned my lesson last year. There's about a dozen sets of everything." I still wasn't sure what it was about hats and gloves that made it impossible for kids to keep track of their stuff, but I wasn't reliving the meltdown of *I can't sled without my hat* ever again.

And that had been Jonas.

I blatantly stared at the circus my house had become.

"You know what I think when I see this insanity?" Zoe asked, coming up beside me with our toddler on her hip.

"That you're good with just one?" I lifted our daughter into my arms through all hundred layers of her fluffy outerwear and pressed a kiss to her nose, which was just about the only exposed part of her.

"So good." Zoe nodded, her eyes slightly wide at the spectacle before us. "So, so, so good."

"You really don't want another one?" I teased. Honestly, as often as I got my hands on her, I was shocked we didn't have four already.

"Ha. Very funny." She shot me a healthy dose of side-eye.

"What do you think, Mel? You want to be an only child?" I reached under my daughter's scarf and tickled her neck.

She laughed, and those emerald-green eyes melted me into a puddle of goo, just like always. "Sled!" The demand was as clear as a two-year-old could make it.

"You sure? It's awfully cold out there."

"Sled!" She stared me down, just like her mother.

"Okay, okay," I agreed as the front door opened.

"We're here!" Naomi called out, her boots heavy on the floor. "The roads are absolute crap."

"Hey, we made it," Jeremiah argued as they came around the corner with Levi.

"Because I drove," Naomi muttered.

"Levi!" Mel tried to reach out, but she had classic snowsuit issues.

"Hey, Melody!" Levi grinned and took her straight out of my arms like the baby thief he was. "I've got her, Uncle Nix. Want to go sledding?"

"Sled!"

"Do you want the pink one or the green one this time?" he asked as he walked off toward the garage, where our sled supply rivaled only the nearest ski resort.

"Geen!"

"You two finish getting dressed," Naomi ordered, following the kids into the garage.

I turned to my wife and yanked her fully into the kitchen, out of eyesight, and kissed her hard and deep. "We could get undressed instead."

"I could get behind that plan," she said with a smile, wrapping her arms around my neck.

Four years of marriage and I still couldn't get enough of her. She wasn't an addiction, not in the way I used to think—she was a necessity, like water or oxygen. My need for her was constant and only surpassed by my love for her.

"Time to go!" Vivi announced.

"Guess we'll have to wait until later." Zoe pressed another kiss to my mouth, then slid out of my arms in search of her boots.

I grabbed the rest of my things and followed my family into the obnoxiously cold day, taking Mel from Levi when the snow came up to his knees at the edge of the driveway.

There was nothing more precious in this world than the woman beside me and the little girl she'd given me. Nothing better than having all of us gather here year after year, carving out the time to be together where the crowd was underage and the only schedule we had to keep was naptime.

Some years, our best hits were written at my dining room table.

Other years, the only thing we wrote were grocery lists when the kids ran us out of milk.

As long as we had the week together, we were happy.

I held Zoe's gloved hand and knew I was the happiest of all.

ACKNOWLEDGMENTS

First and foremost, thank you to my Heavenly Father for blessing me beyond my wildest dreams.

Thank you to my husband, Jason, for getting me through the insanity that has been 2020 and every other year I've been lucky enough to call you mine. Thank you to my children, who never cease to amaze me with their ability to adapt to every new situation—including quarantine—with grace and love.

Thank you to Devney Perry and Sarina Bowen for inviting me into this collaboration and never batting an eye when life went topsy-turvy. You've both taught me so much!

Thank you to Karen Grove, for dealing with my squirrel of a brain. I never worry when I know you're coming behind me with edits. To Jenn Wood for dropping everything to copy edit, and to Sarah Hansen for the phenomenal cover. To my incredible agent, Louise Fury, who makes my life easier simply by standing at my back.

Thank you to my wifeys, our unholy trinity, Gina Maxwell and Cindi Madsen, who always pick up the phone. To Jay Crownover for being my safe place and the wolf to my rabbit. To Shelby and Mel for putting up with my unicorn brain. Thank you to Linda Russell for chasing the squirrels, bringing the bobby pins, and holding me together on days I'm ready to fall apart. To Cassie Schlenk for reading this as I wrote it and always being the number one hype-girl. To every blogger and reader who has taken a chance on me over the years. To my reader group, The Flygirls, for giving me a safe space.

Lastly, because you're my beginning and end, thank you again to my Jason. None of this would be possible without you.

*Enjoy the first chapters of
Books One and Two in the
Hush Note Series*

*LIES AND LULLABIES
By Sarina Bowen*

and

*RIFTS AND REFRAINS
By Devney Perry*

LIES AND LULLABIES

BY SARINA BOWEN

Chapter One

Jonas

Pine boughs scraped against the windows of the forty-five-foot tour bus as it crept along the last half mile of the dirt road. By the time the driver came to a stop outside the Nest Lake Lodge, I was already on my feet. And when the door swung open, I jumped out to taste the Maine air.

This was the moment of truth. I inhaled deeply, taking in the summery scent of lake water and lilacs.

Yes! It still smelled the same. That was a good sign.

Slowly, others began to trickle off the bus behind me. First came Quinn, our drummer. She stretched her legs without comment. But then Nixon, our lead guitar, stepped down and began to laugh. "No shit, man. Really? We drove a hundred miles out of our way for this?"

"Hey! Trust me." I smiled at my two best friends. "Nest Lake is magic." At least it had been once upon a time. And that was why we were here. This detour was supposed to help me remember the last time I'd been truly happy. Before I wrote another album, I needed to convince myself that happiness wasn't impossible.

"Christ." Nixon pulled his T-shirt down over his tattooed abs. "Where's the bar? Where are the women?"

I took a moment to examine my oldest friend, and I didn't like what I saw. A pale, tired face with dark circles under the eyes. 'Twas the season to worry about Nixon.

Most people looked forward to the summertime, but not him. Summer was when Quinn and I watched Nix for signs of a breakdown. From June till September—usually in the midst of a grueling tour—Nixon would trade his beer for whiskey. He would sleep too much and brood too long.

It was only Memorial Day Weekend, and already the man looked hollow. Not good.

I put a hand on Nixon's shoulder. "Think of this as a couple of days off, okay? There's nothing here but trees and the lake. You can thank me later."

He eyed the lodge's low-slung roofline with suspicion. "Have we fallen on hard times? Should I be worried?"

They both stared at me, but I didn't give a damn. "Forty-eight hours," I told them. "No TV, no cell phone service. Just put on a pair of trunks and jump in the lake."

"Shit, I lost my suit in Toronto," Nixon complained. "That sick night in the hot tub with those triplets? I'm lucky I still have both of my balls. Things got hairy."

"Enough about your hairy balls," I quipped. "No suit, no problem. Jump in naked. Or read in the hammock. When the weekend is over, you're going to beg me to stay."

Nix twitched, and then slapped at his neck. "Mosquitoes? Fuck. This is going to be the longest two days of my life."

I'd already begun to walk away, but I turned around to say one more thing to my two best friends. "Listen, team. I wrote seven of the songs off *Summer Nights* about a half a mile from where you're standing. If it weren't for this lake, the words 'one-hit wonder' would appear in each of our Wikipedia entries. So quit bitching about my favorite place in the world."

At that, I turned away. Walking toward the lake, I spotted two canoes parked on the bank, with life jackets and paddles at the ready. I walked past these and out onto the lodge's private dock. The green scent of Maine was strong on the breeze.

"I only have one beef with Maine," said a voice from behind me. "But it's legit."

I didn't need to turn around to identify the speaker. Our tour manager—and my good friend—was the only one who could cast such a huge, bald, muscular shadow on the dock boards. "What's that, Ethan?"

"There aren't any other black dudes in Maine."

I chuckled. "I'll give you that. But it's just a visit. We aren't moving in."

"Color me relieved. You need anything? I'm going inside to divvy up the rooms."

"I'm good. Really good, actually."

"Glad to hear it. Dinner's at seven."

* * *

An hour later, I convinced Quinn to row across the lake with me. "You don't even have to row. I'll do all the work."

"Hey, I'm game." She picked up a paddle and strapped on a life vest.

She tried to hand me the other vest, but I held up a hand, refusing it. "The summer I was here, I swam across this lake most days." I squinted against the glare off the water. "In the morning I'd write. And if I made some good progress, I'd swim and lie in the sun in the afternoon. Otherwise, it was back to the grind after lunch."

"Sounds very disciplined," Quinn said with a sigh. "Maybe I should try it."

"Totally worked!"

Five years ago I'd used that summer to regain control of my life. Secluding myself in the woods had served a couple of purposes. First, it got me away from the crazy Seattle scene. Then, with no distractions and nothing to occupy myself in my room at the tiny bed and breakfast but my favorite acoustic guitar and several empty notebooks, I'd finally written the band's overdue album.

Not only had that album eventually gone double platinum, I'd had the best summer of my life. Because for once, I'd proved to myself that I could get the job done. I didn't have to be just another blip on the music scene—a chump who got lucky with two hit songs before fading into oblivion. I didn't have to be a fuckup. Not all the time, anyway.

Now I steadied the canoe at the edge of the water. "Hop in," I instructed. "You sit up front."

After Quinn was settled on the seat, I shoved off, then stepped carefully into the rear of the boat. Sitting down, I dug my paddle into the water and headed toward the western shore and the tiny town of Nest Lake. After only a few minutes of paddling, the little public dock and the B&B where I'd rented a room that summer came into view.

It had all happened *right* here. The narrow door at the back of Mrs. Wetzle's house had been my private entrance. After a day spent writing, I used to slip on my flip-flops and shuffle down to the dock for a swim. On the Fourth of July, I'd gone skinny-dipping here with my only Nest Lake friend.

Just remembering that night made my chest ache. No wonder songwriters made so much of summertime memories. If I closed my eyes, I could still conjure the potent, warm air and bright stars.

And beautiful Kira. She was the best part of that memory.

"Turn around so I can get undressed," Kira had said that night, her fingers poised on the hem of her T-shirt. I remembered precisely how she'd looked, her cheeks pink from embarrassment, her sweet curves framed against the dusky sky.

Even though I'd been sorely tempted to peek, I'd turned around, obeying her request. Kira was gorgeous in the same way that Maine was—fresh and unspoiled. But she'd been off limits. It had been a rare instance of me staying "just friends" with a girl. And staying "just friends" had been another of my summertime goals.

At the time, I was freshly dumped by my supermodel girlfriend. We'd had the worst kind of pathological relationship, and I'd needed to prove to myself that I could go twelve weeks without relying on a hookup to feel better.

I'd *almost* succeeded.

Funny, but now I couldn't even picture that ex-girlfriend's face. But Kira's was seared into my memory. Her tanned legs and sunny energy had tempted me from the minute I'd blown into town.

But I'd stayed strong. I hadn't watched her strip down that night on the dock. In fact, I hadn't made a move all summer long. Not once. Every time my gaze had strayed from her sparkling silver eyes to the swell of her breasts under her T-shirt, I'd kept my urges to myself.

Of course, *looking* wasn't really against my rules. So after we'd slipped naked into the dark water of the lake, I'd admired Kira's shoulders shimmering in the moonlight and the place where the water dripped down between her breasts. She'd held herself low at the surface, preventing me from seeing much. The mystery had made my attraction that much more potent. I'd floated there, close enough to touch her, while the gentle current caressed my bare skin.

Submerged in the water, we'd watched the fireworks shoot up from the other end of the lake, their bright explosions mirrored in the water's surface. When it was finally time to get out of the water—and after my brain had invented several dozen fantastic ways to appreciate Kira's naked body—I'd asked *her* to turn around while I climbed out on the dock.

Usually, I'm a hundred percent comfortable with nudity. But I couldn't let Kira see the effect she had on me. I didn't want her to know that my mind had been in the gutter the whole evening. Pulling my dry briefs and khaki shorts over my dripping wet body had been difficult with a rock-hard cock in the way.

"Jonas, it really is a beautiful lake," Quinn said, interrupting the movie reel of my memories. "I can see why you'd come back."

"It was the best three months of my life. No lie."

She was quiet for a moment, and I thought the conversation was over. But then Quinn asked a question. "So... Why did you wait five years to come back?"

I rolled my neck, trying to shake the last of the tour-bus tension from my neck. "Because I'm a goddamned idiot," I said, rowing toward the little beach. It was the truth, too. If Maine had lost its magic, it wasn't the Pine Tree State's fault. It was *my* fault. I'd been too stupid to see what was right in front of me.

* * *

When we reached the water's edge, I dragged the canoe up onto the gravelly sand. "We can leave the boat right here. Nobody will bother it."

"Really?"

"Really. That's how it's done here in Outer Bumfuck."

Quinn laughed. "Are you going to show me the town?"

"Of course I am. But it will take about ten seconds."

I admired Quinn's shapely legs as she leaned over to stash her oar in the boat. It took surprising body strength to play the drums, and the muscle looked good on her, especially in her bathing suit and Daisy Dukes.

My drummer and I were truly just friends. We'd met eight years ago at work in a Seattle bar. Years ago—when I was hammered on Jack Daniel's—I once kissed Quinn, in just the kind of dumbass move that can ruin a good friendship as well as a good band.

Luckily, after about five seconds of stupidity, we pulled back and sort of stared at each other. I'd said, "Okay, nope" at exactly the same time she'd said, "Ewww." Then we'd burst out laughing, and never tried that again.

Thank goodness, because I was usually too impulsive for my own good. Quinn and I would've never worked as a couple, anyway. Two moody artists? That's just a bad idea.

Besides, Quinn shied away from romantic relationships. She was happiest when she was scribbling music into her notebook or tapping out a rhythm with the drumsticks that she never seemed to put down.

From the public beach, we made a left toward Main Street. "So…" I gestured like a tour guide. "Here you see downtown metropolitan Nest Lake."

The only living being in sight was a golden retriever sleeping on the sidewalk. As I began to talk, he opened one lazy eye to look at us.

"You have your post office, which is open about a half an hour a day, but don't bother trying to figure out when, because they haven't updated the sign on the door since 1986. And there's the soft-serve ice cream place, the Kreemy Kone. Open until nine. The crown jewel is here—Lake Nest General Store— where I ate dinner every single night for an entire summer, even though it isn't actually a restaurant. And that's it. You've seen the whole town."

Quinn raised a finger, counting the cars. "Four."

"This is busy, actually. A big crowd for Memorial Day weekend."

"Wow." She smiled. "And your fans are about to rush you, I can feel it."

Right on cue, a woman came out of the general store with a gallon of milk. She dismounted the wooden stairs, turning away without giving us a second glance. Then she tucked herself into one of the cars and drove away.

"And then there were three," I said under my breath.

Seeing Main Street brought me into a strange reverie. In spite of the sunshine, I felt as if I was having a very vivid dream. I'd thought about this place so often, and now I was here for real.

Crazy.

"I can see why you came here to write," Quinn said. "But how did you find it?"

"My mom used to come here when she was a little girl. One of the few pictures I have of her is on the porch of the general store."

"Ah," Quinn said. And because she knew I didn't like to talk about my parents, she left it at that.

I'd lost both my parents when I was seven. Coming back here five years ago was a way to try to remember my life before everything had gone wrong.

Did it work? I guess. But the cure was only temporary. Lately I'd been feeling just as lost.

Five years ago I'd come here when my band's new album was overdue. The record label was pissed off at me, so Maine seemed like a good place to hide from their nagging. And my glamorous girlfriend had just dumped me. A tabloid had just run a story about how I'd cheated on her. They used pictures of me with a woman that I slept with the night *after* we broke up.

I was twenty-five years old and already in a slump. So I'd come to this place my mother used to tell me about. It was one of the only details I could remember about her.

I'd needed some magic, and that's what I'd found here in Maine.

"God, it's hard to believe places like this still exist," Quinn said. "Can we go into the general store? And then I want ice cream."

"Lead on." I followed her up the store's wooden steps,

through the screened porch and into the shop itself. What hit me first was the scent. It smelled *exactly* the same inside—musky and rich, like pickles, salami, and sawdust. And it looked mostly the same, lit by old soda lamps hanging from the ceiling on chains, with half an inch of dust on each one.

What's more, Kira's father stood behind the cash register, looking just as grumpy as he had five years ago. The old man proceeded to ignore us both, because he always ignored the summer people. And yet he'd been in business forever, because there weren't any other stores for ten miles.

Two or three years ago, drunk and in a melancholy mood, I had finally picked up the phone to call this very store. It was a call that I'd waited too long to make, and I'd known it was hopeless even before that surly old man answered the phone in his gravelly voice.

"Is Kira there?" I'd asked, knowing it was a long shot. No girl waits two years to hear from the asshole who'd rejected her. Besides—Kira had always said that she was going back to college after our magical summer.

"They moved to Boston," the old man had told me.

Right. That's what I'd expected. They'd moved to Boston.

They.

Hell, I'd expected that too. Kira wasn't single anymore. Why would she be?

Thousands of miles away, in a Texas hotel room, I'd hung up the phone and poured myself another two fingers of scotch. But I'd never stopped thinking about Kira. And I probably never would.

Only one thing in the store looked truly different now. And although I'd expected this, it still made me sad. Her sign was missing. Above one of the back counters, a carved wooden plaque had once hung. KIRA'S CAFE. Her homemade specialty had been a quirky little meat pie, about five inches across. Under an artfully cut-out crust lay curried chicken, or sausage and peppers. There'd been a ham and egg version I'd particularly liked. My first week in Maine, I'd tried a different one each night. My second week, I'd repeated the cycle.

That's how we'd become friends. After I'd eaten her savory pastries nine nights in a row, Kira began feeling sorry for me. So she'd surprised me with some new dishes. I walked in one night to find that she'd made me a big square of lasagna. The next night, she'd grilled up a bacon cheeseburger while I waited.

As the summer progressed, she'd gotten even more creative. The pan-fried lake trout had tasted so fresh I'd almost cried.

"You are the most loyal customer I've ever had," she'd said. By then, I'd memorized the shape of her smile and the flush of her cheek when I complimented the food.

But I didn't hit on her. Not once.

At the beginning, restraint had been easy. I'd come to Nest Lake to be alone and to stop chasing women. I was still bitter about the tabloid article. I didn't need any distractions. I was going to finish that album or die trying.

But by midsummer, my vow of chastity had gotten a lot harder. Literally. The time I'd spent with Kira had evolved from a simple nightly transaction to a real friendship. And every night I went to bed hearing her laughter echo in my head and wondering how her skin would feel sliding against mine.

But I was young and dumb. At the time, I'd written it off as mere horniness. Five years later, I knew better.

Well before Labor Day, Kira's bright smile and intelligent eyes had stolen my heart. And her curvy body turned up in all my dreams. But I never slipped up and made a pass. Not just because I'd been feeling stubborn, but there was something vulnerable about Kira. I couldn't have told you exactly what, but still it held me back. Banging her like one of my fans would have felt wrong.

Besides, if I'd talked Kira into my bed, there'd been a risk that she wouldn't make me dinner anymore. And then I would have been stuck with the miserable fare that my B&B landlady referred to as "food."

Somehow it had all been enough to keep even a dedicated horn dog in check.

"Earth to Jonas," Quinn teased. "Let's pick up a magazine or two, and then I want some soft serve."

I'd been staring at Kira's old counter, memories flooding through me. But where her delicacies once sat, there were now only scary-looking danishes wrapped in cellophane. It was no better than gas-station food.

It was true what people said. You can never go back.

I turned toward the magazine rack, shaking off my disappointment.

DOWNLOAD NOW

RIFTS AND REFRAINS

BY DEVNEY PERRY

Chapter 1

Quinn

"The funeral is Saturday."

I nodded.

"I know you're busy, but if you could come, your father would . . . I know he'd appreciate the support."

Beyond my dressing room door, a dull roar bloomed. Hands clapped. Voices screamed. The beat of stomping feet vibrated the floors. The opening act must be on their last set because the crowd was pumped. The stadium would be primed when Hush Note took the stage.

"Quinn, are you there?"

I cleared my throat, blinking away the sheen of tears. "I'm here. Sorry."

"Will you come?"

In nine years, my mother had never asked me to return to Montana. Not for Christmases. Not for birthdays. Not for weddings. Was it as hard for her to ask as it was for me to answer?

"Yeah," I choked out. "I'll be there. Tomorrow."

Her relief cascaded through the phone. "Thank you."

"Sure. I need to go." I hung up without waiting for her good-bye, then stood from the couch and crossed the room to the mirror, making sure my tears hadn't disturbed my eyeliner and mascara.

A fist pounded on the door. "Quinn, five minutes."

Thank God. I needed to get the hell out of this room and forget that phone call.

I chugged the last of my vodka tonic and reapplied a coat of red lipstick, then scanned the room for my drumsticks. They went with me nearly everywhere—Jonas teased they were my security blanket—and I'd had them earlier, on the table. Except now it was bare, save for my plate of uneaten food. The sticks weren't on the couch either. The only time I'd left the dressing room was when I'd gone to get a cocktail and a sandwich.

Who the fuck came into my dressing room and took them? I marched to the door and flung it open, letting a rage brew to chase away some of the pain in my heart.

"Where are my sticks?" I shouted down the hallway. "Who-ever took them is fired."

A short, balding man emerged from behind the door where he'd been hovering. He was new to the crew, having been hired only two weeks ago. His cheeks flushed as he held out his hand, my sticks in his sweaty grip. "Oh, uh . . . here."

I ripped them from his hand. "Why were you in my dressing room?"

His face blanched.

Yep. Fired.

I didn't allow men in my dressing room. It was a widely known fact among the crew that, unless you were on a very short list of exceptions, my dressing room was off-limits to anyone with a penis.

The rule hadn't always existed, but after a string of bad experiences it had become mandatory.

There'd been the time I'd returned to my dressing room to find a man in the middle of the space, his jeans and whitey-tighties bunched at his ankles as he'd presented me his tiny glory. Then there'd been the show when I'd come in to find two women making out on my couch—they'd mistaken my dressing room for Nixon's.

The final straw had been three years ago. I'd been drenched from a show and desperate to get out of my sweaty clothes. Pounding on the drums for an hour under hot lights usually left me dripping. I'd stripped off my jeans and tank top, standing there wearing only a bra and panties, and reached for the duffel I brought with me to every show. When I opened my bag to take out spare clothes, I'd found them coated in jizz.

So no more men—short, tall, bald or hairy.

"S-sorry," Shorty stammered. "I thought I'd hold them for you."

Beyond him, my tour manager, Ethan, came rushing down the hall, mouthing sorry with wide eyes. Ethan was the peacemaker, but he'd be too late to save Shorty.

In a way, I was glad this guy had snuck into my dressing room and taken my sticks. I needed a target, somewhere to aim this raging grief before it brought me to my knees, and this asshole had a bull's-eye on his forehead.

I almost felt bad for him.

"You wanted to hold them for me?" I waved my hand, Zildjian sticks included. The crew bustled around us, keeping a wide berth as they prepped to switch out the stage configuration. "Were you also going to hold Jonas's Warwick? Or Nixon's Fender? Is that what your job is today? Holding stuff for the band?"

"I, uh—"

"Fuck you, creep." I pointed my sticks at his nose. "Get the fuck out of my sight before I use your head as a snare."

"Quinn." Ethan collided with my side, putting his arm around my shoulders. He gave me a brief squeeze, then spun me around and nudged me into the dressing room. "Why don't you finish getting ready?"

Behind my back, I heard Shorty mutter, "Bitch."

Why was a woman a bitch when she didn't let a man off the hook for this kind of shit behavior? If a guy were standing in my shoes, Shorty wouldn't have dared enter the dressing room in the first place.

"He's fired, Ethan," I shot over my shoulder.

"I'll take care of it."

I kicked the door closed and took a deep breath.

Damn it, why was our tour over already? Why was tonight the last night? What I really needed was a packed schedule of travel and shows so that going to Montana for a funeral was impossible.

Except there were no excuses to make this time. There was no avoiding this goodbye, and deep down, I knew I'd hate myself if I tried.

Somehow, I'd find the courage.

Tears threatened again, and I squeezed my eyes shut. Why hadn't I grabbed more vodka?

After this show in Boston, I'd planned to return home to Seattle and write music. The summer tour was over, and we had nothing scheduled for a month. Except now, instead of Washington, I'd fly to Montana.

For Nan.

My beloved grandmother, who I'd spoken to on Monday, had died in her sleep last night.

"Knock. Knock." The door inched open and Ethan poked his head inside. "Ready?"

"Ready." I clutched my sticks in my hand, drawing strength from the smooth wood. Then I followed him outside and through the crush of people.

The crowd's cheers grew louder with every step toward the stage. Nixon and Jonas were already waiting to go on. Nix was bouncing on his feet and cracking his neck. Jonas was whispering something in his fiancée Kira's ear, making her laugh.

"Are you okay?" Ethan asked as he escorted me toward them.

"Change of plans for tomorrow. I'm not going to Seattle. Can you make arrangements for me to go to Bozeman, Montana, instead?"

"Um . . . sure." He nodded as confusion clouded his expression.

In all the years Ethan had been our tour manager, he'd never had to arrange for me to take a break from the show lineup for a trip to my childhood home. Because since I'd walked away at eighteen, I hadn't been back.

"I want to leave first thing in the morning."

"Quinn, are you—"

I held up a hand. "Not now."

"There she is." Nixon grinned as I approached, his excitement palpable. Like me, he lived for these shows. He lived for the rush and the adrenaline. He lived to leave it all on stage and let the audience sweep us away for the next hour.

Jonas smiled too, but it faltered as he took in my face. "Are you okay?"

Where Ethan was the peacemaker and Nixon the entertainer, Jonas was the caretaker. The designated leader by default. When Nixon and I didn't want to deal with something, like a Grammy acceptance speech or hiring a new keyboardist, Jonas was there, always willing to step up.

Maybe we relied on him too much. Maybe the reason it had

been so hard to write new music lately was because I wasn't sure of my own role anymore.

Drummer? Writer? Token female?

Bitch?

Shorty's damn voice was stuck in my head. "Some guy from the stage crew came into my dressing room and took my sticks. He was 'holding them' for me."

It was better they think that was the reason I was upset. Ethan wouldn't ask questions about my trip tomorrow, but Jonas and Nixon would.

"He's fired." Jonas looked to Ethan, who held up a hand.

"It's already done."

"Good luck, you guys." Kira gave Jonas another kiss and waved at Nixon. She was a little less friendly toward me—my fault, not hers—but she smiled.

I hadn't exactly been welcoming when she'd gotten together with Jonas. I'd been wary, rightfully so. His taste in women before Kira was abhorrent.

"Thanks, Kira." I offered her the warmest smile I could muster before she and Ethan slipped away to where they'd watch the show.

Jonas held out one hand for mine and his other for Nixon's. As we linked together, we shuffled into a shoulder-to-shoulder circle.

This was a ritual we'd started years ago. I couldn't remember exactly when or how it had begun, but now it was something we didn't miss. It was as critical to a performance as my drum kit and their guitars. We stood together, eyes closed and without words, connecting for a quiet moment before we went on stage.

Then Jonas squeezed my hand, signaling it was time.

Here we go.

I dropped their hands and, with my shoulders pinned back and my sticks gripped tight, walked past them to the dark stage. The cheers washed over me. The chanting of Hush Note, Hush

Note seeped into my bones. I moved right for my kit, sat on my stool, and put my foot on the bass drum.

Boom.

The crowd went wild.

Nixon walked on stage and lights from thousands of cameras flashed.

Boom.

Jonas strode toward a microphone. "Hello, Boston!"

The screams were deafening.

Boom.

Then we unleashed.

The rhythm of my drums swallowed me up. I escaped into the music and let it numb the pain. I played like my heart wasn't broken and pretended that the woman who'd supported me from afar these past nine years was clapping in the front row.

Tonight, I'd be the award-winning drummer. The Golden Sticks.

Tomorrow, I'd be Quinn Montgomery.

And tomorrow, I'd have no choice but to go home.

***

"What are you doing here?"

Nixon shrugged from his seat on our jet. His eyes were shaded with sunglasses, and he was wearing the same clothes he'd changed into after last night's show. "Heard you were taking a trip. Thought I'd tag along."

"Have you even been to sleep yet?" I walked to his seat and plucked the glasses off his face, and the sight of his glassy eyes made me cringe. "Nix—"

"Shush." He took the sunglasses from my hand and returned them to his face. "After nap time."

I frowned and plopped into the seat across the aisle. His partying was getting out of hand.

The attendant emerged from the galley with a Bloody Mary. "Here you go, Nix."

First-name basis already? This one wasn't wasting any time.

"I want an orange juice," I ordered, drawing her attention. "And a glass of water, no ice. And a cup of coffee."

"Anything else I can get you?" she asked, her question aimed at Nixon, not me.

He waved her off with a grin.

"Do not get any ideas of taking her to the bedroom," I said after she was out of earshot. "She's probably already poked holes in a condom."

Nixon chuckled. "So cynical this morning."

"Helpful, not cynical. Think of how many skanks I've chased off with my prickly attitude. Think of how many 'accidental' pregnancies I've help you avoid. You could say you're welcome."

He laughed, sipping his drink. "So where are we going?"

"I assumed Ethan told you since you're sitting here."

"Okay, let me rephrase. Why are we going to Montana? You never go home."

I stared out the window, watching the ground crew motioning to our pilots. "Nan died."

Voicing the words was like a hammer to my chest, and every ounce of my strength went to keeping the tears at bay.

"Fuck." Nixon's hand stretched across the aisle, and his fingers closed over my forearm. "I'm sorry, Quinn. I'm so, so sorry. Why didn't you say anything? We could have canceled last night's show."

"I needed it." Of all people, Nix would understand the need to disappear into something for an hour to avoid reality.

"What can I do?"

"Don't fuck the attendant until after you drop me off."

He chuckled. "Done. Anything else?"

"Help me write a song for her. For Nan," I whispered.

"You got it." His hand tightened on my arm, then fell away as the attendant returned with my drinks. She set them on a table, leaving us to relax in the plush leather seats as the pilot came back to greet us and confirm our flight schedule.

When he disappeared into the cockpit, I put on my head-phones and closed my eyes, listening to nothing as we prepared to depart. Nixon saw it as my signal that I didn't want to talk and settled deeper into his chair. He was snoring before we were wheels up, soaring above the clouds.

And I was flying home, dreading the return I'd put off for nearly a decade.

The last time I'd seen Nan, or any of my family members, had been nine years ago. I'd left home at eighteen, ready to break free and chase my dreams. The first year had been the hardest, but then I'd found Jonas and Nixon and our band had become my makeshift family. With every passing year, it had been easier and easier to stay away from Montana. It had been easier to avoid the past.

Except the easy way out had also been the coward's path. I'd missed the chance to tell Nan goodbye.

She wouldn't call me on Mondays anymore. There would be no more cards in the mail on my birthday, stuffed with a twenty-dollar bill. Nan wouldn't boast to her water aerobics class that her famous granddaughter had won a People's Choice Award, then call to tell me exactly what she'd bragged.

Tears welled as the sunlight streamed through my window. I blinked them away, refusing to cry with the flight attendant checking on us constantly, waiting for Nixon to wake up. I turned on my music and cranked the volume so loud the sound was nearly painful. Then I tapped my foot, matching the tempo. My fingers drummed on the armrests of my chair.

I lost myself in the rhythm, like I had last night, only this was someone else's beat.

My own seemed fragile at the moment, like a pane of glass that would shatter if I hit it too hard. I was tiptoeing around my own talent, avoiding it, because lately I'd been questioning my ability to craft something new.

This creative block was crushing me.

Nixon's deepening love affair with cocaine, alcohol and whatever other substances he was putting into his body had hindered his creative prowess as of late too.

Our record label had been hounding us for months to get going on the next album. Jonas was flying home to Maine to write new lyrics. Since he'd found Kira this past year—his muse—most of his recent songs were fluffier than we'd recorded on previous albums. Nixon and I had both vetoed a couple of his drafts, but some of it had great potential.

If we could match them to a tune.

That's where Nixon and I came in. Jonas had a gift with words. Nixon and I wielded the notes.

Jonas's recent lyrics needed the right amount of love in the melody. They needed a hint of angst to keep them interesting and an edge to be rock and roll. Explaining what I wanted in each song was simple. Stringing together something tangible was proving to be a challenge.

Things had been so much simpler when he'd only written about sex.

Now that we had a break in our schedule, I was anxious to get home to Seattle, where I could hole up in my apartment and sit behind my piano until it clicked.

But first I'd spend a week in Montana saying goodbye.

I loathed goodbyes, so I avoided them.

Not this time.

The knot in my stomach tightened with every passing hour. When the pilot announced we were beginning our descent, I shot out of my seat, raced to the bathroom and puked.

"You okay?" Nixon asked, handing me a piece of gum as I emerged and took my seat.

"Yeah, thanks."

"Sure?"

"Just nerves."

Hell, I hadn't been this nervous since Hush Note's early days. I didn't get keyed up before shows anymore, not after years and years of practice. Besides, the moments on stage were the best part of this life. Playing for thousands of people live or playing for millions of people on television, my hands never shook. My stomach was rock solid.

But this? Returning home to my family. Returning home for a funeral. Returning home to him.

I was terrified.

Nixon's hand closed over my forearm once more, and he didn't let go until the plane touched down.

"I don't want to be here," I confessed as we taxied across the runway.

"Want me to stay?" His eyes, clearer after his nap, were full of tenderness.

He'd stay if I said yes. He'd be miserable and bored, but he'd stay. A part of me wanted to use him as a buffer between me and my family, but his presence and fame would only make things harder.

My face wasn't as recognizable on the street as his, and I didn't get half of his attention because I wasn't one of the guys. I wasn't the lead on stage, singing into a microphone as I played a guitar. Nixon had been People Magazine's Sexiest Man Alive three years ago. This year's reigning man was Jonas.

The last thing we needed this week were swooning fans wanting autographs.

I wanted to get in and out of Montana without much fuss. I was here to pay my respects to Nan and then I was going home.

Alone.

"No, but thanks." The plane stopped and the pilot came out to open the door as I collected my things. "Where will you go? Home to Seattle?"

"Nah. I'm feeling somewhere tropical. Hawaii's close."

"Please don't drink so many dirty bananas that you forget to pick me up. Next Monday. Should I write it down?"

"No, but you'd better make sure Ethan has that in his calendar."

"I will." I laughed, bending to kiss his stubbled cheek. "Thanks for flying with me."

"Welcome."

"You're a good guy, Nix."

He put a finger to his lips. "Don't tell. It's easier to get women into bed when they think you're the bad boy."

"Annnd you're also a pig." I frowned as the attendant came over, batting her eyelashes as she handed Nixon a cocktail. When had he even ordered that drink? Maybe I should make him stay with me and force him to be sober for a week. "Don't go crazy. Are you going to be okay?"

"I'm a rock star, baby." He flashed me a smile, the devilish one he saved for his fans and women. It was the stage smile that masked his demons. "I'm fucking awesome."

Lies. He was far from awesome, but I wasn't sure how to help him. Not when he was on a mission to lose himself in sex and booze and drugs like he did every summer.

"Thanks again." I waved. "Enjoy your flight attendant."

"Enjoy your time home."

My stomach pitched at his parting words. I slung my backpack over my shoulder and headed toward the door. At the base of the jet's stairs, my suitcase was waiting with the pilot.

I nodded a farewell and fished a pair of sunglasses from my bag, sliding them on before crossing the tarmac. The path from the private runway to the terminal was marked by yellow arrows on the charcoal asphalt.

The sunshine blazed hot on my shoulders as I pulled the hood on my black jacket over my blond hair. It was the best way to keep from being recognized, and with the mood I was in, it would do no good to be spotted by a fan today.

The summer breeze blew across my face, bringing that clean mountain air to my nose. We'd spent too many days breathing recycled air in buses and planes and hotels. I might have traded my country upbringing for a life in the city and preferred it as such, but this fresh, pure air was unbeatable.

Montana had a wholly unique smell of mountains and majesty.

I reached the terminal door too soon and stepped into the air conditioning. Ethan had reserved a rental car and a hotel suite for me, and as soon as I was checked into my room, I was planning on a long, hot shower. Then I'd unpack and go through the hotel move-in routine I'd perfected over the years.

My toiletries would be lined up beside the bathroom sink. I'd put my clothes in drawers and stow my suitcase in the closet. Then I'd search for a TV channel in a foreign language. I didn't speak a foreign language, but I liked the background noise to drown out any sounds from the hallway.

It was a trick I'd learned in Berlin on our first European tour. These days, I couldn't sleep in a hotel room without the TV blaring some drama in Spanish, French or German.

If it was loud enough, I'd be able to cry without fear someone would overhear.

I spotted the rental car desk, but before I could aim my feet in that direction, a familiar face caught my eye.

The world blurred.

Standing in the lobby of the airport was the boy I'd left behind.

Graham Hayes.

Except he wasn't a boy anymore. He'd grown into a man. A handsome, breathtaking man who belonged on the cover of People beside Jonas and Nix.

He stood motionless with his eyes locked on me. The airport had been remodeled since I'd left, but the spot where he stood was almost exactly the place where I'd left him nine years ago. He'd been standing at the base of a staircase, watching me walk away.

I wouldn't fool myself into thinking he'd been waiting here for my return.

What the hell was Graham doing here? I wasn't ready to face him yet. I wasn't ready to face any of them yet, but especially Graham.

He broke out of his stare and unglued his feet. His strides were easy and confident as he walked my way. His square jaw was covered in a well-trimmed beard, the shade matching the brown of his hair. It was longer than how he'd worn it as a teenager. Sexier. The man he'd become was beyond any version that I'd imagined during many lonely hotel nights.

I gulped as he neared. My heart raced.

This was not the plan. I was supposed to rent a car, go to my hotel and regroup. I needed time to regroup, damn it, and time to prepare.

Graham's long legs in dark jeans ate up the distance between us. The sound of his boots on the floor pounded with the same thud of my heart.

Before I was ready, he stood in front of me.

"Quinn." His voice was smooth and deep, lower than I remembered. He used to say my name with a smile, but there wasn't a hint of one on his face.

"Hi, Graham."

He wore a Hayes-Montgomery Construction T-shirt. My mother had sent me one of the same for Christmas two years ago.

He was the Hayes.

My brother, Walker, was the Montgomery.

The black cotton stretched across his broad chest. I'd spent many nights with my ear against that chest, but it hadn't been as muscled back then. It had held promise, though, of the man he'd become.

The man he had become.

Everything about Graham seemed to have changed, even those golden-brown eyes. The vibrant color was the same as I saw in my dreams, but they were colder now. Distant. A change I couldn't blame on time.

No, that one was on me.

"Let's go." He ripped the handle of my suitcase from my grip.

"I have a car reserved." I pointed to the rental kiosk, but Graham turned and walked toward the doors. "Graham, I have a car."

"Cancel it," he clipped over a shoulder. "Your mom asked me to pick you up."

"Fine," I grumbled, yanking my phone from my pocket. Texting Ethan while keeping up with Graham's punishing pace was difficult, and I looked up just in time to stop myself from crashing into a wall.

Oh, hell. It wasn't just a wall. It was a wall holding a framed Hush Note poster, and there I was, in the center. My hair was thrown back as I pounded on the drums. Jonas was singing into a microphone while Nixon riffed on his guitar.

It was the poster our label had made for tour promo last year, and the airport had embellished it with a banner strung over the top.

Welcome to Bozeman.

Home of Quinn Montgomery, Hush Note's Grammy Award-Winning Drummer.

Graham paused and looked back, likely wondering what was taking me so long. When he spotted the poster, he shot it a glare that might have incinerated the paper had it not been protected behind glass. Then he marched through the door, his strides even faster.

I jogged to keep up but was too far away to stop him from throwing my suitcase into the bed of a truck—an actual throw far more damaging than I'd ever seen from airline personnel.

"Get in." He jerked his chin to the passenger door.

"Okay." I bit my tongue.

Since my rental car was out, my new plan was to survive this ride to the hotel. Graham was upset, and I'd let it blow over. Ten minutes, fifteen tops, and we'd go our separate ways. I was here this week for Nan and causing drama with Graham would have upset her.

So I climbed in his truck and took a deep breath.

Graham's scent surrounded me. As a boy, he'd smelled fresh and clean. It was still there, familiar and heartbreaking, but with a spicy undercurrent of musk and cologne and man. The heady, intoxicating smell wasn't going to make this trip to the hotel any easier.

Before I had my seat belt buckled, Graham was behind the wheel and racing away from the curb.

I swallowed and braved conversation. "So, um . . . how have you been?"

His jaw ticked in response, but thankfully the radio filled the silence.

The Sirius XM Countdown continues with "Sweetness" by Hush Note. A song that's been number one on our countdown for—

Graham stabbed the off button with his finger.

I faced the window.

So Graham wasn't just upset. He was furious. Clearly nine years apart hadn't turned me into a fond memory.

"I have a reservation at the Hilton Garden Inn. If you wouldn't mind dropping me—"

"You're going home."

Right. End of discussion. Graham was doing a favor for my mother since my family would be busy on a Sunday morning.

He'd been sent to retrieve me before I could disappear to my hotel.

Maybe I shouldn't have been in such a hurry to leave the East Coast.

The drive through Bozeman was tense. I kept my gaze fixed outside, taking in the new buildings. The town had boomed over the years. Where there had once been open fields, there were now office complexes, shopping centers and restaurants.

It wasn't until we approached downtown that the streets became more familiar and I was able to anticipate Graham's turns. When we reached my childhood neighborhood, I marveled at the homes. Had they always been this small?

Then we were parked in front of my parents' home. My home.

Finally, something that hadn't changed. Slate-blue siding, white trim, black shutters and Mom's red geraniums planted in a whiskey barrel by the front door.

"Thanks for dropping me off," I told Graham, risking a glance his way. "Just like old times."

He'd always insisted on dropping me off at my house even though he lived next door.

Except back then, he would have smiled and kissed me goodbye.

But that was before.

Before I'd broken his heart.

Before he'd shattered mine.

PREORDER NOW

THE HUSH NOTE SERIES

BOOK ONE: LIES AND LULLABIES

By Sarina Bowen

BOOK TWO: RIFTS AND REFRAINS

By Devney Perry

BOOK THREE: MUSES AND MELODIES

By Rebecca Yarros

ALSO BY REBECCA YARROS

The Flight and Glory Series

Full Measures

Eyes Turned Skyward

Beyond What is Given

Hallowed Ground

The Reality of Everything

Legacy

Point of Origin

Ignite

Standalones

The Last Letter

Great and Precious Things

Coming Soon

The Things We Leave Unfinished

ABOUT THE AUTHOR

Rebecca Yarros is a hopeless romantic and incurable coffee addict. She is the *Wall Street Journal* and *USA Today* bestselling author of over a dozen novels, and the recipient of the Colorado Romance Writer's Award of Excellence for *Eyes Turned Skyward* from her *Flight and Glory* series.

Rebecca loves military heroes and has been blissfully married to hers for eighteen years. She's the mom of six kids, ranging from kindergarten to law school, and when she's not writing, you can find her watching her sons at the hockey rink, or sneaking in some guitar time. She lives in Colorado with her family, their stubborn English bulldogs, a feisty chinchilla, and a Maine Coon kitten who rules them all. Having fostered and adopted their youngest daughter, Rebecca is passionate about helping children in the foster system through her nonprofit, One October.

Want to know about Rebecca's next release? Join her Mailing List or check out www.rebeccayarros.com!

Made in the USA
Las Vegas, NV
21 August 2023

76372260R00184